REAL MEN
KNIT

REAL MEN
KNIT

Kwana Jackson

JOVE
NEW YORK

A JOVE BOOK
Published by Berkley
An imprint of Penguin Random House LLC
penguinrandomhouse.com

Library of Congress Cataloging-in-Publication Data

Names: Jackson, K. M., author.
Title: Real men knit / Kwana Jackson.
Description: First edition. | New York : Jove, 2020.
Identifiers: LCCN 2019044625 (print) | LCCN 2019044626 (ebook) |
ISBN 9781984806505 (paperback) | ISBN 9781984806512 (ebook)
Subjects: LCSH: Domestic fiction. | GSAFD: Love stories.
Classification: LCC PS3610.A3526 R43 2020 (print) | LCC PS3610.A3526 (ebook) |
DDC 813/.6—dc23
LC record available at https://lccn.loc.gov/2019044625
LC ebook record available at https://lccn.loc.gov/2019044626

First Edition: May 2020

Printed in the United States of America
1   3   5   7   9   10   8   6   4   2

Cover art and design by Farjana Yasmin
Book design by Alison Cnockaert
Interior art: Knitting set by Lytrynenko Anna/Shutterstock

For Will
Casting on with you was the best thing I ever did.

ACKNOWLEDGMENTS

Stories, though seemingly made of imagination and magic dust, when ultimately made into book form are no such thing. As the saying goes, it takes a village, and I'd like to give my deepest, most heartfelt thanks to my little village for helping me along the way.

To my family: my husband, Will, and my twins, no longer babies but now young adults who continually take my breath away and fill my heart with pride.

To Ma, James and my not-so-lil brothers, Ash and Semaj, my own Harlem princes. Thank you for always being in my corner and having my back.

To my editor, Kristine Swartz. I can't thank you enough for believing in me and *Real Men Knit*. This is a dream come true and working with you has been a joy. To Fareeda, Jessica and the rest of the incredible publicity team at Berkley. Thank you for riding for *Real Men Knit*. You all are rock stars!

To my amazing agent, the incomparable Evan Marshall. Having you in my corner makes me feel invincible. Thank you from the bottom of my heart.

To Kristan Higgins. Thank you for being my friend and my champion. Who knew superheroes could rock stilettos so well?

Farrah Rochon, Diva, thank you for dragging me over the finish line in the DMs. Your daily words of encouragement and affirmation have been my guiding light. Your friendship can only be described as a gift from God.

To my Destin Divas. What can I say? You all are my home and I love you for it.

Sasha Devlin. My sunshine. Thank you, a thousand times over, for your rays of light. You have always been there with the perfect word and GIF just when I needed it, and boy did I need it!

Penny and Erica, for telling this little butterfly to sit still and focus and for sending encouraging GIFs to make her do so . . . thank you.

To Jamie Beck. Thank you for sharing your expertise. You were right on time at the perfect time. I can't thank you enough, and the same goes for the rest of my Fiction from the Heart sisters: Falguni, Priscilla, Hope, Sonali, Liz, Sally, Barbara, Tracey, Virginia and Donna. Thank you.

To my NYC chaptermate, Sharae, and her wonderful husband, Matthew. Thank you for being so lovely and inspiring.

To Junior. Though you're gone, you're always in my heart, my dear brother, and will never be forgotten.

To my friend and neighbor Mona Swanson. Thank you for sharing your time and knowledge of the foster system. Also, my thanks to the staff at Children's Village for all they do. Words are not enough.

Wendy, thank you for being my friend, my champion and my ride or die. Your friendship is always a source for me.

To my new readers (woot, woot!—so nice to meet you, and come on back now, ya hear?), and especially to my older K. M.

Jackson ones, I can't thank you enough. The fact that anyone takes the time to sit with me and share in my musings is a privilege and one I'm truly grateful for.

Lastly, but this name is always first and foremost, I'd like to thank God, from whom all my blessings come. I don't take any of this lightly, and Lord, in the end I just want to do you well.

1

THERE WAS NOTHING cute about the first time Kerry Fuller met Jesse Strong.

He broke her glasses, she bloodied his nose and they both ended up in a tangle of yarn on the floor in the loft space of Strong Knits being scolded by Mama Joy.

What she wouldn't give to be scolded by the older woman just one more time, Kerry thought as she adjusted her dark-framed glasses and purposefully pushed aside the almost-long-forgotten childhood memory. She glanced over at the front window of Strong Knits, the Harlem yarn shop that had been so much a part of her life growing up.

Any other day Kerry would have loved walking through the doors of Strong Knits. It had been that way since she had first stepped foot in the little knitting shop where she'd worked part-time for the better part of the last ten years and pretty much just hung out for most of her childhood years before that, making it her unlikely sanctuary. A place of calm in the midst of the chaos that was the concrete jungle of upper Manhattan. But this day was anything but normal. Despite the summer sun, warm and glinting off the freshly cleaned windows, showcasing the vintage baskets overflowing with color from the brand-new yarns that Mama Joy had gotten in barely two weeks before, Kerry still felt a chill run through her body that sent goose pimples rippling across her bare forearms.

Even the cute little display to the right of the baskets with fake ice-cream cones made of balls of finely spun cotton in creamy sherbet colors couldn't bring a smile to her lips, when they'd brought her nothing but delight just a little over a week before. But smiling now, and the memory of Mama Joy and those cones, caused Kerry's heart to ache way too much.

When she and Mama Joy had put the display together, it was with much happiness and no idea of the sorrow to come. No, all they could think of then was the smiles of the passersby when they saw the new yarns displayed in the whimsical not quite ice-cream cones. Mama Joy knew the children in the neighborhood would love it. And she was right. They did. Folks came in and immediately asked for those yarns. Little faces glowed when they saw the display and brown eyes lit with delight upon seeing the colorful cones.

But like the dynamo she was, Mama Joy had already been anticipating the next display, looking forward to what they would be doing for the fall. She had been excited about showcasing something even better for the neighborhood kids come the end of August with the new shipments on the way.

Kerry felt a weight suddenly lay heavy on her chest. What would happen to those yarns now? What would they do now that Mama Joy was no longer here to help navigate the changes that the new season would bring? Kerry peered through the glass of the door once more, noticing the darkness in the shop, unchar-acteristic for the hour of the day. If this had been a normal day, the lights would already be on in the back of the shop and right around this time Mama Joy would be stepping forward to unlock the door and wave her in. Kerry let out a sigh as the fact that she'd never be greeted by that wave, or Mama Joy's easy smile, ever again took the air clear out of her lungs.

Oh well, she couldn't just stand here wallowing in her feel-ings. Instead, Kerry swallowed and physically forced them down as she reached out and gave the buzzer on the side of the door three short rings. She waited. One breath and then another. Two more rings. Longer and steadier this time. She moved to the side and rang the bell to chime up at the residence upstairs. *Come on, Jesse, where are you? Noah? Lucas?* She knew Damian would prob-ably not be there, but she thought that maybe Noah and Lucas would have stayed over since they were all supposed to meet up here later anyway.

Disappointment blanketed her shoulders for a moment at the silent response to her ring. Why weren't the brothers together? Especially at a time like this? Sure, Lucas could have stayed over at the firehouse where he was stationed and lived most of the time, and maybe Noah went back to the place he was subletting with the other tour dancers, and knowing Damian, he didn't want any-thing to mess up his usual well-ordered routine so he'd probably gone back to his own apartment. But still, she expected Jesse to be there. Kerry felt her brows draw together. Who was she fooling? When it came to Jesse Strong, who knew what rock he was bur-rowed under this morning? The thought brought with it a sizzle of anger that shot quickly through Kerry's spine, followed immedi-ately by an intense feeling of guilt.

She could at least cut Jesse some slack, today of all days. Yes, her thinking was perfectly logical, but it was uncharitable and uncalled for, nonetheless. Especially since Jesse was hurting just as much as she was—hell, probably even more so—with it being the day after Mama Joy's funeral. She may call Ms. Joy "Mama Joy," like most of the young people in the neighborhood, but to Jesse, Lucas, Noah and Damian, she was *their* mother. The only one that mattered. The only one in this world who stuck around and took the time to truly make them a part of her family. Kerry knew if she was feeling this level of grief and uncertainty, then what must Jesse and his brothers be going through having just lost the only mother they'd ever been able to call their own?

She pressed the shop's buzzer again, then hit the side buzzer one more time. Still no answer. Oh well, she guessed Jesse wasn't there. He probably hadn't wanted to spend last night home above the shop alone. And who knows, maybe he ended up staying over at Damian's. Kerry felt her lips tighten, knowing how unlikely that was, given how well the two of them got along. Nope, more likely than not, Jesse was crashed underneath whatever woman he was currently seeing or hooking up with. She sighed. There she was being petty once again. How was it that thoughts of Jesse brought out the "Call me Petty Patty" side in her so easily?

Reaching into her tote bag to pull out her spare set of keys to let herself into the shop, Kerry hesitated. *It shouldn't be too much of a problem just letting myself in. Right?* Mama Joy had given her the keys ages ago as a backup and Kerry had promised the brothers she'd meet them this morning to help with sorting things out while they discussed the future of . . . well, everything.

Kerry feared that after today the Strong brothers would officially state out loud what she'd assumed after hearing that Mama

Joy had suddenly died. That Strong Knits and all that went with it would be no more. A Harlem institution here and gone in what felt like too short a breath, just like the amazing woman who had made it great.

With a last sigh Kerry finally let herself into the shop. The weight of the old wooden door seemed heavier than ever before. It couldn't be an easy decision for any of the brothers to make. The least she could do was have coffee on for them when they arrived.

As she stepped inside the shop, the light tinkle of the overhead bell made her half smile while bringing a tear to her eye and a painful tug to the center of her chest. She knew it was just her imagination, but it was as if she could still smell the scent of Mama Joy's cinnamon biscuits. The ones she'd make special on Wednesdays for her senior knitting circle, self-dubbed the OKG—Old Knitting Gang. Kerry was their honorary little sister and, in a way, their mascot from early on. She guessed now maybe Ms. Cherry and the rest of the crew would meet at the senior center or one of the women's houses. She made a mental note to get all their contact info so she could still help them with getting yarns online. Not that they'd let her get too far out of reach, mind you. They were just not that type of crew. The OKG felt more *Godfather* than Junior League, meaning that once you were in the family there really was no way out except one, and sadly, Mama Joy had made her way out.

Still, Kerry knew she owed much to both Mama Joy and her friends in the OKG. No, there wasn't much you could get past them, but she and many on the block were grateful for it. Around here, it wasn't always cool to go the "if you see something, say something" route. Not that there was anything wrong with that, but facts were facts, and there definitely hadn't always been the

most amiable relationship between residents and the NYPD. Folks
had to learn a different way to help each other out with neighborhood watches and small groups of friends who became family
when 911 didn't always show up like the cavalry, and at times you
didn't know who was the protector and who was the predator. So
yeah, Kerry owed them and Mama Joy a lot, and it went further
than yarn and double stitches.

At first they taught her to crochet, going from chain stitches to
granny squares, then, as she grew in age and skill, moving on to
knitting scarves and hats, then from there onto anything she could
imagine. But more than the projects, it was the comfort she got
just being welcomed into their group when she'd stop by early
before school and then after school instead of sitting at home alone
for hours on end, listening to the constant fighting between her upstairs neighbor and her horrible husband as Kerry waited for her
own ma to get off work. Or more importantly, during those times
when her ma had her own problematic love she'd dragged into
their lives and Kerry just wanted an escape.

Either way, Mama Joy had long given up on believing or listening to Kerry's excuses for stopping in and just started setting a
biscuit and yarn aside for her, having it all ready, the biscuit
wrapped in a paper towel alongside a cup of sweet hot chocolate
when she was little, and later coffee when her beverage habits
changed in high school.

Kerry closed her eyes a moment. Would she really never hear
Mama Joy's voice again? "Come on in, child, and get you some
nourishment before you pass out. You need this strength with the
way things are out there. A woman's got to have all her wits
about her."

"Damn straight," Ms. June would chime in while not breaking stride in her stitch work.

"Amen to that," Sister Purnell would say, topping off yet another hat or scarf for her church homeless drive or Ms. Cherry's Angel Tree kids.

Kerry smiled, the pain now excruciating. Little did Mama Joy know that just being in those women's presence was all the nourishment that she'd needed. Probably it was all anyone really needed when they took refuge in her little shop. Sure, people may have initially come for the yarns or the knitting or crochet needles or patterns, but it was Mama Joy's seemingly never-ending wellspring of love and sacrifice, which somehow didn't come off as a sacrifice, that kept her and everyone else in the neighborhood coming back.

A small smile or a hug from Mama Joy and, well, you felt like you'd just had the best meal of your life. Cinnamon biscuit or not.

Kerry felt lucky to have been on the receiving end of that hug or whatever Mama Joy was giving out. A fact that in the beginning was both a blessing and a sore spot for her mother. She was a single parent who worked two jobs that barely added up to one. And a young mother on top of it—who, yes, Kerry was sure, she guessed, tried her best to be mature. But at times the dip-and-do bug grabbed her and she didn't really want the responsibility that came with the constant mothering of an introverted kid.

Though Kerry's mother had her reservations about Kerry spending so much time in the shop, when her mother wanted time to herself or the apartment got a little tight for more than two, well then, Mama Joy and Strong Knits became just that much more of a tolerable solution.

Still, the sticking point that brought up problems between

Kerry, her mother and any other neighborhood person with a curious mind and flapping gums was the other elephant in the shop, or four elephants, as it were. Specifically, Mama Joy's four adopted sons—Damian, Lucas, Noah and Jesse—and the fact that they were in and out of the shop while Kerry was spending so much time there.

Kerry thought of her mother, the neighborhood gossips and talk of her and the guys, and snorted to herself. As if her being around ever mattered to the Strong brothers.

Brought in from the foster system to live with Mama Joy when they were all in grade school, the boys ended up being adopted by Mama Joy and taking on her last name of Strong when they were in high school—and by then each was in some way ironically living up to the Strong surname. Kerry was constantly, even still to this day, questioned by her mother and anyone else with half a curious mind about her relationship with the guys and which one of them she was dating. As if any of them thought of her as little more than "Kerry Girl," the shop fixture and a general nuisance to be tolerated.

Though Kerry's mother was fine with her spending time in the shop and learning about knitting and business from Mama Joy, she could never quite get behind her daughter being in constant close proximity to the Strong brothers. Who knew—maybe her mother was right. With her track record for sniffing out heartbreakers and, let's face it, general assholes, she was a bit of an expert in the field. Not that her mother had learned anything, being currently lost in love on yet another potential would-be asshole binge. Kerry prayed that this one would be the last. She'd had it with her mother's disasters and, afterward, having to pick up the pieces. Besides, this last one had taken her ma clear out of state and given Kerry their apartment to herself. She loved her mom, but she loved having her own place almost as much.

It was then that a distinct beeping took Kerry out of her musings. *Beep . . . beep . . . beep, beep, beep.* Speeding up. Oh crap, the alarm!

Kerry ran behind the door to punch in the code. That would be everything she didn't need. She was not in the mood to deal with explaining to the NYPD why she was in a shop that she may or may not still be employed at while the owner was not only not present, but recently deceased. Making sure the alarm was disarmed, she let out a breath, then looked around at the uncommon emptiness. The silence shrouded her as she walked forward and once again locked the front door, her eyes skimming across the flipped-over closed sign that had been in that position for the past week and a half, its possible permanence weighing heavy on her heart.

She shrugged. Nothing she could do about it. Whether the sign eventually flipped back or not was up to Jesse and his brothers. Well, mostly his brothers, really. What would Mr. Party All The Time seriously have to say about opening or closing the shop? What would he care beyond the fact that he'd have to find another place to park it when he was between women? As of late, when Kerry took notice, she couldn't help but observe that he'd been more out of the house than home anyway. Taking longer and longer stints staying with whomever he was seeing at the time.

Still, she thought, it wasn't as if Jesse didn't care. He wasn't that callous. He loved Mama Joy, loved her fiercely, in fact. All four of them did. But she knew they all had separate lives to live, and, thinking clearly, Kerry could not imagine those lives including keeping Strong Knits open. That hard truth said, she had to face the fact that it was time for her to move on and, once and for all, grow up and see her life clearly without the sanctuary of Strong Knits to fall back on.

Kerry headed back toward the small kitchen area, on the way passing some of the plants sent over to the funeral home as tribute. They were shoved over in the corner, as if they were purposely put down somewhere out of the way. Out of sight, out of mind. She could understand that. She caught sight of the peace lily sent from her own mother, who hadn't made it up from Virginia but had sent her regrets, and shook her head. Maybe she'd take that one home and at least get one off the brothers' hands. Or maybe she'd take it to the center when she went there to work later.

Kerry shrugged and turned, finally entering the kitchen and flipping on the lights, going to put her tote down on the counter-top. She suddenly stopped short as her eyes widened. The counter was packed with covered dishes in every imaginable shape and color. Most likely leftovers from the repast after the funeral yester-day. Putting her tote on the counter was almost impossible unless she squeezed it between a mountain of cold chicken and what ap-peared to be a twenty-five-pound ham. *Great.* That was a ham, and no doubt it was honey glazed with pineapple, and it had been out on Mama Joy's counter all night. Why didn't the guys put any-thing away? Kerry shook her head as she opted for placing her bag on one of the old kitchen chairs. She let out a long breath and turned toward the coffee maker. Coffee was very necessary. Now. She'd deal with the ham and the rest of the dishes later.

Purposely without thought, which of course she knew implied thought, Kerry picked up the coffeepot and brought it over to the sink to rinse and refill it with fresh water. She wouldn't look too closely at Mama Joy's knitted dish towels or the multitude of pho-tographs that hung haphazardly on the walls, some in nice frames and others clearly made out of Popsicle sticks and macaroni shells from kids she'd known over the years who'd come into the shop or were from the community center where Kerry now worked part-time. There was even a photo of Kerry from her high school graduation, now eight years past, in its cheap faux wood frame, but hung with loving care. Kerry blinked back tears at the photo of the young woman, her dark hair pressed within an inch of its life, glossy beyond belief and curled to perfection, with shining dark eyes, and full burgundy lips spread wide in a warm, welcoming smile that seemed to say the world was open and full of possibilities for her.

Dammit! She shouldn't have looked. Looking led to feeling, and that was the exact wrong thing to be doing today. But how could she not? There was nothing but feelings all around this old shop, in every seemingly not-well-thought-out nook. And here it was, Mama Joy had gone and hung Kerry's photo right along with her own boys' graduation photos, just as if she were a part of their family too. She and Jesse graduating the same year, Noah the year before, Lucas and Damian just a couple of years before that. Kerry laughed to herself, a wry laugh that grated the back of her throat as she took in the kitchen wall. This whole gallery was so Mama Joy. She was the type of woman who never met a stranger. But that family was no more. Who knew, maybe they never really were in the first place—just something that only existed as long as Mama Joy did. Now would be the true test of that.

Kerry shook her head as a lump gathered in her throat, threatening to be followed by a sob. Nope, not this morning. Not today.

She turned back to the coffeepot, her eye catching on one photo on the way: Mama Joy sitting in her usual spot on the tall stool just off to the side of the front counter with all the boys around her. They must have been late elementary to middle school age. She guessed it was around when they had first been placed with Mama Joy by the people at Faith Hope group home, if she remembered the stories correctly. Though it was an old still photo, Kerry could clearly make out the boys all in motion around Mama Joy while she was intently trying to show them something with her knitting to little avail.

A much younger Damian stood taller than his younger brothers but, as usual, looked bored and slightly exasperated, his dark eyes showing little patience. Lucas, the next oldest, seemed to have gotten his yarn completely tangled, and Noah had put his knitting aside and was instead hopping on one foot, captured mid-spin in the photo. The only one paying any sort of attention, surprisingly, was the youngest, Jesse. He was mimicking Mama Joy's motions and to Kerry's astonishment had a pretty good-looking scarf started and a look of pure wonder in his soft green eyes.

What happened to that little boy? Kerry wondered, then snorted as the answer came almost as quickly as the question. She knew exactly what happened. *Boobs.* Sure, she shouldn't say "boobs," but that was what he and his brothers were calling breasts back then, and she could just about pinpoint the time that Jesse turned. It was when he put down the knitting needles and instead wrapped his hands around his first pair of boobs that it all changed.

Kerry stilled and found herself inadvertently looking down at her own perfectly adequate pair. She shrugged, then rolled her eyes before looking for the coffee filters in the mess of covered dishes. Who could blame Jesse? It wasn't as if he had to fight for the boobs to come his way. Hell, it wasn't as if any of the Strong brothers had to fight in that department. Since each of them had hit puberty and shot past six feet, they were like four boob magnets with eight good hands between them. As if all it took for the girls to come flocking was height, muscles, sexy eyes . . . oh hell. Who was she fooling? It honestly didn't take too much more than that. Not once a person got a look at them. Not that she was magnetized or anything. It's just that some girls were metallic in that way.

2

JESSE STRONG WAS having a good dream. Well, maybe it wasn't a dream, because when you were dreaming did you actually know it was a dream? Weren't dreams supposed to convince you of their own reality? Thinking on it that way he irrationally reasoned that this wasn't a dream. More like a waking memory, one that he was more than happy to hold on to, since it was a memory of a warm body, smooth-as-silk skin, dark curly hair, bright eyes and full lips that seemed to only know the word "Yes."

"Yes." His most favorite word ever.

But the dream started to change. The inviting "Yes" turned to a dark, whispered "No." The warm body and bright eyes turned cold. Dead. No. She can't be dead. Mama. Mama! You can't do this to me. Don't leave me, please. Not again!

"No! I said no."

Jesse frowned.

"I'm sorry, no, we're closed today."

He frowned deeper as the opposite of his most favorite word hit his ears, bringing him out of the bliss of his waking memory of

Tamala from three weeks ago—or was this memory of Erika from last week? No matter. The delicious memory was already fading, bringing him too close to the edges of the all-too-real present that he was not ready to face. Shit. Why did days keep cropping up every twenty-four hours? It seemed no matter how much he tried, drank, partied, fucked, whatever, he couldn't seem to just sleep through and skip one. Skip just one day. Preferably the last day. Or days.

Jesse groaned as he ran a hand across his face and opened his eyes, wincing against the sharp rays of the sun that had the nerve to slip through the blinds and make it past the part of his curtain that wouldn't shut all the way without a pin to hold it closed.

Screw you, sun. Shining bright on a day like today.

What the hell time was it anyway? Six? Seven a.m.? He contemplated just turning over but went on full alert as the sound of a bang from downstairs hit his ears. What the hell? Did that come from the shop? But they were closed today. They were now closed every day. Not to mention the fact that it was the damned crack of dawn.

More shocking than the sun, just then there was another sound, something like a crash, and he bolted upright, hitting his bedroom floor at top speed. They *were* closed today. Closed, and Mama Joy was . . . well, she was definitely not down there where the crashing sound was coming from. Jesse hit the stairs at a run, though not before he grabbed his old high school baseball bat, kept at the ready behind the back of his bedroom door.

Bat raised, heart pounding, Jesse was filled with more than annoyance when he rounded the corner to the shop's back kitchen area only to meet the wide eyes of Kerry Fuller. Her fearful and shocked expression of having him come at her with a baseball bat raised quickly turned to clear anger as her eyes narrowed and she gave him a slow up and down.

Suddenly, Jesse was fully aware of the fact that he was clad in nothing more than his gray striped boxer briefs and an early-morning predicament that was totally normal but not one he was sure their sweet Kerry was used to. Though the look she gave him when her gaze came up once again and their eyes locked said, well, maybe she was, and maybe she thought he didn't quite measure up?

Jesse snorted to himself. *Yeah right. As if.*

He watched as Kerry's eyes shifted from him to the bat in his hand and then back to him again. "You plan to do something with that or is it just for show?"

Jesse felt his brow quirk as he fought hard to control his other extremities from doing the same and he let out a low groan. "Dammit, Kerry, what are you doing here so early? You scared the hell out of me and almost got your head knocked off in the process."

Her look, followed by the low snort that came after, let him know she was completely unfazed. "Early? It's past nine, and you knew I'd be coming by this morning. I was practically laying on the bell before. Didn't you hear me?"

"Obviously not," he said with a shrug and a slight wave of the bat.

The movement once again seemed to bring Kerry's awareness to his near nakedness and he watched as her eyes roamed over his chest, but then she seemed to think better of it, turning away and walking toward the coffeepot. She poured herself a cup, and as the aroma hit Jesse's nose—or maybe that was her smell, either way it was both sweet and smoky—he felt his brain starting to come to life, apparently catching up with his body.

"Don't you want to head back upstairs and put some clothes on? Make yourself decent?" she said.

It took a moment for the comment to click in his brain. Once again, quicker body than brain situation. *Decent.* That word was so Kerry that Jesse couldn't help the smile that tugged at the corner of his lips. In the midst of everything changing it was good to know some things never did. "No, not so much just yet," he said, while reaching over her shoulder to take the cup from her hand. "What I want right now is some of this coffee."

The quick turn and frown from her was just the reaction he was looking for. "Jerko," she hissed. "There's a whole pot here. Why do you have to take my cup? Can't you make your own?"

Jesse took a sip and grinned. "I can, but yours is always perfect. It just tastes better. Besides, who says I'm not decent?"

Kerry shook her head before turning away from him. She grabbed another mug from the plastic dish rack by the coffee maker and silently made herself another cup. Jesse watched as she took a dainty sip before looking up. He knew he was being kind of an ass, screwing with her like he was, drinking her coffee while in his drawers and staring at her in this old kitchen that held too many memories. He paused and frowned. But he also knew that this moment was way more comforting than he was willing to admit out loud. Hell, he was happy to have somebody there, anybody, just to not be alone with his thoughts.

Not now. Not today.

So instead of moving, Jesse watched intently as Kerry brought the mug to her lips again.

The mug was yet another from their mismatched set. They had many that Mama Joy had acquired over the years. A mug from here, a plate from there—like everything else, nothing went with anything quite right in this old brownstone, yet it all seemed to fit together. It was how Mama Joy said she liked it. Things didn't have to match up perfectly to fit, she'd always told him and his brothers. When he was still young, half-impressionable and full of hope and longing, he'd say—he didn't know why, maybe just to see her smile, because she always did when he said it—"Like us?" "Yes, like us," she'd answer back and kiss him on the forehead, warming him from the top clear to his toes.

Jesse closed his eyes for a moment against the sight of Kerry as the image of his brothers came to his mind. Four boys from different makeups and ethnic backgrounds, brought together by their shared need of, first and foremost, a home, but probably more so the love that the seemingly irreverent single Black woman had given them. They now had the nerve to call themselves brothers, so much so that they'd taken that woman's name to seal the deal. But now she was gone, so what would they do with the legacy she'd left them when it was all said and done? Did any of them even know what the word "legacy" meant?

He opened his eyes and looked at Kerry again. They'd be here soon and Jesse didn't have a clue how he and his mixed bag of misfit brothers would get their shit together and work it all out. Like the mugs in the house, there was nothing about them that really could place them one with the other. There was him, the youngest, or the baby as Mama Joy used to say, though being a baby was something he could never remember, not even when he reached back to his furthest memories. And now at twenty-seven he could definitely not call himself anywhere near a baby anymore. Still, he was the youngest of his bothers, a mixture of Black from his biological mother and something else, maybe white, maybe not, from his father, who could be just about any middle-aged guy with green eyes and a take-no-responsibility attitude.

Then there were Lucas and Noah, who were at least partially from a matched set since they were the only two out of the four of them that actually shared a blood connection, having been born of the same Asian mother, though they had different fathers. Lucas, the older of the two at thirty, was full—or "ish," because who really knew what without a DNA test—Korean, and Noah, the younger at twenty-eight, was half Korean and half Black—or Black-ish, because once again, DNA. Jesse had only been able to piece together parts of their past from what they had shared over the years, but what he did gather was that their mother died in a fire, which was tragic and more than plenty to mentally parse, given the fact that Lucas ended up being a firefighter. But Jesse got it, he guessed. Demons being what they were and all.

And lastly, though firstly, at least in age and his own ego-inflated mind, was Damian. He was a year older than Lucas and at least twenty when it came to general pain-in-the-ass-ness. Damian was Afro-Latino and, once again, "ish" like the rest of them, with a sketchy, not quite fully put together past, and the self-proclaimed leader of their little motley crew of misfits. As if anyone was fighting him for the position. Nope, not at all. Damian could have it.

As he drank Kerry's coffee, Jesse's mind continued to wander back in time, for the most part to when they were first brought to Mama Joy. After the shock of being in a new place, with a single mother and a yarn shop, he remembered the relief of being out of the group home and cautious joy over not being in yet another foster home where the kids were treated like little more than a

potential source of income. He remembered the mistrust and wea-
riness on his brothers' faces and how long it took for those looks to
go away. How long it took them all to stop with the territorial
jockeying for positions and turn into the brothers they were today. That took years. Years of arguing, screaming, yelling, pun-
ishments, but also love and patience. And he—no, they—owed all
that to Mama Joy. They were unruly messes, each of them, but
somehow Mama Joy, already at what some would consider past
her prime in age, was able to whip them into shape and turn them
into so much more than the system ever expected them to be.

He would always consider when Mama Joy agreed to take them
on and adopted them as her own the best day of his life. The boys
no one wanted had found a forever home with a single woman
who ran her own yarn and knitting shop. Sure, most everyone
told her she was half-crazy, but the way Jesse figured it, it was that
wonderful crazy half that was just what she needed to keep the
four of them in line.

Jesse felt something in his chest tighten as he watched Kerry
bring the cup away from her lips once again. Her round brown
eyes were soft and full of an understanding that made him feel
like she'd been reading his thoughts, and he was suddenly more
naked and vulnerable than his stupid underwear made him out to
be. He cleared his throat. "You're right," he said. "I think I'd better go and get dressed. Before you know it, Damian will be here
barking orders and trying to run things, so I need to be ready."

Kerry just nodded, which somehow made him feel worse. More
than anything, in that moment, Jesse wanted her to give him some
of her usual dismissive admonishment. What he needed today was
a Kerry-sized kick in the ass, not her sympathy. "You go and do

that," she said softly, and he caught a small hitch in her voice. "I, uh—" She turned and pointed to the back table, which, he noticed for the first time, on top of being packed with the leftovers from yesterday, also now held two large shopping bags. "I'll sort out this food. I don't know if you heard, but Mrs. Hamilton was here this morning and she dropped off more. I'll pull it out, and if you want me to, I can bring some up and put it in the fridge upstairs."

Jesse frowned. "I don't know where. The house fridge is full of leftovers from the repast too. That's why this other stuff is still out down here. We can try and stuff it or split it between all of us when the guys get here. Maybe Lucas can just take it to the firehouse. He's there most of the time anyway."

Kerry nodded again. "That's a good idea. I'll start dividing it up. But I'm afraid we'll need more containers. Mrs. Hamilton was probably only the beginning. You can expect plenty more where this came from. Knowing the neighborhood ladies, they will want to keep you well fed." She gave his chest and bare stomach a look then that was deep and penetrating and had his abs quivering on their own. "Besides, Mama Joy wouldn't want you losing weight."

Jesse shook his head and groaned. "No, she wouldn't." He sighed and looked again at all the food. "Mama Joy was definitely loved."

"That she was." Her voice cracked again.

Oh hell. Why did he go and say that? Jesse looked down and caught the tears that had sprung to Kerry's eyes.

Shit. "I'm sorry, Ker—" he started, going to reach for her.

But she put her hand up, halting his words before they could continue out of his mouth. "No. Don't say that. You have nothing to be sorry for. I should be here as a help to you and your broth-

ers. Not blubbering like some fool and adding to your troubles."
She quickly swiped at her eyes with the back of her hand, pushing
up her glasses and looking so darned cute and vulnerable. The image reminded him of catching her crying in the loft of the shop so
many years ago, way back when they were in junior high.

"You're not a fool." He lowered his voice. "And you're never
trouble. You're family, Kerry. And you loved Mama Joy just as
much as any of us. Just as much as she loved you."

There was a loud hiccup sound as her tears came on full force.
"Well, damn, Jes. You went and did it now," she said, putting
down her mug and reaching for a paper towel.

As if on autopilot, Jesse stepped forward and took her into his
arms. Her shoulders and back were awkward and rigid, but within
seconds she softened, and he felt the delicate quaking of her muscles against his body as she sucked in uneven breaths between
sobs. He held her there. Taking in the warmth of her softly twisted
braids against his bare arms. Soothed by the light smell of laven-
der and musk as her twists tickled his nose as she heaved and let
her sorrow out. Jesse swallowed down hard, blinking back his
own tears as he fought to calm his hard-pounding heart.

He would not cry today. Jesse reminded himself of his vow once
again. He had told himself yesterday that he'd shed enough tears
and he was done. Mama Joy would want it that way. She wasn't
one to go in for a lot of sorrow. She'd have told him to have his
moment and then move on. To think of her from now on with only
joy and happiness in his heart. And that is what he would do.
Once he got his damned mush of a heart in line to listen.

But then a damned lump formed in Jesse's throat, and it completely pissed him off. He didn't have a right to have a lump. He

didn't have a right to any more tears or wasted time. He'd done his crying and carrying on at the funeral yesterday, and that was enough. It was clear as day from the looks and comments from his brothers this past week and from all the neighborhood friends and acquaintances who had shown up: He was a fuckup, and as per his usual he'd fucked up and was a disappointment to Mama Joy right till the very end. Not even being there when she'd needed him at that critical moment. Wasting time and not living up to his potential, whatever that was. How could he continue to disappoint her now that she was gone?

Sure, it was a pattern for him, but it was one that he was now determined to break.

Mama Joy was the only one who'd ever seen potential in him, and she'd indulged him from the very beginning. Doing what she called "cultivating his creative spirit," all the while working herself into an early grave. Truth was, he was nothing more than a selfish bastard, taking what he could and never giving back in return. Not even when she clearly needed him to help more around the shop and relieve her of some of her heavy burden.

Kerry sniffled loudly and Jesse swallowed down hard on the determined lump, willing it away while ignoring the wayward tear that slipped from the corner of his eye as he held her and gained strength from her pain. He mentally paused and took the moment in. Yes, he was a bastard, in the kitchen in his drawers holding this woman and once again letting someone else do the hard work for him. He couldn't even grieve right for Mama Joy, so instead he just stood there and let Kerry do the hard work for him while he held on for all he was worth. But Kerry did feel hella good. Maybe he'd just hold her a little longer . . .

"What the hell, Jes? This is a goddamned business, not your

bedroom. Mama Joy is in the ground one day and you're seducing a woman in your underwear in her back kitchen!"

Fuck. Damian's voice pierced Jesse's ears like a hard two-by-four to the skull. Leave it to his annoying older brother to make his entrance at exactly the wrong time.

3

"OH, IT'S JUST you, Kerry."

Kerry stepped away from Jesse's dangerously comforting embrace and turned. Damian's voice was as bland and cold as his gaze.

Yeah, it's just me. Gee thanks, Damian. Dismissive much? But she didn't let her thoughts out of her head and off her tongue. What did it matter anyway? How many times over the years had she heard those words, or some version of them, from one of the Strong brothers?

An off-the-cuff "Oh, it's just you." Or, worse yet—no comment at all. As if she was just another fixture in the shop. Like the coffeepot or the old farmhouse table in the main room that was used for classes and weekly knitting circles. Kerry squelched back a sigh as she stepped back and out of Jesse's arms and looked over at Damian, who had come into the kitchen through the back door. She quickly swiped at her wet face, noticing that Jesse's chest was probably even wetter. Shit. It was bad enough that Jesse saw her weak and crumbling. She didn't need to go falling apart in front of Damian too.

"Yeah," she started, trying her best to keep her voice even and calm. "It's just me. I was having a moment and, uh, Jesse was kind enough to offer some comfort."

She watched as Damian's sharp brows knit tight and his angled jaw tensed. He gave a glance Jesse's way, no doubt taking in his state of mostly undress. "Comfort, huh? I bet he was."

Kerry's eyes went skyward as her tears were, for the moment, forgotten and the brothers gave each other one of their usual stare downs. For brothers, Jesse and Damian could not be more opposite. Their differences had little to do with their lack of shared DNA and more to do with, well, just about everything else. Jesse was all light in his looks and demeanor, with his lightly tanned skin, his mossy green eyes and his shoulder-length sandy-brown locs, which fit his Bohemian vibe. And then there was Damian, who pretty much was the definition of darkness. With his cinnamon-hued skin, close-cropped dark hair and onyx eyes that could singe a person's soul, he walked around most of the time with a smoldering aura that perfectly fit his whole quick-tempered, brooding persona.

And no one put Damian into a temper quicker than his youngest brother, Jesse. Maybe it was that Jesse fluttered between his vocations like he fluttered between women. A fact that bugged straitlaced Damian to no end. The vocation part—not the women, probably, since Damian was a low-key player himself. Still, Jesse couldn't pin down whether he wanted to be a DJ, a bartender, or "use his liberal-as-fuck communications degree for something besides charming the shit out of women," as Damian put it. While she was alive, Kerry knew, Mama Joy had to break up plenty of arguments between the two of them.

Damian, a corporate financial analyst, was the picture of a wannabe Wall Street raider the way he strutted around in his perfectly tailored suits. Kerry was sure seeing Jesse in the kitchen nearly naked was just the thing to piss him off. And she knew that Jesse was sure of it too.

"You can keep your judgment to yourself, Damian," Jesse said. "Whatever is going on between me and Kerry is between me and her."

Kerry balked. "There isn't anything going on."

Jesse shot her a look. "Of course there isn't, but what business is it of his?"

Yeah, of course.

Damian let out a snort. "I can see you're just as mature as ever, little brother." He stepped farther into the kitchen and reached around Kerry to pick up a coffee mug out of the dish rack. Helping himself to a mug of the steamy brew, he took a sip of it, black, then looked back at Jesse. "So, are you going to go and get dressed, or have you decided to add 'nudist' to your list of useless extracurriculars?"

"Seriously, are you starting with me today?" Jesse said, crossing his arms as if instead of being mostly naked, as his brother had pointed out, he was dressed in the height of fashion. "Could we at least have one day that isn't shrouded in your self-righteous bullshit?"

Kerry watched as Damian put down his mug and puffed out his chest, taking an ominous step toward Jesse while Jesse unfurled his arms and postured. His already wide chest became even wider and he jutted out his chin, looking his older brother directly in the eye.

"As if you know anything about self-righteousness or self-determination or anything to do with any type of work-related adjective," Damian said.

"Listen, I'm not in the mood to take your sh—"

Kerry shook her head and took a step forward. She threw both hands up. Her palms stopped in midair, inches from each of the men's faces, silencing them immediately. Having gotten the response she was looking for, she slowly put her hands back down and turned her head, shifting her gaze back and forth between the two, looking them both in the eye.

"One day—" she said, her voice so low that it was almost a whisper, and for a moment she wondered if they could hear her clearly. Kerry cleared her throat and spoke up, a bit louder this time. "One day is all it's been that Mama Joy has been in the ground, and already the two of you are at it as if you're elementary kids on the playground fighting over a toy. What would she think?" Kerry waited a beat as that question was answered with silence.

Jesse's gaze shifted guiltily, while Damian clenched his jaw tighter.

She decided to twist the screw a little more. "I'll tell you what she'd think. She'd be damned disappointed in the two of you. And she'd tell you both to straighten up and get your acts together and behave like the men"—she paused there—"no, the brothers that she raised you to be."

It was then that Damian opened his mouth as if he was about to say something, and Kerry raised her hand once again, shocking herself with her forcefulness and silencing him. Her eyes shifted to Jesse, stopping whatever flippant response he was conjuring up. She gave him a quick up and down. "Now, I suggest you head upstairs and get yourself dressed, because I'm sure Noah and Lucas will be here soon, and you all have plenty to work out. Not to mention you don't want any of the neighborhood ladies coming by with casseroles and getting an eyeful, do you?"

Jesse's eyes went skyward before landing back on her mischie-vously and giving her a half smile. "Well, I don't know—do I?"

She looked at him deadpan and they stared at each other in a mini-standoff for about three seconds.

Jesse blinked first and sighed. "Well, I guess I've gotten my orders," he said to Damian before looking back at Kerry with what could have been a hint of admiration. "Look at you, Kerry Girl."

Maybe not. The Kerry Girl comment skated on the edge of grating, but she'd let it pass, for now. Instead of stinging, for the first time that damned nickname actually soothed her in a weird kind of way. Still, she raised a brow. "It would seem you have, so get going. The day isn't getting any longer."

Jesse turned and headed out of the kitchen and back up the stairs while Kerry forced herself not to focus on his alluring back view.

"Who would've thought you had it in you?"

Damian's words came smooth and matter-of-factly from over her shoulder but hit like a shot.

Kerry turned. He was leaning casually against the counter, coffee cup back in his hand as he sipped, and stared at her with those penetrating eyes of his. "Had what?" she asked, picking up her own, now cold, coffee and going to place it in the microwave. She pressed a few buttons and awaited Damian's answer. "Well?"

"Had so much gumption, I mean. In all these years I've barely heard you utter more than a few words put together, and never with such forcefulness. What's gotten into you?"

Kerry fought to get ahold of both her composure and her thoughts as the microwave dinged. What had gotten into her? What should it matter to her if the brothers fought? That was their business now. Mama Joy was gone and today they were getting together to decide how to handle her affairs. She was, or in a short while would no longer be, the hired help. She internally winced, but she knew she needed to be real now, at least with herself.

There was a lot to consider. Or, correction, the four guys had a lot to consider. Though the property was small, being a four-story brownstone storefront, the fact that it was prime Harlem real estate gave the brothers plenty to think over. In the end, the brothers would most likely close the shop, sell the property, and split whatever was left after the bank got their cut between the four of them. Each going their own way, only to get together every once in a while, on the odd birthday or holiday.

Just thinking of it brought a painful ping to Kerry's heart. There would come a time in the not-so-distant future where they would be nothing more than a fond memory to her. And, well, who knew if they would ever think of her at all, fondly or not. She blinked quickly, careful not to look Damian's way.

She wouldn't cry again. She was determined not to. So instead she took a gulp of her coffee and ignored that its taste had gone sour and thanks to the microwave it was now way too hot. She swallowed the scorching brew anyway. Anything to counter these feelings, and right now a burning tongue beat a teary eye.

"I've talked plenty over the years," she said between hot sips. "It's just that you all weren't listening. Not that it matters." And it didn't, she thought as she put the hot coffee down and busied herself by now shifting the never-ending dishes on the counter, opening and closing the fridge, playing an odd game of jigsaw, then finally pulling out a platter to use for serving later. Calmer and more composed, when she next spoke, it was with a lower tone. "Look, I know it's not any of my business, but I do know that it would make Mama Joy—"

"Mama Joy is dead," Damian said, cutting her off.

"Well, her memory, then," she gritted out, "happy if you guys would just get along. Especially now. As brothers, like she always wanted for you all. More than anything, that meant so much to her."

She looked up when all she got from Damian was silence.

He stared at her for way longer than was comfortable before finally speaking. "What the hell is all this talk about memories? What good will that do any of us now? She was here and now she's gone. Anything more than that doesn't matter."

She stared back at him, then snorted. The snort came out purely by accident, but he was being classic Damian right now. His wall was up and, he thought, firmly in place. But she could see the cracks. With him there was always a crack. "If you say so. But does it matter what you say or what you can see? We all know what she believed and what she wanted."

Once again, Kerry found herself playing a game of chicken.

Shit. She didn't sign up for all this drama so early in the morning. Finally, he blinked. "Well, hey, at least you put a low fire under the unmovable Jesse." He gave her a salutatory nod that was still condescending. "And for that I have to give you credit. It would seem that you learned a lot more from Mama Joy over the years than just knitting. I guess I can call a truce at least for that."

He was being a total ass, but Kerry smiled, the memory of the old shop's proprietor seeping into her mind and telling her to give him this one. "You'd be surprised at what I've picked up."

Just then the front buzzer chimed, and they both turned at the interruption. Two men stood outside. They were light and dark, almost mirror images of each other. There was Lucas with his pale creamy skin, sharp nose, rosebud lips and heavily lidded, deep-set eyes, which most days he kept covered by either shades or his long bangs when he was not on duty at the local firehouse. Then there was Noah, his younger brother. Noah had about two inches on Lucas in height and was two shades deeper in color. Though he wasn't a weight-lifting gym rat like his brother, he did his working out on dance rehearsal floors, so neither of the two were slouches in the body or looks department. The funny thing was that most people never put the two together as biological brothers even though they looked practically the same. Still, even in this day and age, their skin tone difference tripped many up and they placed the brothers as nonbiological just like Damian and Jesse.

"It would seem your brothers are here," Kerry said.

Damian growled. "Why didn't they just come around the back or use the residence entrance? What's with ringing the bell as if this is some damned chateau? I bet they see me here."

"How about you let them in?" Kerry replied. "I'll freshen up the coffee and bring out some of this food. Then I'll go to the storeroom to take care of some inventory and get out of your way. You know, just to make things a little easier while you all, um, talk things out."

Damian nodded, and for a moment Kerry thought she might have seen his impenetrable facade drop. "Thank you," he said, his voice low and steady.

"For what?" Kerry asked.

Damian placed his hand across her forearm, the gentleness of his gesture oddly prickly. "For being here. And for always being here for Mama Joy. I know you meant a lot to her, and that means a lot to me." He blinked. "Well, to all of us."

His out-of-the-ordinary tenderness put Kerry off kilter and she waved a hand. "No need to thank me. Mama Joy was good to me, and I'll always be grateful for that."

Damian nodded as, once again, Lucas and Noah rang the bell and now added a knock to the outside door. "Come on, open up," Noah yelled. "You want us to wait out here all day?"

In a blink, it was as if Damian's wall came up as his eyes hardened and he groaned.

"You better go and let your brothers in before they cause a scene, and I should get to work," Kerry said, thankful for the interruption herself.

Damian started off toward the front but stopped and turned back Kerry's way. "And don't worry, Kerry, we will definitely pay you for your time this week while we settle up."

His words—no, the way he brought up money out of the blue hit Kerry in the chest like a physical blow. She took a small step back and narrowed her eyes. "Did I say anything about money?"

He looked at her, his expression slightly shocked. "No, you didn't, but despite our circumstances and yours, rents still must be paid and lights must stay on. Besides, correct me if I'm wrong, but you don't live on good deeds alone, now, do you?"

Damn that Damian Strong, always bringing things down to the bottom line. Of course she didn't live on good deeds alone. And she hated the do-gooder rep she'd acquired with the Strong brothers. But the one thing she'd learned over the years from working in the shop and seeing how Mama Joy ran things was that what she gave out usually came back, and whether Kerry was paid or not, she would make it, she guessed . . . well, somehow.

Kerry gave herself a mental shake. Of course she would make it. Screw Damian and his stuck-up dollars-and-cents hard-ass logic. Yes, Mama Joy was suddenly gone, but Kerry's life was still on track. She was going places. Besides the totally tragic and sucky unfortunate death of her mentor and sounding board, Kerry knew she still had ample reasons to celebrate. Or at least that was what Mama Joy would be saying right now.

Kerry sure as hell didn't feel it. But it was true there were reasons, slim as they were. She'd finally obtained her degree in children's counseling and art therapy. She was working at the center this summer part-time but hoped for a full-time position as soon as funds opened up, which she'd been assured they would. Well, moderately assured. She and Mama Joy had happily talked about the day when she'd finally stop working in the shop for good. Though those talks for her were always bittersweet. She could admit now that though, yes, she loved working with the kids and, yes, enjoyed her work at the center, she never was in all that much of a hurry to leave the shop. It was as if she was torn between the wonderful warmth of the cocoon of Strong Knits and the reality that was the rest of the world that she knew she had to face but was never quite ready. Ridiculous, but there it was.

She internally snorted. Now *here* it was. The world was here, right in her face, and she suddenly had no choice but to go out and deal with it, whether ready or not. Though, under the worst of circumstances now, she could see clearly that all those extra years Mama Joy had acquiesced and given her hours that fit easily with whatever school or part-time center schedule she had was not really for business purposes but most likely for both of their comfort. Fact was, they were just used to each other. Kerry would tease Mama Joy, saying she'd never truly get rid of her, that no matter what job she got she'd pay Mama Joy to let her show up and put in a few hours a week in the shop. Little did she know that Mama Joy would beat her out the door first. That wasn't how it was meant to be. Mama Joy was supposed to always be there. Happy and in her shop, a sanctuary for them all from the outside storms.

Finally, Kerry gave Damian a sharp look. "Like I said, did I say anything to you about money? Go and let your brothers in. We all have a lot of work to get through. There is plenty to get cleaned up and cleared out around here. No use in any of us wasting any more time than necessary."

SCREW YOU, DAMIAN, Jesse thought as he angrily tugged on his jeans and then pulled his T-shirt over his head. He was still fuming after a quick shower that had done nothing to cool his mood. Of course his brother would show up at just the wrong time and assume the absolute worst about him. That was always Damian's way. Hell, that was everyone's way when it came to him. They always assumed the worst.

Jesse, the family fuckup. Jesse's so lazy. Jesse has no ambition. Jesse the player. Well, that one maybe he had to own, but yeah, he knew how they each thought of him, and it wasn't too highly. Jesse let out a sigh and slipped his feet into his well-worn Chucks. He ran his hand through his locs, untangling them as best he could, finally giving up and searching the top of his nightstand for a band to pull them back and out of his face. He didn't need his more straitlaced brothers railing at him about his hair today.

Letting out a long breath, he then sucked in deeply, preparing to go downstairs and face his brothers for the first time without the backup of Mama Joy as a buffer. For so many years he took for granted the calming strength of having her at his back. Though in many ways the Strong brothers were their own little mini crew. A source of silent protection from the ever-looming threat of all that could harm them: the system stacked against them, judgment, their race, police, gangs—the list sometimes felt endless. But Mama Joy was his true protection within the house, or at least he had thought so. Jesse snorted. Probably all his brothers had thought the same thing. Mama Joy had that way about her.

Still, she was the one who got *him*. She was the only one who did. Understanding his creative quirks. She never judged or expected more from him than he was willing to give at any time. Jesse paused as he thought over what had just run through his mind. *More than he was willing to give.* Damn, he really was a selfish bastard.

Swallowing hard against the image of Kerry that came up and swam before his eyes, Jesse fought against his emotions. But Kerry was right in what she'd said in the kitchen—Mama Joy would be disappointed with how they were acting. How he was acting. It was as if nothing had changed and he was going about business as usual, disappointing her in death as he had all his life.

He looked over at the baseball bat, now back behind his bedroom door. What had he been thinking anyway? Running downstairs in his underwear like some fool, then standing there in front of Kerry like a broke-down Calvin Klein model? Yeah, he knew it was only to mess with Kerry and get a rise out of her. But it wasn't fair, and she didn't deserve it. He was clearly being childish and deflecting from feelings he didn't want to face. The thought of her teary and warm in his arms made guilt rise even higher. No, it wasn't fair. Bringing his pain to her. No matter how close they were or how good and perfect she felt, Jesse knew it wasn't right.

Besides, Kerry wasn't one of his normal hookups or even close to a potential hookup. No, she was different. She was more like family—well, as far as not being any relation could be like family. But then again, that was pretty much his whole family. Still, she didn't deserve his teasing, not when she was there to help them.

Kerry deserved better, and he knew Mama Joy would have wanted him to be better. Jesse let out a sigh and looked toward the hall stairs as he heard the sounds of what must be Lucas and Noah joining the fray. He swallowed, then stepped out into the hall and gave a glance to the closed door of Mama Joy's room on the opposite end of the hallway. Better or not, it was time to face the music.

Decisions must be made, and it was time for him to finally step up and take his place once and for all to be the type of Strong brother that Mama Joy always wanted him to be.

"ARE YOU OUT of your damned mind?" Of course, this question that wasn't really a question but more of a statement of fact was coming from Damian's lips.

"No, I'm not," Jesse said, trying his best to stay calm. It would do no good for him to yell or, hell, show much emotion for that matter. Not when it came to sparring with Damian. Even though his decision and, he knew, even those of his brothers would be purely based on emotion if they ended up going his way.

"In what world does it make sense to keep the shop open? Shit, Mama Joy was barely able to keep it hanging on all these years," Damian said. "How she made do, we'll never know, since she never shared her financial problems with us. Not even with me. But I'm sure a large part of it was from city grants, subsidies and some of her magic luck, which, now that she's gone, is also gone right along with her."

Jesse thumbed his hand toward Damian and looked at his other two brothers. "See what I mean. An asshole. And worse, an asshole with no vision or faith."

"Oh, come on with that bull," Damian said. "How far is some

crap like faith really going to get any of us? Besides that, when have you ever had vision?"

Jesse raised a brow and gave his brother a knowing look. "Really? I can't believe you're going there."

Damian threw up his hands. "You know what, I'm not. Because this conversation is ridiculous. The fact remains that none of us know anything about running this place. Not that we'd have the time even if we did." Damian snorted and gave Jesse a side-eye. "All except you, that is."

"He's right," Lucas piped in as he pushed back and got up from his seat at the large farmhouse table, on the way snagging another one of the muffins that Kerry had put out. So very Lucas. He would not be goaded into rushing his words and instead took the long way around. He pushed back his bangs, which had grown long over the past week, with Mama Joy's death and the funeral arrangements. Jesse knew he'd trim them soon before going back to work. He watched as Lucas leisurely walked around the display of new yarns that Mama Joy had set up in the corner by the front window the week before last. With his muscular but still trim firefighter frame, Lucas could barely fit around the tight display and had to take it sideways. Still he looked comfortable as he picked up a skein of marled wool in shades of blue and held it up, inspecting the various tones, giving it a caress before placing it back in the basket. He took a bite of the muffin in his other hand and looked at Jesse as he chewed. The long, dark, assessing stare gave Jesse not a clue about which way his brother would go. Finally, Lucas spoke. "Come on, Jes. Though it sounds like a nice idea in theory, Damian is right."

Shit. Not the way Jesse was hoping.

"None of us really know anything about the shop or the day-to-day running of it. This was Ma Joy's domain," Lucas said, using the sweet endearment that the four of them sometimes called her, before he continued, "and pretty much just our pass-through on the way upstairs to our living quarters."

"You mean our home?" Jesse countered, and watched as Lucas's jaw tightened. "You know as well as I do that this place has been way more than just a pass-through. And even though you're at the firehouse most nights now, you still pass through here plenty. We all do." Jesse turned toward Damian. "You included, whether you want to admit it or not. It's not like you totally gave up your room-slash-closet. But using it as just storage space, I'm sure, makes giving it up easy for you."

Damian glared. "Of course giving up our home isn't easy. How can it be an easy decision?" For a moment Jesse thought he may have seen a flash of pain come across Damian's features. "But how can it be considered our home without her?" They all fell silent and the air went impossibly still. Damian shook his head. "No, it's too much. And I don't think you can handle it. She could barely handle it. You would be in for some really hard work, pretty much for the first time in your life. And we each have our own lives. We can't be here to bail you out when you fuck it up."

Jesse clenched his fists. "I'm not going to fuck it up."

"How do you know?" Damian countered. "Do you know how many businesses fail in a year?"

"But this is an established business with a built-in clientele and reputation."

"And I'm coming to you all now saying we could sell and have cash in hand. There are already buyers who have been getting in touch with me," Damian countered.

Jesse shook his head. "Really? It's been one day since the funeral and you expect us to believe that? You really are the worst. Are they getting in touch with you or are you getting in touch with them?"

Damian glared at him. "Believe what you want. You will anyway. You've always been a dreamer and in your own head. Mama Joy went along and fed into that, but it's time for it to stop. Buyers have been getting in touch with me and Mama Joy for years. And like back then, I wouldn't entertain them, because doing so would feel like betraying Ma by turning my back on you. So how about you shut up and listen for once."

"Okay, this is getting a little off topic, and we need to calm down," Noah said by way of cooling the room.

Jesse breathed deeply. Noah was right, and he knew he wouldn't get anywhere with Damian. He also knew he had to get it together and get ahold of himself. It was time to change tactics. Letting go and overplaying his hand would do him no good. So instead he focused and mentally centered himself before standing.

"Come on, Noah," he said changing plays and switching brothers. Noah thought differently than Damian and Lucas. He always had, though he traveled a lot now as a professional backup dancer and was about to go on tour again. He'd only recently gone in on a sublet, and Jesse knew he didn't want to lose the assurance their home here gave him. Just like his brothers, Noah still kept the bulk of his memories stored in the fourth-floor space he shared with Lucas. Looking into Noah's eyes, Jesse could see how torn he was. If Jesse had any real shot, it was probably through getting Noah on his side.

"Noah, you get what I'm talking about. You know how important the shop—this space and our home is." He decided to add a little hard reality to the emotional side of things. "Not to mention, you're only subletting now. You"—he looked at Damian and Lucas then—"as well as all of us know that there are no guarantees in life. Your tour will be over pretty quickly. Apartments, rents and landlords are unstable as shit. Do we really want to give up on our home so easily?"

There was a satisfying grunt from the Damian corner of the shop with that one, and Jesse continued his campaign on Noah.

"Hell, half your skill, talent and control you learned from Mama Joy here knitting."

Noah shrugged. "I wouldn't go that far. I do have some talent of my own."

"Of course you do, but you were able to focus it because of what you got through her. That you can't deny. Now, how can we just let what she built go so easily?" Jesse watched as shame clouded over Noah's face. He afforded himself a breath of relief as he looked at each of his brothers. "We all learned valuable lessons from Mama Joy in this very room, and everything she taught us made us who we are. It helped center me and fixed the focus problems that I had in school."

"Yeah, too bad it never helped focus you on any sort of career path," Damian quickly countered, his voice full of snark.

Jesse sighed. "Seriously, do you list 'professional shithead' on your Tinder profile? Because if not, you could be sued for false advertising."

"How about I come over there and show you just how much of a shithead I can be?" Damian snapped back.

Lucas stepped between the two of them. "Enough. We don't have time for this. Decisions need to be made." He looked at Jesse. "Listen, Jes, I get what you're saying. And keeping the shop open, I know, would mean a lot to Mama Joy. But I really don't see any way that can be done. Noah's got his tour, Damian's got his work, and I've got my schedule at the firehouse."

"And?" Jesse asked.

"And what?" Lucas replied.

Jesse was exasperated. Exasperated and furious. Did they really think so little of him? "Are you all seriously not even going to consider me to run the shop?"

He watched as his brother did little to shield the disbelief that ran across his expression. Lucas's tone when he spoke was slow and placating, as if he was talking to a small child, and it did nothing but infuriate Jesse more. It was made all the worse when he placed his hand on Jesse's shoulder. "Like I said, Jes, it all sounds well and good, but I don't see how we can make it work." Jesse didn't miss the emphasis Lucas used on the word "we." Why was he using "we" when he was talking about "he"? He shrugged hard, pushing his brother's hand away.

"Well, if *we* can't make it work, what about *me*? I'm asking you all to consider me for once. Think of what I can do here."

Lucas was shaking his head when Jesse heard Noah shift. He turned then and caught the self-satisfied smirk that was plastered across Damian's face. "I think we're done with this subject," Damian started. "Now let's get down to business and talk about how we're going to liquidate the inventory, divide the insurance while paying off any debt and take care of dividing the rest of the estate. There is still plenty to take care of and lots of paperwork to look into. Mama Joy wasn't the best when it came to record keeping, so the sooner we get on it the better."

Jesse looked around the shop as Damian droned on as if his previous speech had never even happened. Of course Damian would take over. Since he was the oldest, the one with the highest degree and the resident financial advisor, it made sense that he'd be in charge, but it didn't feel right. Nothing about this felt right.

As Jesse's gaze roamed, all he saw now were the colorful remnants of Mama Joy's dreams, and the idea of packing them up and sending them off made a hollow cavern form deep in his chest. He felt rage begin to smolder, the first small embers of a low, burning heat that licked at his toes and worked its way up his legs, quickly taking over his entire body. He banged his hands down hard on the wooden table, causing his brothers to turn in shock.

"Shit, bro! You're losing it!" Noah said, coming over to his side and clapping his hand on Jesse's shoulder. "Calm down, Jesse. I know this is hard. But understand, it's hard for all of us. You have to see that this decision is for the best."

"The best for who?" he asked, pushing Noah's hand away and hitting them each with a challenging stare. "It's not for the best, it's just the easiest. You all are up in here acting like a bunch of goddamn wimps, and Kerry was right when she said earlier that Mama Joy would be ashamed of us. How can you just close down her life's work at the first hint of adversity? Didn't she teach us anything? What was all her sacrificing for?" Jesse ran a frustrated hand over his forehead. "Dammit. She gave us so much. What if she shut down when things were hard with us? Without her, where would each of us be?"

He paused for breath then, and instead of being met with an argument, he was met with silence. Though he didn't know exactly where they would be without Mama Joy, he sure as hell knew it wasn't in as good a position as they were in now. Even though, at eight, he was young when Mama Joy took him in, he was already a handful, and he knew after having been in and out of two foster homes pretty quickly that he didn't have any place else but back to the group home to go when she took him in. He also knew that Noah and Lucas were on the verge of being separated when Mama Joy took them in as a pair. And as for Mr. Know-It-All Smart-Ass, he had been this close to juvenile hall or worse, and he knew it too.

Finally, Jesse cleared his throat and spoke again. "Not to mention this shop is an institution in this neighborhood. We close and what's gonna take its place? Some chain coffee shop or another goddammed CVS? This is one of the last family-owned businesses in Harlem. We owe it to her and to the neighborhood to at least try to stay open."

"That's your problem right there, Jesse. You are too sentimental, and sentimentality won't get you anything but heartache. It sure as hell won't pay the bills or keep food in your belly," Damian said.

Jesse looked at his brother. "You mean like it did for you most of your life?"

Damian glared at him, or maybe he was glowering. Whatever. He probably thought he was being all scary and shit, going his intimidation route. And on anyone else it just might work. He was sharp, that brother of his, so well put together—every part of him exuded downtown corporate businessman. Yep, his brother had cleaned himself up so well that no one would suspect he was an abandoned kid originally from the Bronx, shuttled from foster home to foster home until finally Lady Luck smiled upon him and he ended up just like them, in the arms of Mama Joy. No, no one would know that Mr. Dapper-Dan Mind-on-His-Money-and-Money-on-His-Mind Strong, as it were, when he first came here, was two grades behind for his age and labeled a discipline problem who would never even make it out of middle school, let alone get a scholarship to one of the best business schools in the country. Jesse knew though, and worse yet, Damian knew that Jesse knew who he was and where he came from. Not that his story was all that unique. At least not in this house. They all had one like it, or close to it. And they all owed what they had now to the love and teachings of Mama Joy and the neighborhood that had taken them in as one of its own.

Damian looked like he was about to protest again when there was a knock on the shop's door. The four of them turned in unison toward the interruption with what may have been a bit of relief. But the relief turned to surprise when they saw the intruder was a young kid of about ten. He was medium-brown skinned with short-cropped hair, extra faded on the sides and a little higher on the top. He wore basketball shorts that were slung low, though maybe that was mostly due to his thin frame and not to his trying to make any sort of fashion statement. The boy had paired the shorts with a white tank top, which also looked at least one size too big. He looked at them through the door with wide brown eyes while one hand clutched a brown paper bag.

Lucas pointed at the sign on the door. "Sorry, we're closed," he said through the doorway.

"I know," the kid yelled to the door. "Um, yeah. I know you're closed. I was just hoping I could come in for a moment."

Lucas turned around and looked at Jesse. "You know this kid?"

Jesse took a step forward. He didn't recognize the kid, but he did recognize the shakiness in his voice. Jesse shook his head. "No, I don't. But he's young and looks harmless. Open up to see what he wants. Maybe he's selling candy bars or something."

"As if we want or need some candy bars?" Lucas said.

"I could use a candy bar," Noah countered.

Jesse shook his head. That was his brothers. Ready to go to blows over something serious one minute, and minds on candy the next.

Lucas sighed. "Fine. Lemme see what he's got. If he's got the ones with almonds, we can get some."

Damian snorted from over to his left while Lucas opened the door. "What is it we can do for you? Are you selling candy or something? I've got two dollars, but I don't want any if you don't have the ones with nuts."

The boy shook his head and swallowed. "Um. You're one of the Strong guys, right?"

Lucas grinned, then flexed. "I've been told I'm all right."

The boy gave him a "Really, are you serious right now?" look that made Jesse's morning, then shook his head. "I mean you're one of Ms. Joy's sons, right? The Asian fireman one."

Ouch, kid. Jesse could only imagine Lucas's face at that one. He hated being singled out as 'the Asian one' out of the four of them, having gotten plenty of it most of his life. It barely let up now that he worked for the FDNY. But it seemed to be the kid's day because Lucas gave him a pass. "Yeah, I guess I've been called that. Though 'firefighter' is good enough."

"You've been called worse," Jesse yelled, and got a sharp look from Lucas that had him quickly turning back to the boy. "What can we do for you?"

"You're another one," the boy said.

"The one without a job," Damian mumbled.

Jesse then noticed just how tightly the boy held on to the brown paper bag in his hand. He clutched it at his side, crinkling the top, while he twisted his feet over on the sides of his sneakers nervously. "Yeah. That's right. I'm Jesse, and these are my brothers."

The boy looked up and around at the other three men with what seemed like awe and a bit of fear. Still, he swallowed and continued to talk. "I'm Errol Miller and, well, I just wanted to tell you that I'm very sorry for your loss." The boy swallowed again, and Jesse could tell he was now fighting back a tear.

"Thank you. We appreciate that. Did you know Mama Joy well?"

The boy looked at all of them nervously once again and it seemed as if he was wondering how much was safe to say. "Well, not all that good. I had just started to come here with the summer program. And I, um, I liked it. So, she said I could come back anytime. I did, well, a few times. She was nice. I heard some of the kids talking about what happened to her and it made me sad." He got a hitch in his voice. Jesse looked at Lucas, catching his brother's eye over the boy's head. "Real sad," the boy continued. "So, when I told my mom about it, she said it would be okay if I came by and gave my condolences. That it was the right thing to do."

It was then that Kerry walked by the back kitchen opening, and she paused at the doorway. "Errol! What are you doing here?" she said, stepping into the main lounge.

The boy brightened at the sight of Kerry, his entire face opening up and his demeanor changing as he smiled at her. But then, as if remembering his mission, he quickly sobered. "Hi, Miss Kerry. I just wanted to come by to say how sorry I am about Ms. Joy."

Kerry stepped forward and took the boy into her arms in a hug. "Oh, Errol. Thank you so much. That is so kind of you."

Errol pulled back and unclenched his fists from the bag he was holding. He looked up at Kerry with a sad longing in his eyes and Jesse could see he was debating a question. "Will the shop be open again for us kids to come in for a lesson?"

Kerry looked around at Jesse and his brothers, then back at Errol. "Errol, I'm not sure. The family has to do some figuring out about that."

Errol let out a breath and looked at Jesse. The boy nodded soberly as if he fully understood, despite his young age. Once again, he clenched the brown paper bag tightly.

As if she knew he wanted something more, Kerry questioned him. "What you got there, Errol? Is it anything I can help you with?"

Once again, Errol looked at all the brothers, and it was then that Jesse could see the embarrassment as it bloomed across his features. He looked at Kerry and put his shoulders back before reaching into his bag and pulling out a small set of circular knitting needles and what appeared to be the beginning of a hat cast on, though Jesse could see he had gotten himself into a tangled mass of dropped stitches. "I think I've made some mistakes here and could use some help, so I was hoping there would be another class," Errol said.

Kerry's smile was warm and nonjudgmental as she gently rubbed the top of his head. "Yes, it looks like you do have a little bit of a mess here."

She looked across to each of them, a hint of warning in her eyes before they softened. Lucas, then Noah, then Damian and finally stopping on Jesse. "But don't worry, it's just a few dropped stitches. In knitting there's never a problem that can't be fixed. It's only yarn. Now, why not come back to the kitchen with me and let's see if we can't work this out."

Jesse watched as the boy let out a breath and seemed to brighten, as if the weight of the world was lifted from his shoulders. He followed Kerry to the back, and Jesse could hear her as she gave the boy a snack and then began to patiently teach him how to fix his mess.

Jesse turned to his brothers. "Just give me a few months. Let me try to keep the shop open for a few months—six months to a year at most—and see if I can't keep it afloat. The shop is our legacy, and one that meant too much to Mama Joy and the community to just let it go. Not without giving it a try at least. Hell, it's our last name on the awning," he said, pulling his hole card by bringing up the Strong name they all collectively took on when Mama Joy became their official adoptive mother.

"Yeah, but how can you do it alone? The fact remains that we all have jobs we still have to do. You said it's *our* legacy—it wouldn't be fair for you to be the only one working here, taking this on all alone," Lucas said.

Just then Kerry stepped back into the main room with Errol. She walked the boy to the front door, letting him out with a wave, then flipped the lock. Turning to all of them, she looked at Jesse, then switched her gaze to Lucas, breaking the silence and rocking their world. "He won't have to do it alone," she said. "I'll stay on and work with him, at least until he gets the hang of how the shop runs."

Jesse blinked. The woman standing before him was Kerry, but suddenly she bore little resemblance to the quiet, shy Kerry who had always hovered in various corners of the shop, a shadow to Mama Joy. No, this woman was all confidence and intelligence underneath her curly twists and thick-rimmed eyeglass frames. He looked at her deeper. There was something new and different behind her all-knowing chestnut-brown eyes. The corner of her lips quirked up, twitched ever so slightly as if the secrets of the world were hidden behind their full lusciousness just itching to escape.

Wait. Luscious lips? Secrets? What was he thinking, and what was she talking about, staying on? This was Kerry. Their Kerry Girl. Why was she doing this? And how could he let her? She had just finished school—a few years late, but she'd received her degree and now had her own plans and dreams lined up. This was her chance to get out. To move on. Why wasn't she taking it?

It was Damian who voiced Jesse's concerns out loud. "Why would you do something like that? You've just finished school, Kerry, you've gotten your degree. Why would you put your plans on hold to help us?"

Kerry was quiet as she seemed to be thinking while she looked around the shop, her already soft brown eyes growing wistful and slightly sad before she focused back on them. The look she gave Jesse went through him and seemed to reach down deep, past his heart even, all the way to his soul, before she blinked and turned to Damian to answer his question. "Maybe it's like you said. Maybe I've learned a lot more from Mama Joy than you all even know. And I think it's time for me to share that before I take the next step and move on. I know it's what she would have wanted."

4

S HIT! DAMMIT, AND shit once more!

Kerry couldn't believe what she'd committed to.

What if Damian was right? She found herself still wondering hours later as she made her way to her afternoon job at the community center. Though she didn't want to admit it, she was putting a portion of her life on hold for their needs. Or were they her needs? Wait, who truly needed who in this convoluted situation?

The whole thing made little to no sense, and if she had any sense at all she would have just kept her trap shut and stayed out of their business. Mama Joy was gone. And during the woman's life, though she had given lots of her time and energy to Kerry, Kerry had been just as good to her. It wasn't as if there was some sort of karmic debt that she had to pay, so why was she still so intent on inserting herself into the Strong family's life?

"The daughter I never had," she'd heard plenty of times. Kerry knew she'd made Mama Joy happy in life. And now that Mama Joy was gone, in a way it did feel like Kerry had lost what was essentially a second mother to her. The woman had helped raise her in ways that her own mother hadn't and maybe could not. But if she really wanted to make Mama Joy happy, she'd not hold her sons up in their moving on, and she also wouldn't hold her own life up. She'd take her degree, go harder on LinkedIn, Monster, Indeed and every other redundant-ass app and site out there and up her job search. Kerry let out a huff. Not that she hadn't already been doing that. But come on, it wasn't like they were dropping dream positions from the sky into overdue do-gooder graduates' laps.

Kerry frowned. When she'd started on her degree work, it did seem like all she thought she wanted, but somewhere along the way things started to get muddled. Yes, she still had a passion for the kids, and sure, there was still a simmer of a dream in her heart of doing more, getting out of the shop and making things better for the community. However, after working at the center and seeing firsthand the setup and system of things, the frustrating bureaucracy, the way it—dammit—felt like every freaking deck was stacked against Black and brown kids, she wondered if she could truly be effective. And honestly, she wondered if she'd ever feel as fulfilled as when she was giving knitting classes to the children side by side with Mama Joy.

But would this make Mama Joy happy? Kerry knew it sure as hell wouldn't make her mother happy. Both she and Mama Joy agreed on the fact that her degree would take her out of the shop, and if her mother had it her way, further than their Harlem neighborhood. It was her mother's dream for her. Not that it was something new. A version of that dream was dreamed by just about every low-income mother from every low-income urban neighborhood. But why was that the ultimate dream?

Kerry frowned. She knew she couldn't stay outside in the heat mulling over it all much longer though and made a swift turn at the corner of 145th and Eighth Avenue and started up the hill, breaking into even more of a sweat. The comfortable morning had morphed into an uncomfortably hot afternoon, and perspiration crept down the center of her back. Kerry shifted her tote from one shoulder to the other to prevent the digging from making too deep a mark in her flesh as she let her questions and uncertainties rattle around in her head.

She didn't know what had made her walk out from the kitchen like she had, nor what had caused her to make her declaration in front of the brothers. It was as if she was hopped up on some sort of superwoman ego trip. Marching in there in the middle of the four Strong brothers and making her declaration like she was some sort of female supreme ruler. She shuddered. Just thinking about it gave her a slightly heady feeling. Still, she must have been out of her damned mind.

Who knew? Maybe it was the emotion of the past week, the photos in the kitchen that morning, little Errol Miller, or maybe it was Jesse and those dammed body-hugging briefs. Either way, all of it worked together and put her in the uncomfortable position of not wanting to let go of her present life without at least some sort of fight.

If only Mama Joy had had the same option. Kerry stilled as the memory of Jesse and his brothers arguing that morning came back to her. Who knew, maybe the dead woman did, in a weird, round-about kind of way. Kerry felt it when she heard Jesse fighting so hard against his brothers and all their reservations. His strong words and fierce determination were what gave her the final bit of courage she needed to step out from the back of the shop and pro-pel herself forward to the front.

Still, she couldn't help but have serious doubts. Doubts and at the same time a strange sense of hope. When she'd gone into the shop that morning, she'd thought the brothers would surely make the decision to close. That Jesse would be the main one behind that decision. To her, though she didn't doubt his love for Mama Joy, he seemed the main one who would want to take his share of the proceeds, then cut and run. Go on to sunnier, possibly more beachy pastures. The type where the women were plentiful and wore fewer clothes in the winter months. Hearing him talk about Mama Joy and what she meant to them, as boys and as men—it touched her in the most profound way.

The fact that Jesse still felt a connection to the shop and the more unbelievable fact that he'd rallied so fervently for the things that Mama Joy had worked so hard for stunned Kerry. She could admit it hit her hard. Harder than she ever expected. And, at the same time, it had softened her. Softened her toward Jesse in a way that she honestly didn't want to be softened. In a way that probably wasn't quite safe.

It had her thinking about all the years she spent trying to ignore the feelings she had for him while she watched him flutter in and out of the shop on his way to meet this girl or hook up with that one. And it had her thinking of all the lost hours spent daydreaming about him as she mindlessly knit one, purled two and imagined him tangling his fingers between her own as he took the yarn from her hands and pulled her into a kiss.

Ugh. What a dummy she was. Stupid girly dreams wasted on a boy who never even looked her way. And now here she was, a grown-ass woman and still in the same space, giving up her time for his dreams. She was sure once her mother got wind of the situation, she'd parrot back some form of those exact same words. Not that her mother had a leg to stand on, but still, it wasn't a conversation Kerry was looking forward to.

She let out a frustrated sigh as she opened the door to the community center. But then relief washed over her as the cool blast of air from the newly installed air conditioner hit her mercifully in the face. Maybe she'd just let that whole conversation wait as long as possible. She'd only committed to a short time at the shop, just long enough to get them on their feet, and after that she'd be free to pursue her own track. She might be on to another job by the time her mom was any the wiser.

The sound of children's laughter mixed with the occasional low conversation permeated Kerry's ears as she made her way through the community center's halls. A little girl came running out of one of the classrooms at top speed, her high pigtails bouncing. "Whoa! Slow down, Imara." Kerry held up a cautious hand to the child. "You know running in the halls is not allowed," she said softly though sternly.

The little girl looked up at her with wide, dark eyes. "I'm sorry, Miss Kerry. But I really gotta go. I was holding it for so long before Mr. Watkins saw my hand."

Kerry nodded and stepped out of the girl's way. "Okay, well then, be off with you. But take it slow and be careful."

"Yes, miss," the girl said as she made her way down the hall, this time not running but shuffling at a fast run/walk pace.

Kerry shook her head. Poor Imara. She probably really did have to go. Mr. Watkins was getting up there in age and was usually so focused on his set lesson plan that, honestly, he barely noticed when the kids were trying to grab his attention. He, along with many of the other teachers, desperately needed an assistant in the classroom for just that reason. But the center was happy to have teachers like Mr. Watkins, who, though they could have retired a few years back, stayed on to teach in the communities they knew and loved for the children who needed them the most.

With the upcropping of charter schools that went year-round, the parents of the kids who went to public schools had been desperate to find ways to supplement, as best they could, their children's learning. Hence this year-round after-school and summer learning center where Kerry worked part-time. It was one of the places she had considered moving on to since completing her degree—though she hated to admit that the lack of adequate compensation as compared to the private sector made it difficult to keep working there high on her list. She couldn't stay on part-time forever, and as of now, there were no full-time positions open with the salary and benefits she needed to cover her rent. No matter how much she wanted to stick around, she still had to be somewhat practical. *Yeah, rich from the woman who just volunteered to continue working at a knitting shop that will most likely close within three months.* She shook her head at her own folly.

Just then one of her coworkers, Alison, peeped her head out of her office. Alison was an ESL specialist and the assistant department program director. Everyone tried not to be too salty about the fact that she had achieved this title at twenty-four, but Alison on her best days made that challenging. Throwing off clearly non–New Yorker airs while using extravagant hand gestures that mimicked early-nineties B-boys and bordered on gang signs, she whined constantly about the problems in her whole-assed two-bedroom condo in a new building on 138th Street that used to be affordable housing but was no longer.

"Hey, gurl!" Alison drawled, or said in what she believed passed for a drawl.

Gurl?

"Hello, Alison," Kerry said, quickly screwing her face to look like she was both interested but also in a rush to get to her class.

"How are you?" The drawl switched to a pout as she jutted out her arms as if she wanted Kerry to come in for a hug.

Kerry looked at her and blinked. Today, Alison wore a linen one-piece jumper that was about three sizes too big for her slim frame with a tiny yellow tee underneath emblazoned with an owl wearing huge glasses. Her brown hair was center parted and plaited into two French braids. Kerry and her friend Val had previously had to politely explain that *No, ma'am, they should not be called boxer braids.* She looked more like a summer camp CIT than anybody's director of anything, but whatever. Alison waved her hands and Kerry realized they were still outstretched. Kerry nodded and, instead of a hug, coughed, and watched Alison's hands go down.

"Are you okay? I didn't expect you today with the funeral and all. I thought you'd take the week. I was prepared to cover for you."

I'm sure Val would have loved that, Kerry thought, thinking of her friend who she often co-taught with.

"Thanks so much. But I'm good. Or I will be. I appreciate the concern and the offer of help. Now I'd better get to class to set up."

Alison nodded as she poked her bottom lip out farther. "All right then, but let's do drinks soon. We are neighbors and all."

Kerry screwed her good face on tight. "Yeah, that we are."

Alison grinned. "Harlem world!" she whooped as Kerry caught sight of Emily, Alison's assistant and another ESL specialist—well, the real ESL specialist, who grimaced and gave Kerry an apologetic look.

Poor Emily, Kerry thought. First, there was the fact that despite funding and the need for specialists in the classrooms, she'd been saddled with the job as assistant to Alison, which essentially meant she did all the real work that Alison failed to cover in the classroom. And on top of that, Emily being the nice—maybe too nice—white person with a diversity-challenged boss, she felt the need to constantly apologize for said diversity train wreck. It was as if the woman walked around with a constant but silent "I'm with Stupid" tee on.

Kerry gave her a "Stay strong" look to counter her "I'm so sorry for this disaster" lip bite before continuing down the hall.

"Harlem world! So we're doing that today?" Kerry's best friend, partner in crime, homegirl and all that came with it, Valencia Gibson, said as Kerry walked into the arts and crafts room.

"Oh stop, she tries," Kerry said.

"You stop. It's not as if you were not thinking the same thing," Val responded. "That Lil Miss Sweet act can fool some of the girls, but not this one."

Kerry smiled, but her eyes rolled to the ceiling, betraying her true thoughts. "You got me. Yeah, Harlem world by way of Stamford. I so cannot."

"But Ms. CIT did have a point with asking what you're doing here today. What's the deal? I would have covered for you. Even if I had to deal with her. You didn't have to come in."

"I told you I'd try and come in today. I knew it would be busy and the kids would be riled up after returning from swimming. I didn't want to leave you shorthanded," Kerry said, storing her bag in the drawer on the side of the desk.

Val frowned, the small furrow barely wrinkling her smooth mocha-toned skin. Still she continued with what she was doing, sorting construction paper by color to prepare for the next project before the kids came in. "Sure, but I didn't think you'd actually do it. With today being the day after the funeral and all. I know how close you were with Mama Joy. Plus, I thought you'd be helping out over there, getting them straight."

There was a pause, and Kerry could practically feel Val's wheels turning. Kerry knew her friend would have plenty to say when she found out about Kerry staying on at the shop, and honestly, she didn't know what side of the fence Val would be on. Either way she'd be sure to give Kerry an earful.

Val continued. "She sure will be missed. The kids are so disappointed they won't have the occasional trips to her shop anymore or their knitting sessions with the two of you."

"I was already over there this morning doing what I could," Kerry said. "And the children shouldn't give up hope just yet." She moved to help sort and lay out colored pencils.

Val's brows went impossibly higher, arching even more suggestively as her full lips twisted up with a smirk. "Oh, were you now? Over there this mor-ning." She was busy accentuating her words, then suddenly stopped when she caught on to the rest of what Kerry had said. "What do you mean not give up hope?"

Kerry shook her head but couldn't help the quirk in her lip. She was used to getting teased by Val about her work in the shop. It was mildly annoying, but right now she'd take mildly annoying over hugs and sympathy. She'd had enough of that over the past week and plenty of it heaped on her yesterday. She'd seen enough tears and shed more than she thought possible herself over the death of Mama Joy, so right now, even teasing from Val was a welcome distraction. But still, maybe she should have kept the hope comment to herself until she'd squared it all in her mind and double-confirmed with Jesse that the shop would remain open. "No need to get all twisty," she said, trying to keep her voice matter of fact. "You know it's nothing like that."

"Nothing like what?" Val asked, doing her quick-witted loose-thread-finding thing and giving it a tug. "If it was nothing like that, then you wouldn't know what *that* I was talking about. But since you know what *that* I am talking about, then I'm going to assume that *that* must have clearly crossed your mind." Valencia gave her body a little shake. Today that body was clad in stretch jeans rolled at the ankle and a flowing blouse that did little to hide her shapely figure, but Kerry was sure Val thought it was demure enough to be considered downright churchy for a teacher.

"I'm talking about the *that* that you're talking about. And that *that* has not crossed my mind," Kerry said, then frowned at her outright lie as the image of Jesse in his underwear flashed in her mind. She waved her hand in front of her face. "What are we talking about anyway? This is getting silly."

Val laughed. "Well, it's good to see you smile either way." Her friend's expression got serious as she looked Kerry in the eye. "I know how hard this has been for you, and I know it's going to be a long road, but I hope to see you smile more in the future. It will take time, but you will get through this." Val got a wistful look as her eyes went slightly skyward. "Lord knows I'm still overdue to take my time with my grandmother."

Kerry stepped forward and gave her friend a hug. Val had lost her grandmother two years before, and though for the most part she continued to soldier on with a smile and a wink, Kerry knew how hard the loss was on her. "I know, hon, I know."

But in true Val form, her friend quickly shimmied out of her embrace and looked up at her. "So, tell me, were all the brothers in attendance today? Over there being just as wickedly fine as they ought not to be?"

Kerry cocked her head to the side, then continued walking around the classroom as she placed colored pencils down. "They were and they are," she gritted out.

"Woman, you say that like it's a bad thing."

"Well—" Kerry paused, looking at Val cautiously. "I'm not sure it's a good thing. Not the 'fine' part. That's neither here nor there."

"Well, they can put it over here. Any of them and all of it. Especially that Lucas—or is it Noah, or maybe it's Damian? Oh, what do I care? Either, any or all of them will do—" Val interrupted herself. "But are you talking about the fact that they've made decisions on the shop? Sorry, hon, but you knew that was coming. Without Ms. Joy—well, even with her—how long did you expect the shop to go on?"

Kerry twisted her lip as she heard the sound of their kids coming up the hall. She knew that in a matter of moments they'd be inundated with the clamor of thirty-four children bearing down on them, ready to take part in the creative assignment of the day. She looked at Val and decided to blurt it out. "That's just it. They are not closing the shop. At least not yet. They decided to try to keep it going for a while. Jesse convinced them of it."

Val paused in her work and looked up at Kerry with a shocked expression. "Jesse? Lazy Jesse?"

"Hey, that's not fair."

"Sorry. I didn't mean 'lazy.' How's this: 'fine as hell but chronically without gainful employment' Jesse?"

"He keeps a job!"

"Not a steady one. How did he convince them to keep the shop open? Now, I know you've been pining for him since you've been old enough to get your pine on, but come on. Let's get real. Doesn't he seem like the most unlikely candidate? He is the one who's always fluttering from this project to that, not to mention from this woman to that. He doesn't seem the type to want to settle down with the running of a knitting shop. How did he convince his brothers?" Val asked.

Kerry let out a long breath and gave Val a hard look. With anyone else she probably could have argued Jesse's case, but she knew she couldn't bullshit Val. Might as well just get it out. Besides, she could hear the kids getting closer. "He told them he'd be able to make a go of it as long as he had some help," Kerry said with as much conviction as she could muster.

Right then the class started to file in and take their seats. Kerry smiled as she pointedly ignored Val. She gave the kids directions to not start drawing until they were properly advised of today's assignment—which was a waste, since three were already at it.

She was just about to admonish one but practically jumped out of her skin when Val suddenly appeared behind her with a hard tap on her shoulder, causing her to turn around and face her friend eye to eye.

"Help, huh?" Val arched her left brow high.

"Well, it seemed like a good idea at the time," Kerry said, wanting to look anywhere except for into her friend's shrewd eyes. She watched as those eyes narrowed.

"Just like I said, each one of them finer than they ought to be. You'd better watch out, Kerry Girl."

Kerry rolled her eyes. How was "Kerry Girl" suddenly taking off as the catchphrase of the day when she was a good and grown-assed woman?

5

JESSE WAS ONCE again left alone with nothing but the silence of the shop, and it terrified him. He took a swig from his beer and noted the taste was more bitter than smooth. Why did he even open his big mouth about keeping the shop going in the first place? He looked around, taking in the dream, the legacy that was everything Mama Joy. Floor-to-ceiling wood shelves overflowing with colorful yarn, sourced from where, he didn't know, but he did know that it was from all over and it would now be his job trying to figure out the wheres, the hows and the whys.

Shit. Where would he even begin?

He looked up at the loft where the patterns were kept and hanks of wool were spun into balls and thought of all the times he'd run up there as a kid to hide out when he'd done something wrong. He laughed at the thought but coughed on it as it got stuck halfway. Not that his hiding ever worked. Mama Joy knew every nook and cranny of this old building. And there wasn't a spot in it where he or his brothers could hide if she really wanted to find them. Sure, sometimes she'd humor them. Let them have their moments thinking they'd gotten away with something, but really it was only time enough for them to sweat and stew about what they'd done and possibly get hungry enough to smell whatever deliciousness she had conjured up for dinner. More times than not, they'd come out on their own and take their punishment, whatever that may be, knowing it was well deserved and somehow grateful that she cared enough to dish it out anyway. There were plenty of others who wouldn't waste the time or, worse, would take the swift route with a hard smack or a quick kick.

Jesse pulled out his phone and stared. He thought of calling one of his brothers but quickly changed his mind. He wasn't in the mood for more conversation with or confrontation from any of them at the moment. Better to quit while he was—Jesse paused, stuck on what to think. "Ahead" was not a word he'd use for what he was. Idling, maybe? At the starting gate. Damian had gone back to his place downtown and Noah to his in Brooklyn. Lucas was on call tonight at the firehouse so he'd be staying there. The silence in the shop, despite the cars roaring outside, the people, the music, still felt overwhelming.

He glanced at the loft again as a vision of a young Kerry came to his mind. So many times in the past he'd longed for this type of quiet. He guessed she did too. To be alone but not quite lonely. He'd often find her up there in the loft having beaten him to just the place he was going to go and hide out. She'd be quietly sitting in the corner, her back against the large wardrobe, knitting without a sound as if she had somehow sprouted there in that very spot. Like a girl-shaped bush with big round eyes behind her even bigger glasses and her multiple braids twisted in opposite directions.

She'd give him an annoyed look but never much more. Then

she'd move over and quietly make space for him to sit and knit beside her, as if he was some puppy or a cat that didn't need much by way of acknowledgment, only space to just be. Those were the good days, the peaceful days. The other days he'd bound up, still get that same look from Kerry and, though he knew she'd not say a word, he'd put his fingers to his lips and give a "shh" gesture as he'd hide out behind the cupboard until the shock of his report card had worn off and Mama Joy had turned her ranting down to a low roar.

Like their first meeting. He hadn't expected her to be up there when he was running from his brothers, but there she was. He thought he was getting out of the way of a sure beatdown at the hands of Damian over messing with his stuff when, in the end, after tripping over Kerry and falling on top of her, he'd ended up getting the smackdown not from his brother but from her. Then, after, another from Mama Joy for causing such a ruckus. It was amazing Kerry ever let him near her after that. He had thought for sure with the way she'd whirled on him she either A) was scared of him or B) just flat-out hated him. But he guessed in the end he was someone she moderately tolerated. And by the way she always hung around the shop and was never really out like the other girls in the neighborhood, he suspected she also chose that place as her refuge from the outside world.

That's what it had been like with Kerry all these years. She was there seeking refuge and, in some ways, being a source of refuge even if she didn't know it. He guessed he should feel relief over the fact that with Mama Joy's passing, Kerry wasn't just abruptly leaving too. Honestly, until that morning and the real possibility of the shop closing, he hadn't gotten his head around it. But if he was honest with himself, the thought of her leaving scared him.

Scared him, but at the same time, brought on no small measure of guilt.

Was Damian right? Was he just using Kerry? Jesse shook his head and stalked off toward the back stairs. He couldn't think like that. Kerry was no longer that little girl from the upstairs loft who he'd used for cover and safe passage. She'd made her decision freely without any coercion from him. Besides, judging by the way she had handled herself today, she was definitely no longer a young woman he could just shush and easily move along from.

No, she was grown. Well and fully grown. He could tell that by the way she felt and fit in his arms earlier that morning. A feeling that was too perfect and one he knew he could not act on. Still, it was altogether surprising and definitely not unwelcome.

But no, he couldn't think about it. Shouldn't think about Kerry in that way. Number one, they were close, way too close. Close in that way where Kerry could look at him and see straight to the heart of him as only a person with way too many years under her belt could. She knew his strengths, but worse, she knew his weaknesses. Which, of course, was a clear reason why she'd more than likely never consider him. But on top of that, there was reason number two. Kerry was a woman way too good for the likes of him. He knew it, and more than likely, she knew it. Why even waste the time, risk the potential heartache, when the outcome was inevitable? Jesse had already disappointed one—no, two women in his life. He wouldn't screw up by getting entangled with Kerry and adding her to his list. She'd be one of those whom he wouldn't be able to forget.

Better to stay on his p's and q's and finally do something worth making Mama Joy proud and not wind up on the receiving end of disappointment in Kerry's big brown gaze.

Suddenly the shop's front doorbell rang, followed by three firm but—he could tell—feminine raps. Jesse frowned, looking up at the window. Though it wasn't yet dark, it was well past seven, and the closed sign was still on the shop door anyway. He let out a groan. It was probably more food from some of the neighborhood women. How much did they think he could eat? But his lights were on upstairs, as well as the back light, so there was no way he could get out of not accepting it by pretending he wasn't there. Besides, they were just being nice. Going in and acting rude would not fly. He would be haunted, if not by Mama Joy then by all the neighborhood talk, enough to make him feel as if she'd come from the grave. Jesse started back down the stairs, his mind fighting to get into business mode and focus on all he needed to attend to and discuss with Kerry come the morning.

He'd get right down to things, showing her and his brothers just how serious he really was. There were questions about timing, how long she thought inventorying and cataloging everything would take. Maybe they'd close the shop for three or four weeks while they got it all together and then have a grand reopening in Mama Joy's honor, though it would be better if they could cut that time even more.

With these thoughts, for the first time, Jesse felt like a little bit of a weight was starting to be lifted from his chest and he could actually focus on something positive instead of the overwhelming abyss of dread that had consumed him since Mama Joy suddenly passed away. True to his form, he'd been filling his time and his mind with all the wrong things: sleeping late, picking up bartending jobs, then leaving with a bottle and drinking heavily on his way home, women, more drinking and, hey, more women. But with this go at the shop, maybe Mama Joy would be proud of him working to turn things around. Not running, but facing life head-on for once.

Jesse went to the door and looked out, focusing his gaze. Opening it, he tried to keep his mind on neutral as he took in Erika Taylor, his sometimes bedmate for the last couple of weeks and at most a convenient distraction. Still, he felt a familiar heat begin to rise as his eyes scanned her body. She was wearing black strappy high-heeled sandals and a barely there little black dress that just made it to the top of her mahogany-colored thighs and dipped low in the front, showing off her full breasts. It being early evening, he couldn't tell if this was an outfit she'd worn all day or something she'd put on to come over to see him. Since he didn't quite know what she did for a living, he couldn't make an assumption either way. She flipped her head, and her wavy hair cascaded over one eye to perfectly highlight how expertly she'd worked her makeup. Her full red lips broke into a wide smile as she held up a large bottle of wine and waved it at him.

Erika looked past him and into the empty shop and then back at him, her smile brightening when she saw he was alone. "I was guessing that you probably had a long day and could use a little bit of company." Her words came out as more of a statement than a question.

Jesse looked at her as his mind whirled over all the business he had just told himself he had to get done. There were notes he wanted to get to, plans to write. "Thanks, Erika, but it has been a long day; yesterday was long too. I'm kind of exhausted."

Erika's expression fell, and a bit of her bravado went with it. "Yeah, I'm really sorry I didn't make it to your mom's funeral. I figured I didn't really know her like that, so it wasn't quite my place."

REAL MEN KNIT   71

He looked at her, surprised that she would even consider it, since even though they had been sleeping together for a while, they hadn't gotten as far as meeting people in their usual day-to-day. Their hookups thus far had been at her place and at motels up in the Bronx. She seemed fine with it. But now, with the look in her eyes and the way she'd looked around the shop, Jesse wondered just how fine she was. "It's okay," he said. "It was more of a family thing."

Erika twisted her lips and tightened her grip around the bottle. Shit, even he could admit that was cold. He sighed. "Come on in. You know what, it's been a long day but, um, you're right, I could use some company."

Erika looked up at him and smiled again, the brightness coming back into her eyes. She shimmied past him and he caught sight of what little there was to the back of her dress. Her behind was perfectly shaped, just like the bottle she was holding. Jesse looked around the shop once again and more than anything wanted to block it all from his mind.

He quickly closed the shop door behind Erika and made sure that the closed sign was still flipped. He put his hand on the small of her back and ushered her through. Past the cash register, the baskets of needles, and the displays of yarn. Past the farmhouse table and all the remnants of Mama Joy's world. He led her up the stairs toward his own room, snagging a couple of glasses and a takeout menu along the way. "You hungry?" he asked close to her ear as she went up the stairs before him.

Erika turned around and wrapped her arms around his neck. Pulling him in close to her full lips, she gave him a sexy smile. "That all depends," she said, her voice low and husky. "What are you offering?"

6

IF JESSE WASN'T up yesterday, then he probably was still in bed this morning too. Kerry knew his patterns, but she guessed sometime today they would have to have a talk about store hours and whether it was fine for her to be opening the shop, but in the meanwhile, with time of the essence, she didn't have any of it to waste. If they wanted the shop back up and running quickly, they needed to get a move on. There was no time to wait on a sleeping beauty like Jesse Strong to arise at ten-ish or whenever he felt like it. By this time Mama Joy was usually up and almost ready to greet customers, if not already chatting with a few passing neighbors.

Making her way into the shop, this time Kerry quickly disabled the alarm, not wanting a repeat of the scare she'd had the day before. But then she turned and ended up in shock anyway over the state that Jesse had left things in both the work area and the kitchen.

Kerry felt her jaw clench tight as she tried her best not to out-and-out howl over the mess. *Dammit, couldn't he at least take out the trash?* she thought while heading toward the coffeepot. Today was recycling day, not Kerry clean up and put out the recycling day. Yep, she was going to have to have a serious sit-down with him about her job description, because rinsing his empty beer bottles was definitely not going to be a part of it. Hell, she was doing them a favor, and him most of all.

She found herself stewing over all of this and then some as she rinsed. Shaking a bottle over the sink, she looked up toward the stairs and expelled air in a hard blast out of her nostrils. What did he and his brothers get up to after she'd left anyway? She knew they were distraught, sure, but this was not the way to start things off.

But then the image of the four of them sitting around drinking, all wishing they were together under different circumstances, pulled her up short. She let out a sigh as guilt grabbed her. She could empty a few beer bottles without complaint just this once if it was what they needed. At least they were bonding, and that was something. She hated to think of Jesse staying alone in the house upstairs without Mama Joy's laughter to fill the empty spaces.

Just then Kerry heard the sound of steps on the back staircase to the residence. She smiled. Good. Sleeping Beauty was finally awake. She rinsed the last bottle and, despite her earlier thoughts, knew she couldn't let Jesse off that easy and decided to still give him some ribbing for the mess and drinking so heavily with his brothers. "What the hell, Jes? Did you guys have a party over here last night? You could have at least invited me if you were going to leave all this crap for me to clean up," she said, turning and fully expecting to meet his hazel gaze.

"Sorry, hon, but it was more like a private party. You know, just for two. I'm afraid you would've been a third wheel."

Kerry froze as her eyes met dark-brown ones instead of the soft green hue she was expecting. This tall female bottle of sex was definitely not Jesse, and yes, she was right—Kerry knew immediately she would have been a third wheel. Though the woman finished her little speech with a smile, neither showing her teeth nor meeting her eyes, Kerry quickly caught her full meaning.

"Would you mind adding this to recycling?" the woman said as she pushed an empty liquor bottle toward Kerry. It was ornate and highly decorated with fake crystals and gold overlays to make it seem expensive, but Kerry knew the brand, and it was nothing but overhyped cheap hooch. She felt a frown come on—unbidden, but it came nonetheless—before she caught herself and nodded, cracking the slightest smile.

"Sure, no problem," she said, taking the bottle from the woman's hands, noticing the sparkly tips on the woman's nails and how they perfectly matched the tips of her toes. How she would soak the rhinestones off her toes was beyond Kerry. Or how she could comfortably fit her feet into a pair of sneakers. It didn't matter. Those were not feet for sneakers.

The thought of where those feet had been the night before came to Kerry's mind and she turned away, quickly rinsing the bottle and dropping it into the recycling bin with a hard clang. The woman behind her chuckled, her laugh both throaty and coy at the same time, and it made Kerry feel like she somehow knew exactly what she'd been thinking about where her toes had been, and the thought pissed her off.

Why was she still here?

Shit, Jesse. Late-night-party picker-upper and booty-call cleanup crew were definitely not part of her job description. And would never be. Kerry bent to pick up the recycling and take it out front. Maybe if she left the woman would get the hint.

"If you'll excuse me," Kerry said, going to step around the woman, but was surprised when she didn't immediately move out of the way. Kerry stilled and looked her straight in the eye. Okay, this was cute for a moment, but she no longer had the patience for it. Jesse's women were his deal. She would not be taking on that baggage. Kerry blinked at her. "Is there anything I can help you with? If not, feel free to follow me out."

There, that should surely give her enough of a hint. Too bad if Jesse didn't give her the formal goodbye she was looking for, but she'd not get coffee, a kiss and a send-off this way. Kerry stepped around her, hoping the hint was caught and the woman would just follow, but then she looked up the stairs just in time to see Jesse barefoot in sweatpants, a shirt in hand as he was making his way down. He stopped, eyes wide when he saw her.

"You here already, Kerry? I didn't expect you to show up so early since we're not officially opened yet."

Kerry glared at him. "I gathered. So is this morning's surprise going to be a thing with you? Because it really shouldn't be. News flash, this is the time I usually come to work. It's the time most people start their days and we get ready to open. Maybe you should get used to it—that is, if you're up to it."

Jesse frowned as he pulled the shirt over his head and shoved his arms through the armholes. Kerry shifted her eyes toward the door, trying her best not to stare at his chest like she had yesterday.

"Of course I'm up to it. Didn't we get that squared away yesterday? This is me," he said, his voice full of earnest determination. "Here I am, up and ready to work. I'm all about the business."

Kerry cocked her head to the side. "Yeah, my arms are full of how much you are all about the business."

Jesse frowned, then seemed to notice for the first time the trash in her hands. "Okay, I get it. No need for the extra commentary," he said, taking the bin out of her hands. "I'll take this trash out and then we can get to work. And don't worry, things might've gotten a little out of hand last night; that won't happen again. The new me is with you and totally ready to focus."

Kerry raised a brow. "Yeah, you're all about the focus. I can sure see that. Nothing gets past you."

"What are you talking about?" he asked.

Kerry shrugged, and at the same time the woman with the legs made her presence known. She sauntered up to Jesse slowly, her hips doing a little separate dance that somehow defied physics. She did that throaty laugh again as she caught sight of Jesse's shocked expression. Kerry frowned, wondering just how much he had drunk and how soundly he'd been sleeping.

"Just a one-night thing, huh?" the woman said, and nodded as she bent to fix the strap of her sandal, though Kerry could tell it wasn't in any way out of place. She looked back up at Jesse. Kerry couldn't tell if Jesse's openmouthed expression was over the surprise of seeing the woman still there in the light of day or over the fantastic show of cleavage she was putting on display. She came back up and gave him a little shrug. "It's no matter, sweetheart. With the work you put in last night, I'd consider it enough for one night and then some." She leaned over and kissed his cheek. "We can call ourselves good for—what? A week? Or will it be two days before I'm hearing from you?"

"Um, I thought you had left, Erika. Last night, as a matter of fact." Jesse chuckled awkwardly and looked between Kerry and Erika. Wait, was he actually giving her a signal for some kind of help?

Kerry frowned, scrunching up her nose at him. Pretty-faced,

horny bastard. She suddenly felt sorry for Erika, with her weighted-down toes.

Erika gave Kerry a sharp glare as if Kerry was about to steal her candy. Hmm. Maybe she didn't feel that sorry for her. Kerry cleared her throat. "Jesse, the recycling. You don't want to miss the trashman."

Erika's look went through Kerry, then all the way to the back of her skull. Damn. She was rough. But Kerry would not flinch. She stared back.

Jesse coughed. "Yeah, um, Erika, let me take this out. I've got to get to work."

Erika turned to Jesse and put on a little pout. "I thought this was your shop."

His brows went skyward. "It is, and I have to work," he said, heading for the door. This time she got the hint and followed, gliding gracefully, though Kerry could see the toll the night and the height of her sandals had had on her feet.

At the door, Erika, though not acknowledging Kerry, made a show of doing just that by expressing herself loudly enough for her to hear. "Well, I had a great time. I'm glad I could be here for you when you needed me, baby." She smiled at him. And though the "baby" was kind of nauseating, Kerry noticed her smile looked bright and genuine, making her quite pretty in the process.

Kerry turned away, not wanting to watch the two of them anymore—or, who knew, maybe not able to. Why watch anyway? Jesse's grief fucks were his business and his alone. The woman was right; Kerry was definitely a third wheel in this party for two.

"Let me walk you out," she heard Jesse say, finding his voice along with his legs.

A real prince. So now he was all manners. The tan knight and the used-to-be man of her dreams, and there he was walking out his last night's stand while she was cleaning his kitchen like a broke-down Cinderella.

She was an idiot. But an idiot who still hadn't had her coffee. Kerry was just about to flip the switch on the pot when she heard the door chime and the sound of Noah's voice. She turned to greet him, but when she saw Jesse coming in behind his brother, she stopped short.

"So was that Erika Taylor leaving the shop this early in the morning?" Noah asked in a loud and ribbing voice.

Jesse looked from his brother to Kerry and then shrugged, putting his hands in his sweatpants pockets. It was a gesture Kerry had seen him make countless times when he was trying to get his story straight in his mind before blurting it out to Mama Joy. "Yeah, she was, she, um, was here to, uh, give her, um, condolences."

"Condolences, huh?" Noah said. "Lucky you. She definitely looked condolence ready in that little black dress. I swear I don't know how you do it. You get condolences that look like that and all I get is pound cake and countless prayer hands on the 'gram."

"What y'all talking about?" Lucas asked as he entered the shop.

"Jesse getting condoled all night long by Erika Taylor."

Lucas cocked his head to the side, looking pensive for a moment, before he grinned. He then let out a long breath. "I'm sure there are worse ways to grieve."

"You're telling me," Noah said, then gave his brother's hand a solemn tap.

Kerry growled, and all turned her way as if finally remembering she was there. "Oh, hey, Kerry," Lucas said, his smile turning from devilish to sweet at the drop of a dime. "I didn't see you there."

Kerry nodded. "Yeah, I'm guessing not."

He pulled a sheepish face and she rolled her eyes.

Though she would probably admonish the hell out of them for the subject of the convo, seeing the three of them together and laughing in the shop like this so early in the morning would make Mama Joy happy. More than anything their late mother was the happiest when she had "her boys," as she called the strapping men, all together under her roof. Kerry understood that. She remembered conversations—short, passing mumblings, really—when she was sitting and knitting with Mama Joy or during Mama Joy's talks with the Old Knitting Gang about how much she feared for each of them out in the world. Mama Joy wasn't much of a sharer when it came to her own fears and worries, and the only thing that got her tongue loosened was when her needles were flying. But Kerry got it. Whether biological or not, they were "her boys," her children, and she loved them fiercely. She talked about her dreams for them and how much she feared that by their just being who they were, men of color in this world, those dreams could be stopped short in the blink of an eye.

For that, Kerry was grateful for this moment of laughter, but still, she'd had her fill of talk of Jesse getting condoled by heavy-toed, long-legged Erika Taylor to take care of her for the rest of the day and then some. "Are you all staying for coffee?" Kerry asked. "If so, I'll put more on."

Both Noah and Lucas shook their heads.

"Sorry, Ker, I have rehearsal," Noah said. "It's getting close to crunch time. I just came to pick up a few of my things. But I'll be back later. There are still a couple of weeks before the tour starts, and I'll give you all as much time as I can up until then."

Kerry noticed the thickness in Noah's voice and walked over to him, taking him in a hug. Not knowing if she'd gone too far, she pulled back and looked up into his expressive brown eyes. She knew instantly she was fine. "Don't be like that, Noah. I know you're feeling some kind of way about going on tour right now, but it's going to be great. Sure, the timing sucks, but we'll hold down the fort." She clamped down and looked at Jesse and Lucas, then back at Noah. "I mean your brothers will."

Noah blinked at her, then looked around, his eyes roaming the shop and landing on the spot where Mama Joy usually sat. He was smiling softly when he looked back at her. His deep-set eyes were shining. "I know you all will," he said. "But I also know when I come back, nothing will be the same."

"No, it won't be," Lucas said. "Though she won't be here, we still will. Waiting for you."

"Yeah, we'll do whatever it takes to make sure our home and our business are still secure," Jesse added.

"So in the meantime you gotta go out and dance your pop lock-ing ass off and show the world what you've got. You've worked hard for this moment, bro," Lucas said, giving his younger brother a look that said there was no other option but to go out and do his thing.

"Don't worry, you've got this, and we've got you," Jesse said.

Noah nodded and blinked away unshed tears while Kerry tried hard to hold on to her composure. She couldn't take it when they were like this. She didn't know if she liked it better when they were at each other's throats. Sometimes that side of them just felt easier than this loving, bonding side. This side was enough to make a woman melt into a puddle of goo on the shop floor just to have them trample right on through.

Kerry cleared her throat. "Seriously, why are we acting like this is goodbye right now? You'll be back later to help us get ready for the opening," she said. "Go rehearse, then get back here to work some more when you can. We'll cry over you leaving when the time comes. For now, there is work to do."

Noah's smile this time was much closer to his real one. "Yes, ma'am, Kerry Girl."

"Good. That's all I want to hear."

The coffee done, Kerry was surprised when she came out of the kitchen to find Jesse alone with no Lucas or Noah in sight.

"Where did Lucas go?" she asked. "I thought he was staying for a while."

Jesse turned from where he was standing by the door and looked at her. His smile was soft and endearing, and for a moment she was taken back to early days and soft squishy dreams of him and hopes of some sort of butterfly future. But then he looked away. He shuffled his feet, and as he started to speak, he couldn't quite meet her gaze, and all Kerry felt was ominous despair. "He went upstairs to grab something. Listen, Kerry, about Erika earlier, it wasn't like you might've thought."

Kerry frowned. Why did he have to go and bring up Ms. Sparkle Toes again? "Um, excuse me, Mr. Out of the Blue, it's not like I was asking. The question on the table was where is Lucas?" She gave him a headshake and turned to go back the way she came, mumbling to herself, "It's not like you owe me any sort of explanation."

"But I kind of do."

Kerry stopped short and turned back his way, crossing her arms. "Why?"

He looked at her, confusion clouding his face.

"Why what?"

"Why would you think you owe me an explanation and why would you think I thought anything at all?" she asked. "It's not like I spend all my time, or any time for that matter, thinking about you and your nighttime activities, Jesse Strong."

She didn't know if her words came out a little more clipped than she had intended them to, but it seemed her sharpness hit a mark. "But still—" he started, and Kerry held up a hand.

"No buts. You don't owe me any sort of excuse or explanation. We're friends and coworkers. No more than that. What you do during the nighttime hours is your business." Kerry paused, thinking of her next words. "Though I would suggest possibly showing any of your other sympathy givers the way in and out of the residence entrance so that they don't have to come through the shop. I'd also like to make it clear that this is the last morning that I'll be cleaning up after your nighttime carousing. It's not part of my job description."

She glared at Jesse and he stared at her, then finally burst out laughing.

"Did you just say 'carousing'?"

Kerry let out a groan. "So what? It's a word."

He pulled a face. "That it is, Kerry Girl."

"Oh, screw you with the Kerry Girl. Commenting over my saying 'carousing' while you were busy last night with old claw-foot."

Jesse stilled. Then burst out laughing again. "Good one. The toes were a bit much."

Kerry shrugged, trying to stay serious, but a snort escaped anyway. "I'm not saying, but I'm saying. They were heavy. Just layered to all hell. Your poor sheets are probably shredded." She frowned then. Dammit, she didn't need the image of Jesse shredding sheets with claw-toed Erika or anyone else running through her mind. She could take a lot, but that was maybe too much. "Seriously, could you be a little more circumspect? We are trying to focus on the shop and building on the legacy Mama Joy started. I don't recall while she was alive there ever being any sort of tradition of young females coming in and out at all hours of the morning and night."

Jesse stared at her a long time before he nodded and then turned away, mumbling under his breath, "Don't worry. I know all about her legacy, and I'm glad to know I've got you keeping track now too."

Kerry bit her tongue. Literally. It was better than making an ass of herself by saying the wrong thing. Again. Why did she have to go in and add that last part about the women traipsing in morning and night? What did it matter to her if they traipsed or not-traipsed? "That's not what I meant, Jesse. All I meant was that I was just thinking of the good of the shop."

He turned to her and nodded, a half smile making his already beautiful face just that much more so. "Don't worry, I've got it. I get exactly what you are saying. All I was trying to let you know was that Erika isn't anything serious. My mind is where I said it was yesterday: on doing what I have to do to keep this shop open and afloat. You won't see Erika, or anyone else for that matter, again."

Kerry felt her brows tighten. "And once again, Erika or any other women you get on with are none of my business and it's not like I care. Are we clear?"

There was a knock immediately followed by the door chime. In that moment Kerry didn't think she could welcome an interruption more. Though the air had been turned on, she was starting to break out in a sweat with this conversation. Thank goodness for

Tracy and the UPS delivery, she thought. But just that fast her mind went awash with grief. Tracy? The delivery? Oh hell. There hadn't been any deliveries since Mama Joy passed, though Tracy was kind enough to stop by the day after and give condolences as soon as he'd heard the news from the other shopkeepers in the neighborhood.

He was a nice guy, quick and efficient, and always had a kind word, but Kerry could barely find her voice this morning thinking of what must be in the package he was holding. It was most likely the long-overdue yarns Mama Joy had been waiting for from the weavers in Oregon. She'd so been looking forward to it and now here it was and she wasn't here to open it. Dammit. "Hey, Tracy," Kerry finally said, giving the big guy with the soft brown eyes a weak smile.

"Morning, Kerry. Once again, I'm so sorry for your loss. Ms. Strong will truly be missed." He cleared his throat and looked at her earnestly. "You both will." Jesse shifted, drawing Tracy's attention his way. "I mean you all will. The neighborhood won't be the same without this shop here."

Jesse frowned. "The shop is here and will be here."

Tracy gave him a look for a few seconds, then nodded. "I'm glad to hear it. Well then, I have a delivery for you all." He turned back Kerry's way. "You are still taking deliveries for her, right?" Kerry felt her brows furrow. Tracy was friendly, but this was starting to feel like friendly with three ellipses hanging out on the back end. He was sweet, but not that sweet.

"Yeah, you can give that to me," Jesse suddenly blurted out from over her shoulder. "I can take it. I'll be accepting on behalf of my mother."

Tracy looked over Kerry's shoulder, and his eyes narrowed

into a "What's up with him?" look. But Kerry quickly took the package from his hands and shook her head. "Don't worry, I'll sign for it," she said quickly, scrolling the electronic pen across the little keypad. "This is one of Ms. Joy's sons, Jesse. He, along with his brothers, will be running the business."

Tracy's eyes narrowed further, showing signs of skepticism. But he nodded his head. Then, out of respect, he immediately said to Jesse, "I'm sorry for your loss. Like I said, your mother will be missed."

Jesse's eyes were sharp, and his voice was clipped. "That she will be." He took the box from Kerry's hands. "Thanks. We won't hold you up any longer. I'm sure you have a schedule to keep."

Kerry frowned. Damn, rude much? It wasn't like Jesse at all, and Tracy was just being nice. But she kept that to herself and smiled Tracy's way. "Thanks, Tracy. You have a good day. We'll be seeing you."

At the sound of the door closing again, she turned to Jesse. "What was that all about?"

Jesse looked up from where he was opening the box, softly fingering the beautiful gradated yarn. "What? I was just letting him know that we'd be open and that I would be here when he came with deliveries."

Kerry frowned, walking over to inspect the delivery. They each reached for a skein of the pretty blush-colored wool blend at the same time, their fingers brushing across one another; crap if a current didn't go from Kerry's two pinky fingers right down to her toes. She pulled back and looked at Jesse. His expression was cool and unaffected as he fingered the yarn, inspecting it carefully, twisting it under the harsh beams of morning sunlight streaming through the front window. "Sure you were," she said. "Sure you were."

————✎————

AFTER REFRESHING HER coffee, Kerry came back out to the front of the shop and caught sight of the back of Jesse as he stood behind the large oak counter, leaning on Mama Joy's stool. He was looking out onto the street beyond the store's paned glass. She had to admit he looked somehow right, but at the same time out of place, in the spot Mama Joy frequented. Kerry looked closer, catching the hint of worry in his eyes and the tight set of his lips. Did he feel the same displacement that she was seeing?

She cleared her throat. "So what are you thinking, boss?" Kerry frowned. The "boss" moniker definitely didn't fit Jesse.

He shook his head. "Don't call me 'boss,' Kerry." Jesse looked her up and down in a way that probably should have been more distasteful than seductive, so she pushed it to a back corner of her mind, chalking it up to her imagination. "It's . . . weird," he finally said. "It's easier to think of us more like coworkers. I'm not your boss. Besides, you're helping me out here. Now, what I'm thinking—well, hoping—is that it won't take us too much time to reopen. The faster the better. The quicker we get some revenue flowing back in here, the better for me with keeping my brothers quiet."

Kerry agreed. "Okay, I hear you. I think I can get you up to speed pretty fast with how things have been running so that you can get going. Sort of a crash course, since there's a rush." She let out a low breath and looked around. The shop was in good physical shape, as far as an establishment of its size and age went. Mama Joy did a great job keeping it clean and tidy. Though it was maybe just a little outdated, if she was being honest and considering the updates of the newer establishments of the neighborhood. But she didn't know about bogging Jesse down with all that right now. "Let's see if we can do a surface cleanup and I'll take you through what I know about Mama Joy's organization systems. We should be able to get back up and open right away, and in no time you'll be running things and I can get out of your hair."

"Hold it," he said stopping her. "I do want to get going fast, but maybe just making do won't do."

"What? Didn't you just say we need to open ASAP? With this plan, the money won't be rolling in, but at least you'll have something coming through." She paused, thinking of the current traffic flow. "Well, hopefully. I'm sure there are more things we can do to drum up business as time goes on."

Jesse frowned. "Yeah, but don't we want to do better than that? I don't think it's going to cut it. Not for Damian. We need to push harder."

Kerry was surprised. She thought she was making it easier for him; frankly, she had expected him to just go along with what she was saying. She took a sip of her coffee and put it down on the worktable, careful to grab one of the knitted coasters that Mama Joy insisted everyone use. "What do you mean?" she asked. "You're starting to lose me, Jesse. Is getting the shop open as quickly as possible your priority or not?"

He was quiet for a moment as he looked at her, his stare doing nothing to ease her feelings. She swallowed, then remembered she hadn't taken another drink. Quicker was better. Opening and getting running quicker would mean her moving on and getting out of his hair and their lives just that much faster. There was no reason for him to be against this plan.

"It is," he finally said, "but if I'm going to do this, then I want to do this right. A surface clean and just going with the status quo won't cut it. Not now. In order to make a splash and turn this into a business that, at the least, makes enough for us to stay in this location, we've got to amp things up."

Kerry looked around the shop again. Crap, he was right. And it wasn't like she wasn't just thinking the same thing. Besides, continuing on with things just as they were in the shop and without Mama Joy to pull in the customers, they would probably be out of business in six months, if not three. "Okay, I'm listening. So tell me, how are we going to do both?" She was nervous. Though Jesse was right, he couldn't go too far and sink them further. She could easily imagine an all-out war between the four brothers if the shop failed.

Jesse moved from where he was behind the counter and walked toward her. He reached out his hand, coming at her faster than she expected, and her instinct was to dip back and out of the way, but for some reason she didn't. Not even a flinch as he softly pressed his thumb across the middle of her brows and gave her a smile. "Stop with the hard looks and the frowning so early in the morning, Kerry. You don't want these frown lines to turn permanent, now, do you? Because if you end up getting somebody's bootleg Botox and it goes wrong, I can't promise not to laugh right in your face."

Kerry slapped his hand away and stepped back. Could the man stay serious and focused for at least a ten-minute stretch without making her the brunt of his jokes? And why didn't she duck away from his stupid lethal touch?

They looked at each other for a few tense beats, expressions suddenly more serious than with their normal back-and-forth banter. The tension in the air was now swirling around like fine dust. Finally, Kerry found her voice, if not her full senses. "As if this melanin would need Botox. Wait! You think I need Botox?"

With her comment Jesse's eyes softened; of course he was just messing with her. She watched as the sparkly hazel went all mossy and soft. She liked it when his eyes went soft like that. She coughed again. Hold up, she should not be thinking about his eyes. Soft, hard, in any way. It was bad for business and bad for her heart. She knew she could take a lot off Jesse. The teasing, ribbing, even the pain of long-legged women with heavily adorned toes exiting his bedroom in the early-morning hours. Those things were almost welcome because they kept her at the distance of right where she needed to be. But when his eyes went soft and his smile turned true—she sucked in a breath. That she couldn't take. That was her kryptonite.

A soft Jesse stripped of his usual mask was truly a dangerous thing.

His gaze went roaming down to her lips, her neck, her collarbone and back up again to her eyes. Kerry swallowed as he licked his plump, peachy lips and grinned. She felt like an idiot, but dammit if she wasn't waiting with bated breath for the next words that were about to come out of his mouth.

"What is this about Botox? Kerry, you better not do anything to that pretty face of yours. Besides, if they jack it up, you know we're all gonna laugh at you, and then we're going to have to kick the doctor's ass on top of it," Lucas said as he bounded around the corner from the back staircase.

Kerry let out the ridiculous breath that she was holding as she turned toward Lucas, who had changed into black sweatpants and a sleeveless black cotton tee that showed off his taut, lean but well-honed muscles. He had his baseball cap turned backward, signaling he was ready to get down to work. But then she noticed the duffel bag he'd dropped on the floor by his feet.

"I swear, if you two jerks aren't related by blood, you should be," she said. "I wasn't talking about Botox." She looked back at Jesse, then gave him a frown. "This is just your brother once again trying to be a smart-ass." She turned back toward Lucas. "So are you sticking around to help out today, or is that getup for work or working out?"

"I'm sorry," he said with a tilt of his head and an apologetic smile. "We've got exercises to go through at the station. I could get the time off but I think I should save the days for when I'm really needed to work here." He looked at Jesse. "I have a feeling it will be often."

Jesse shook his head. "Chill with that, Superman. Go out and do your save the world thing. I've got this covered."

Lucas gave Jesse a "Sure you do" look, then turned back to Kerry. "But make a list of the things you need me to do to help. I'll come over on my day off." His expression got a little more serious this time as he looked back at his brother. "You try to keep a level head. I know you want to do a lot around here and make everything grand for Mama Joy, but remember we're trying to get out of the red. Not further into it. Don't go overboard."

"When do I ever go overboard?" Jesse replied.

For that, all he got was a pointed look. "Like I said, a level head. If you need a reminder of what that means, just text me."

Jesse frowned. "Your Damian is showing. Now go. I don't need a reminder or a minder. But thanks."

Lucas sighed before turning to Kerry. "Sorry to run out and

leave you with this one, Kerry, but I promise when I'm back to work here, you'll have all my hands and then some."

Kerry grinned. "You make it sound like a promising promise. Now, don't worry about things here, you just get on with your training and lifesaving. We've got this."

"Bye, bro," Jesse growled out. "We've got this."

7

A PROMISING PROMISE? Kerry's words to Lucas were still echoing through Jesse's mind as he made the walk south and crosstown to meet his friends that night at Bird's, a local restaurant and bar.

Had she been actually flirting? Nah, she couldn't have been. Kerry wasn't the flirting type. She had to have been just making conversation. It was banter, of course. Kerry Girl type of banter, and he was just reading it wrong.

But what was up with that delivery dude, Tracy? The way he looked at her you'd think he was angling for a forty-percent tip and an excellent service survey write-up. It was UPS, not freaking Uber Eats, man.

Jesse told himself to chill. This was just the normal running-a-business stuff that went along with the day-to-day of the shop. And Kerry clearly was not being flirty—maybe. So him thinking she was being flirty was just due to the fact that he'd never really been in a one-on-one situation with her for such a long length of time. Never gotten to observe her in this way. Not that this type of observation was in any way a hardship. More like a revelation, really. And not a bad one at all. It was just, well, surprising.

Little Miss Surprising Flirt or not, Kerry's knowledge of the shop and Mama Joy's running of it was undeniable. She was everything he needed and perfectly highlighted all he didn't know. Wools versus cottons versus blends and the proper storing of them—and they still had to get into the nuts and bolts of cataloging, distribution and sourcing. Thank God for her. If she hadn't stepped up and he had been stupid enough to just let her walk out the door, they would be sunk. The woman was practically a yarn encyclopedia and, as such, invaluable to him.

Invaluable. The thought exhilarated, scared and embarrassed him all at the same time. It scared him because he didn't want Kerry to be invaluable to him. She had her own life and she didn't need the obligation of being saddled to the shop or him for any length of time. It embarrassed him because, as Mama Joy's son, the one without any definite career path or responsibilities, he should've known more about her systems and the running of the family business. He was a knitter and knew some yarn fundamentals, but listening to Kerry, it was clear his knowledge was sorely lacking. She was perfectly spotlighting how well he'd wasted years fluttering from idea to idea and job to job on the pretense of finding himself. What an ass. As if he was ever going to find himself in any of the lame jobs he had been picking up anyway. Mama Joy must have been so disappointed in him. The fact that she faced his half-assed ways of playing at adulting with a constant unflappable positive energy was beyond him.

Nope. Kerry didn't need to be stuck with the responsibility that Mama Joy had of taking care of a slacker like him. And she wouldn't be. At least not for long. He'd get his shit together. Finally, once and for all, and take the responsibility he should have taken years before.

He thought of Kerry and her patience when explaining a pricing structure to him earlier. He could see she was being extra cautious, as if she were teaching one of her elementary students, which probably should have annoyed him, but honestly, he knew he needed just that type of step-by-step handling right now. Hard as it was to admit it.

"You have to understand," Kerry had told him when they were getting into yarn pricing, "these yarns are more expensive for lots of reasons: the material, which is rarer and harder to come by, the strength and wear. Of course, we have less expensive yarns and stock them to have a full range to serve the community, but putting more volume into cheaper yarns I think would be a mistake."

When he was about to argue further, being nervous about the amount of stock they had in these more expensive yarns, she shook him off, anticipating what he was going to say before he said it. "I know what you're about to say, and yes, cheaper yarns can theoretically bring in more sales volume, but we can't compromise there. If folks want that, there are the bigger discount stores to serve them. People do, and hopefully new customers will, come to us for the specialty hands-on experience."

Jesse coughed as his body unexpectedly heated. Kerry should not be using expressions like "hands-on." It made his fingertips itch and his throat dry.

She continued. "There's just no way small shops like this could ever beat the big craft stores when it comes to discount yarns. So Mama Joy made a concerted effort to put most of the inventory in higher-quality specialty yarns from small, mostly independent contractors."

"Hence the high bills without a lot of revenue," he said.

"Hence the satisfied customer squealing over the idea of making a one-of-a-kind piece with a specialty yarn," she shot back.

"I totally get that," he said. "But I can't help but think we could probably get more people in the door if we had a lower-cost selection."

Kerry's full lips tightened a bit as she grimaced. "I understand that cost for the crafter is always an issue, which is why we have to give them a reason behind each of the yarns we sell."

"Yeah, but we also have to get them in the door. We need to find a way to get in plenty more of those squealing customers if this business will end up staying afloat. With just a quick look over the books and listening to Mr. Sunshine Damian, if we keep operating the way things have been going, we'll end up in the red every month." He sighed and hated the defeatist sound of it. "But he's right. There's no way I'll be able to lobby to keep the place open." Jesse looked at the beautiful specialty yarns and knew their worth both monetarily and emotionally to those who would eventually create with them. "Not like this. They will end up wanting to sell for sure."

"Don't worry about that," Kerry said, though the look in her eyes let him know that she was just as worried as he was. But then her look suddenly changed, her eyes taking on a surprising depth and sensuality that wasn't there a moment before. Finally she broke her gaze and looked around the shop, getting up and pacing. "The old customers will be happy that we're still here to serve the community even though Mama Joy is gone."

She gave him a saucy grin and a look that suddenly made him

feel more naked fully clothed than he had the morning before. "I have a feeling once the word gets out that it's you and your brothers who are keeping the shop open and taking over the business, well, you won't have that much trouble getting in those squealing customers."

Jesse raised his brow. "Why do I get the feeling that we're not talking pricing and inventory, but now something entirely different?"

"Not entirely—let's just say my mind has flipped to branding. And I'm not talking a full revamp or anything too far from the shop's foundations and roots."

Jesse gave her a hard look. "So what are you talking about?"

She raised a brow at him and grinned. "You know how Mama Joy would always go on about using what you've got to get what you need? Well, you guys have got needs. So it's time to use what you've got."

Jesse suddenly covered his chest with his hands and gasped. "Now I know we're not talking about yarn and inventory."

The discussion and her ultimate laughter were at the top of his mind as he finally stepped into Bird's. At first he'd said no to Craig's and Ziggy's texts to come out. But after Kerry left and it was just him feeling how large the small shop felt when it was empty, it suddenly seemed like too much to bear. Yeah, he knew it was mad sketchy of him to run away from his feelings once again, but it was what he did best. Besides, at least with this run he wouldn't end up with another Erika-in-the-morning situation. His letting that happen showed just how off his game he was.

But there would be no games tonight. Just some food to fill him up and a quick drink to send him off. That was all he needed.

Besides, Bird's was a no-brainer distraction. An old Harlem

spot, it had recently been remodeled to cater to a younger clientele. Thankfully it hadn't gone too far with its updates and still kept most of its original charm. Folks were even more thankful that they had kept their original cooks, because Bird's had some of the best wings in Harlem—still at a half-decent price if you could catch them on special, and Jesse was still in time for wing hour.

There were no pretenses at Bird's. No bouncers or red velvet rope out front. At Bird's there was none of the pressure to put on a performance just for a drink and a decent hot wing. It was a good thing too, because Jesse didn't think he had it in him to put on a show tonight. The day had taken enough out of him already with Kerry taxing both his brain and his body. Stepping in the front entrance and looking into the assessing eyes of the night's hostess though, Jesse quickly realized that maybe he might have to do a little two-step, as it were.

"Hey, Jesse," the hostess said. She tilted her head with a certain amount of suspicion and then ran her tongue over her front teeth. "Good to see you. It's been a minute."

Jesse looked at her, trying to keep his gaze steady and not give away the fact that he was trying to piece together the puzzle forming in his mind. Quick images of lips, tongues, breasts and thighs came to him, and he gave her a cautious smile, careful not to overplay his hand as he recalled the quick make out session they'd shared two months before.

But his smile faltered when her eyes took on a hard edge of sharpness. "I had hoped to hear from you but maybe you lost my number after we last saw each other."

Shit. Why hadn't he remembered about her working here when he agreed to wings at Bird's, and why couldn't he remember her name? He searched his mind, bringing up their encounter. Her lips, her neck, thighs, breasts, panties, silk, blue silk. Blue! "Sorry about that, Blue," he said, his eyes softening as he sighed, relieved to have remembered her name. "I've had a lot on my mind lately and then, well, there have been some personal things going on."

Her harsh look eased and she put her hand to her mouth. "Oh my goodness, I'm so sorry. I'm sure you have had a lot going on. I should have started with giving my condolences."

Jesse shook his head. "There's no need. It's not like you met my mom." He knew immediately the moment the meaning of his words struck her. She nodded to cover it up and it only made him feel worse. This was the second time that he was callous over what should have just been a kind acceptance of words of comfort. For some reason, hearing the words from women he never even brought by to meet Mama Joy just felt false. Why act like they were something more than they were now? Yeah, it was cold, but that was the truth of it.

He and Blue had made out. Not so much as a proper hookup, or even halfway to it, and he was sorry to disappoint her, but no, he hadn't called her. But look at the other side—it wasn't like she'd called him either. What year was this? It wasn't like he was that hard to look up. Try as he might, being Jesse Strong made it hard as hell to go completely ghost in the little village of Harlem. Jesse gave a nod to Blue but kept his smile reserved. He looked past her, checking out the crowd. It looked like there would be a wait for a table, and the bar was three or four deep in some spots. Finally, he spotted Ziggy at a booth in the back.

"I see my friends over there and they already have a table," he said to Blue. "It's been good catching up. Maybe we'll get to do it again soon." Again? What had he just told himself? Damn, habits were hard to break.

Blue's smile went wide and she shifted, popping a hip and pumping out her breasts. "Sure," she said. "I believe you have my number."

He nodded and started toward the back of the restaurant. "I'm sure I do."

Yeah, he had her number and Erika's and so many others. But he didn't have time for that now. Not with all he had to do to get the shop reopened. Not to mention working with Kerry. It took just about all he had to keep his head on straight. Making that mistake with Erika was bad enough, but having Kerry greet her in the morning—well, it was downright embarrassing.

Not that it should make any difference who Kerry caught in his kitchen, but still, it somehow didn't feel right. Kerry in there with Erika or whoever it might be. That was Mama Joy's domain. His brain did a mental freeze. Mama Joy's domain. He guessed he'd have to change his thinking on that, and soon. But shit, it had only been a little over a week, and he wasn't quite ready to make space in the kitchen or his heart just yet.

Having woven through the tables, Jesse pushed his wayward thoughts to the back corner of his mind as he greeted Ziggy with a dap and moved in to sit.

"Where's Craig? I thought he would be here by now, especially with seventy-five-cent wings being over in thirty minutes."

Craig came up behind them just then. "What are you talking about?" Craig said. "As if I'd miss wing hour. I've already put in my order for twenty. I suggest you get yours in before it's too late. You know how they are here. Once the time is up, the price goes up."

Jesse nodded and raised his hand, hoping to get the attention of their server. Thankfully he came over quickly, a young guy with deep-brown skin and a serious expression. Way more serious than the job and the venue called for, but who was Jesse to judge? He'd spent most of the day brooding in a yarn shop, so he wasn't one to talk.

After putting his order in, he leaned back, letting the energy of the room, and the fact that he was out, take over his mind and body. It was good to be out and not think about the shop for a little while. Not think about his life two weeks ago or his life twelve hours from now. Right at this moment, he just wanted to be in the moment.

"So, how are you making out?" Ziggy asked, breaking into his zoning.

Jesse tilted his head and thought about the question, not sure he wanted to answer and not sure he had an answer.

"You held it together pretty good during the funeral. I have to hand it to you. I don't know if I could have been as strong as you were. Must be something to do with your last name. Your mother was an amazing woman. She definitely passed a few things on to you and your brothers," Craig said.

"That she was," Jesse agreed, and he didn't have any words to add besides. "Strong" wasn't the adjective he'd use to describe himself or his brothers these past two weeks. Honestly, he didn't know how he'd found it in himself to even fight for the shop the way he did. Everyone had thought he and his brothers were so together. Four misfit princes of Harlem—but lately they had been more misfits than princes. Barely talking and only meeting in passing, except when it was time for Mama Joy's weekly dinners. Now, without her and those dinners, when would he see his brothers?

Who knew, maybe that was part of why he fought so hard to

keep the shop open. How could he lose her and them too in one fell swoop? He knew he couldn't take it.

When he came out of his own thoughts both Ziggy and Craig were staring at him, as if he maybe had stopped talking midstream and they expected him to say more. He hoped like hell that he hadn't expressed any of his thoughts out loud, but he didn't have to worry about it much because just then their server came over with their drinks and Craig's order of wings, along with Ziggy's.

Craig was all about the wings and immediately dug in, but Ziggy wasn't ready to let the conversation go. He'd picked up a wing but still pointed it at Jesse. "So, you didn't answer. How you holding up?"

Jesse shook his head and took a sip of his beer. "I'm like you see me here. I'm okay. Don't I look okay?"

Craig slipped him a look, then nodded. "You look all right. Still a little too pretty, and I'm not sure why I hang out with you. But yeah, alright." He stared at him a little harder. "But you're not sleeping worth a damn, are you? You need to get some rest. That pretty face won't last forever."

"Aww," Jesse said, and reached for one of Craig's wings. Craig's horrified expression was priceless. "Thanks for your concern, Auntie."

"Shut the hell up and be prepared to give me one of yours when it comes or shoot me a dollar."

"A dollar?" Jesse said. "It's a seventy-five-cent wing."

"Interest, my man. Interest. And wing hour is about over anyway."

Jesse laughed, feeling kind of glad to have come out now that Ziggy had broken the mood. "Okay, so wings aside, what's up with you and Erika Taylor? You and her getting serious?"

Jesse's laughter quickly faded. Dammit, word traveled quick.

"No, we're not getting serious. Nowhere near close to that. She may have stayed over at my place, but it was a onetime thing."

"A onetime thing?" Craig asked. "Damn, you pretty mother-fucker. That's a smooth-ass drop right there. Slipping in about Erika Taylor staying over and then a onetime thing. Your lucky ass been tipping with her about a minute, pissing off half of Harlem and the Bronx, and now you're talking a onetime thing." Craig shook his head. "You really are worse off than I thought. Here, have another wing. You need a refill on your drink too?"

"More like a few-times thing, but her sleeping over at my place was a onetime thing. She knows this," Jesse said. "Just like I told you. And I gotta keep my mind on my grind right now."

"Oh, Erika can keep a brother's mind on his grind. That's for damn sure," Craig said as he and Ziggy clinked glasses.

"So what's the grind?" Ziggy asked. "Did you and your brothers decide how you're going to close up the shop?"

Jesse felt the tension that was just starting to dissipate rise up again. Even his boys didn't give any thought to him keeping the shop open. Nothing like a high dose of no one believing you've got any ingenuity to bring a guy down. Still, he faced his detractors head-on. "No, we've decided to keep the shop open. Or rather, I have. My brothers will help me out when they can."

The looks the guys were giving him had him thinking for a moment that he was speaking another language. Even Craig had stopped chewing. He decided to continue on. Go remedial and maybe they would understand. "We figured it's what Mama Joy would have wanted. She cared about the shop and what it means to the community. I figured I need to at least try."

Craig and Ziggy continued to stare.

"Jeez. Why are you both looking at me like that? Is my reputation that bad? Don't I always come through whenever either of you needs me?"

They frowned and looked at each other skeptically, no doubt thinking of all the times he'd been late to a party or hadn't shown for an event at all. "Come on and cut me some slack," he said. "This is going to work out."

Finally, his friends nodded. "We get it," Ziggy said. "We were just a little shocked is all."

"Yeah," Craig agreed. They were turning into quite the little act as they shook their heads and confirmed their comments with their wings. "You know," Craig said between bites, "though, sure, you can do whatever you want and put your mind to, it's just the idea of you and your brothers running a knitting shop is a little shocking. Do you plan on converting it into some sort of other kind of business? Like do some sort of play off the Strong Knits name. Say Strong Brothers Bodega. Or go the ironic route and do Strong Brothers Vegan Snacks."

"Vegan snacks? This from the wing happy hour champion? Besides, Harlem doesn't need another redundant or useless business with a short shelf life."

Craig shrugged. "You got a point there, don't go vegan. If it was me, I'd do a chicken and rib shop."

Jesse made a face. "Didn't I just say we don't need redundant?"

Craig nodded. "I know it sounds that way. But with chicken and ribs it's all about the sauce, and I've got a helluva sauce."

Jesse knew there would be no getting Craig off this particular bone, so he just let him go with it. "When you open that rib shop, I'll be first in line," he said. "I know you can burn. Until then, I plan on doing my best with the yarn shop I've already got. Besides, I've got a plan, and luckily Kerry is staying on awhile to continue to help out. Between the two of us, with the way she keeps her nose to the grindstone and her mind on her work, we shouldn't have any problems."

Zig frowned. "Mind on her work? If you say so."

Now it was Jesse's turn to frown. "What's with the 'If you say so'? You all know Kerry. She's the girl who worked in the shop all these years helping out Mama Joy." He shook his head. "Maybe you didn't notice her. Brown skinned, glasses, kind of unassuming, but a nice smile."

Ziggy laughed. "Oh, we noticed her all right. We been noticing her. Just like half the guys over by the bar right now. I don't know what's wrong with your eyes—that woman is no girl."

Jesse spun around quick enough to catch a crick in his neck, but still didn't see Kerry.

Zig laughed. "You don't see her because she's got guys on each side of her jockeying to buy her a cheap drink. Look to the right. She's with that friend of hers with the ample assets and the dimples."

It took another second, but then he spotted her. There was Kerry, and just as Zig had said, she was flanked by more than a few dudes and her friend Val. She'd changed from the simple jeans and loose top she'd been wearing earlier and was in really tight jeans paired with a tank top that showed more than it hid. She wore her twists up high, showing off her long neck, and large hoop earrings made her skin glow with a kind of iridescent invitation.

Jesse felt his heart begin to thump with a wild beat. Why had he never seen her like this before? Why was he suddenly seeing her in all sorts of ways that made little to no sense? He stared. This woman holding court at the bar was definitely not the shop's Kerry Girl but some alternate of her morphed into his dream and night-

mare. This woman was Kerry Fuller and more than he could probably handle.

Jesse polished off his beer and put it down with a thud as he
turned to his friends. "I could use another drink. What about you
guys? Next round's on me?"

Ziggy and Craig looked at each other with caution then back at
him and shrugged. "Well, if it's on you, then yeah," Craig said as
Jesse got up. "Just make sure you only get the drink. Don't go
over there starting shit. She's off the clock, so not your employee
tonight."

But he was already on his way to the bar, their voices growing
distant. Right now it was as if he was being pulled by an invisible
thread straight toward Kerry Fuller.

8

KERRY WAS PISSED as well as a little buzzed when she stripped off her clothes to shower that night.

It was moments like these when—though she missed her mother since she'd up and moved to Virginia, following behind the hopes of yet another love—Kerry was at least grateful to have their tiny Harlem apartment all to herself. This way her mother wasn't home to cast judgment on her condition, not that Kerry hadn't seen her more than way past buzzed more than a time or three. Also, Kerry no longer had to sleep on the old pullout in the living room, since the apartment was only a modest one bedroom.

Still, being both pissed and buzzed made Kerry slightly uncomfortable in her own skin as she went through the motions of taking off her hoops and putting them in her jewelry dish, then lathering makeup remover on her already smudged-beyond-belief eyes. She added more of the oil-based cleanser to her lips, working it in to get off the deep berry stain that had looked so good when she'd first left with Val for drinks but over the course of the night had turned dry and cakey. Like so many other things, not living up to advertised expectations.

She stared at herself as the makeup came off but still couldn't quite settle herself, no matter how she tried. This low-grade out-of-body thing she was experiencing was probably welcome to some, but to her, it just felt off. It made her wonder if it was the drinks or scarily something more. Usually she was a one-and-done type of girl, preferring to stay fully in control at all times. Buzzed was not a feeling that appealed to her. But for some reason just one drink hadn't cut it tonight. Not with Jesse Strong all around her. In her mind and then in the flesh.

And as for being pissed, though it was not entirely new, of course, she hated that feeling all the more, especially seeing where tonight's unsettling pissery came from.

Damn him, he was putting her off her game. Messing up the well-crafted persona she'd spent the better part of her adolescence and twenties creating for herself. Kerry liked to think of herself as a calm spirit and wanted others to think of her as one too. It was part of her armor. And it worked for her. Some did the whole tough-bravado thing. She did the sweet-unflappable-sensitive-caregiver deal. She'd worked hard to create a safe space in her mind where everything stayed calm. But now with Mama Joy gone, and taking on the shop with Jesse, it seemed that space was under constant attack. So much so that she couldn't even go out, feel uninhibited for just a moment and have a good time without the reminder of her troubles, the shop and how they wove too closely together. Yes, Kerry could easily admit, at least to herself, that she cared about the Strong brothers. All the Strong brothers. But damn Jesse for taking her feelings and things too far tonight.

She turned on the shower and debated whether to make the

water extra hot or extra cool, wondering which would regulate her mood in its current state. Sure, she was being flirty but she was also, as usual, on alert while at Bird's, being extra careful given the energy of the restaurant that night.

Kerry was no fool. She wasn't about to just take a drink from any stranger on the street. Man, woman, hot or not. But the offers hadn't been bad. At least it was interest, she'd first embarrassingly thought. No one was looking at her tonight with pity or, worse, tolerance. No, she wasn't just a fixture. She was a living, breathing woman, and for a while she liked it. So Jesse, helpful as he may have been, had a lot of nerve swooping in like he did and ruining her good time when he didn't even know about the situation.

There she was, politely refusing the kind of pushy—okay, maybe a touch swarmy—dude with a beard, neck tats and ridiculously dry lips, judging by how he couldn't stop licking them. Yeah, he needed to move back and out of her personal space. And yeah, no matter how much she shimmied backward on the barstool or angled her back, the swarmy guy was still too close.

Kerry shivered, trying to shake off the good feeling Jesse's fake claim had given her. She felt her body heat as she remembered the damned comforting warmth of his body when he was suddenly solidly by her side. But the fake part was what she had to remind herself of. His pretense of acting like she belonged to him was about as real as that jerk of a swarmy, dry-lipped guy telling her how amazing she was. How she was a dream, a snack, a dime piece, and all he ever desired. She didn't believe that asshole, and she damned sure didn't and couldn't believe Jesse.

Kerry knew she shouldn't be too mad though. Not at Jesse. The dry-ass lip licker was a lot. The person she should be mad at was herself, and she'd add Val to the mix for coaxing her out and into that particular meat market when she'd told Val there was a rom-com with her name on it.

"Why you playing hard to get on my boy here?" Lip Licker's wingman had said.

Though flattering at first, their lines were getting old, and Kerry just wanted a table.

"Come on, Shorty," Lip Licker said. "Why you acting like that?" The host called a name, and he got a tap on his shoulder from an-other of his friends. "Look, our table is ready. Why don't you two come and sit with us?"

Kerry shook her head. "No thanks. We're fine. We've got our own drinks and our table is coming."

Val gave her a little nudge with her knee and a nod of agree-ment. Though her friend was the original persuader in getting her out earlier—"You need a break," Val had said, "and I need some dick"—even she wasn't open to what these dudes were offering up. Instead she looked at Lip Licker's wingman. "Yeah, we're good. We've got this, but you guys enjoy your night."

Lip Licker, not happy with the dismissal, changed his tune to a decidedly darker note. As if angry and bitter would somehow be the game changer that instantly had Kerry wetting her pants for him.

"That's the problem with women nowadays, don't know how to take it when a man is just trying to be nice. They always got to be too fucking independent for their own good."

"And thank God for it. I for one can appreciate a woman who can take care of herself." Kerry heard Jesse's voice come from over her shoulder as he reached around to take the glass out of her hand. He looked her in the eye as he casually took a sip of her cocktail.

"But seriously, Ker, independence is one thing—these sweet drinks are another thing entirely," he said, making a face.

When she just stared at him, he tilted his head. "So what's up, Ms. Independent? You buying?"

She let out a sigh. "Don't you wish." But then she noticed Lip Licker starting to flex and changed her tune. She didn't need unnecessary drama, and even more so, Jesse and the shop didn't. She looked at him, and though his posture was relaxed and he had his usual smile on, she knew it was fake. There was that subtle hint of tension in his jaw, and when she saw his nostrils flare as he looked at Lip Licker, Kerry decided defusing the situation would be best.

"I do enough," she said. "Don't you think? How about you clean out your pocket for a change?"

"I don't know what's going on, but I thought you were coming to sit with us?" Lip Licker said, his delusions grand indeed.

"Um, no. That's not what we said," Kerry started, but was cut off by Jesse's familiar arm around her shoulder. For the life of her she didn't know why she didn't push it away but wanted to lean into him even more. He looked at the guys as he directed his words to her and Val. "Okay, ladies, let's go. I've got wings cooling over there, and I hate my chicken cold."

"Damn right." It was Jesse's friend Craig, who, it seemed, had assessed the situation from where he was and decided to join them. "Let's go. My last order is up and I'm not missing out." Just like Jesse's, Craig's words, though seemingly meant for her and Val, were weighted and sent Lip Licker and Wingman's way. Kerry looked at Craig and didn't know which idea was scarier: him going at it with this guy or him being mad over his wing-a-thon being interrupted.

She started to get up, nudging Val along with her.

At the table Ziggy scooted over to make room, but Jesse quickly pulled her down and over to his side of the booth. Val took a seat next to Ziggy, and after some shifts, Craig perched on the edge next to her. "Cozy" would be a nice way to describe their seating arrangement; "tight" a more honest one.

THIS WAS NOT the way she'd expected her night to turn out. Not that she had expected some grand evening, but after the past few days with Jesse, being in such close proximity to him at night was a bit much. As were the looks she kept getting from the hostess from the moment she sat at their table. The man really got around.

Not that it had been entirely uncomfortable, Kerry contemplated as she lathered up her body and recalled the surprising moments of comfort she had enjoyed while squeezed next to Jesse in the booth at Bird's. It was unnerving how right it had felt sitting close to him. Even with the boisterous friends, the wings and the envious stares, sitting next to Jesse always felt right.

Well, almost right. If it were truly right and things were as her overactive imagination dreamed they would be, she wouldn't be home showering alone just like all the others who'd come up to bat, batting their lashes and shaking their asses his way that night.

Kerry sighed. At least she'd gotten slightly better treatment than the total strikeouts. Though not by much. Val had miraculously disappeared only five minutes after Craig made his exit once the final wing was gone, and the group was left staring at a sad pile of bones. The three of them, her, Jesse and Ziggy, were left staring at their phones and the "had to dip" messages from Craig and Val, and Jesse ushered Kerry out to a cab to ferry her home.

She probably should be pissed at Val, leaving her like that, but she couldn't blame her. Her friend had come out with an agenda to ease her three-month-long sexual drought, and good for her, ticking boxes off her sexual to-do list. And besides, Val didn't just flat dump her. She'd texted her and cash-apped her share of the bill, so there was that. But Craig? Kerry pulled a face. The way he'd gone in on those wings had her skeptical about his technique. It could be either very good for Val or an altogether disaster.

Kerry tilted her head back and put her face under the shower spray, careful not to let any water get under her shower cap and hit her braids. It was way too late and she was way too tired to get into the laborious drying process her twists would entail. Still, the water felt good, even if it did nothing to cool her off now that she'd gone and thought of Val getting over her drought and the fact that her own seemed positively Sahara-esque.

How good it would be to have more than her pillow or her own hands between her legs tonight. Jesse with how he looked in his T-shirt that fit him just so and those jeans that scooped his ass and hugged his thighs. Not to mention how he'd smelled when he'd first pulled her in at the bar, that heavy mixture of rugged musk and sweet sleep that he always had lingering on him. She couldn't help but imagine what it would be like to have a whole night with that scent surrounding her while she wrapped her legs around that perfect ass of his. Looked into his eyes, finally got a taste of those full lips.

Shit, maybe she was more than a little buzzed, she realized when she stopped lathering and noticed where her hands had gone.

Damned Jesse. A ruiner of her days and now her nights. Freaking bastard. Knowing him, he'd probably put her in the cab and gone back to pick up the hostess who was giving out all the yes signals. Either her or some other woman. It wasn't as if he didn't have his pick or was that discerning. That was, until it came to her. Clearly she was not his type at all.

Kerry tightened her lips and clamped a guilty hand over her mouth. It wasn't right. Mama Joy was dead, and though most of Kerry's assessment of Jesse was spot on, she shouldn't be judging him so harshly, at least not under the circumstances. She had no claim on him. Nor he on her, despite his acting tonight to the contrary.

Starting to prune and also getting tired of the circular thoughts going on in her head, Kerry began to rinse off. As she was just about to turn off the water, she heard first a small clink, followed by a much louder clang and then an outright bang.

She looked up at the showerhead and ducked just in time as water came spewing out of the pipe joint full force. Hopping out of the shower, she reached back in to turn it off, but still the water spewed. What the hell? At this rate the shower would start to overflow soon and she'd have a flood. She grabbed a towel and slid the shower door closed right when there was a loud crack and even more water spewed, this time from both the showerhead and the wall, brown and murky. No freaking way!

She looked up at her ceiling and the gushing water. "Is this what I get for thinking impure thoughts about your baby boy, Mama Joy?"

There was another loud bang and, at the same time, the lights suddenly went out.

"Oh shit!" she yelped. Maybe it was what she got.

No, she definitely was buzzed and needed to get it together, she thought, still dripping wet and towel in hand. Enough was quite enough.

An explosion? A water main break? Should she call 911, 311 or just Con Ed? She didn't know what to do cold, wet and alone in the dark.

Clothes. First she had to get on some clothes.

Feeling around and grabbing her cell, she flipped on the flash-light app and found some leggings and a tee to put on in her basket of not-yet-folded laundry. Turning to look for her sneakers, she jumped at the sound of a loud banging at her door. At the same time, her lights came back on and she heard the water stop. Oh, good, a triple save! Or a double. Who knew who was at the door.

Kerry looked out her peephole and was surprised to see Lucas looking back at her. She opened the door in confusion. What was he doing there looking all official in his fireman waders, suspenders and all?

"Come on, Kerry, you've got to go," he said without any fanfare.

"What do you mean I've got to go?"

He looked at her seriously. "There was some sort of explosion. We don't know if it was underground or from the building next door, but we're evacuating just to be safe while it gets checked out. I'm sorry. You've got five minutes." He looked up the stairs. "I'm hitting the other apartments and will swing back this way."

"Mrs. Robins?" Kerry said, thinking of the older woman who lived next door.

"We've informed her. Don't worry, we won't miss anyone. Now move. Throw something in an overnight bag. You can't stay here."

And just like that he was gone. *Can't stay here*. Well then, where was she supposed to stay?

Phone first. She thought of calling Val, but dammit, how could she interrupt her friend at peak watering time? What sort of homegirl would that make her?

She didn't know what to do, so instead, she would figure it out on the street. Lucas had said five minutes, and now she could hear her frantic neighbors making their way out into the hall. Hell, maybe this was really serious.

Kerry found her duffel and threw some clothes in the bag, along with her laptop, cell, chargers and toiletries. Surely she didn't need all that much by way of clothes. She'd be back in time to get ready for work at the center and the shop. Kerry frowned before throwing in another top and a sundress and two extra pairs of underwear. This really sucked. Here she was all packed up and not a place to go.

By the time she hit the street she saw that old Mrs. Robins was already there. The older woman looked none too worse for the wear. Her pin curls were perfectly covered with a flowered bonnet and she was wearing a trench coat over her good housedress. She didn't have a duffel or anything so crass but instead a cute little red-and-gold pullie carry-on that made Kerry wonder if she always had this to-go bag packed and also made her think on her life and how woefully unprepared she was for just about everything.

"Are you okay, Kerry dear?" Mrs. Robins said. "Did you call your mother?" Oh God no, a middle-of-the-night freak-out from her mother was not the cherry she needed on this sundae. "Do you have somewhere to go? You are welcome to come out to Queens with me if you'd like; my daughter will be here to pick me up shortly. They are saying something about housing over at the shelter, but I don't know. I'd rather not think of you in one of those beds alone this time of night."

"Don't worry, Mrs. Robins. She'll be fine," came a deep voice from over Kerry's shoulder.

Kerry turned and met Jesse's gaze. "What are you doing here? How did you even know?"

He made a face. "It was a full-on explosion, Kerry Girl. You could hear it all the way to the shop." He said this as if she was the dingiest of bats out there.

Mrs. Robins chuckled.

"Well, still, that's far off."

"It's not that far," he answered. "And besides, Lucas called me. Said something about you needing to be rescued." He grinned wide. "Twice in one night? Don't let me find out you're going to make a habit of this."

Kerry balked. "Listen, I didn't need your rescuing then, and I surely don't need it now."

He looked at her and blinked but nodded in the affirmative. "Okay, so you've got somewhere to go? Is somebody picking you up?"

It was on the tip of her lips to say "Val," but shit, he had probably gotten some form of the same sexy-times text from Craig that she had gotten from Val.

"I hear they are setting people up in the shelter. A night should be fine."

"Kerry?" This came from Mrs. Robins, and it was posed as a question but had all the feeling of a warning.

Shit. She knew when she was good and stuck. Kerry smiled at the older woman. "Don't worry, Mrs. Robins. I'm not staying at the shelter. I'm fine."

Mrs. Robins gave her a long look, then looked over at Jesse. She finally cracked a slight smile and walked away with her little to-go bag when Jesse gave her his own nod, as if he was somehow taking over and handling the situation. *What the total hell was that?*

He let out a breath. "You know, Kerry Girl, sometimes your stubbornness can go just a little too far. Why you scaring the old lady like that?"

"And why are you being such a Neanderthal dick?" she grumbled under her breath, afraid to talk too loud, not for Jesse's sake but in case Mrs. Robins might overhear.

Still, Jesse leaned forward and took the duffel from her hand. Kerry wanted to pull it back but felt lighter as soon as he took the weight from her.

"Come on, then," he said, then paused and reached out his hand, going for Kerry's head. This time she ducked, but Jesse was fast as he pulled the wet shower cap from her head. The sprinkling droplets splashing her face, surprising her. Crap, she'd forgotten she had it on.

"Did you even dry off?" he asked, looking down at her body. Suddenly the coolness of the night air and being under his perusal put her braless nipples on full alert.

He shook his head, then sighed. "Of course you didn't. Let me get you back to the house before I have to hurt somebody out here."

"What are you talking about?" Kerry said.

Jesses raised a brow, then leaned in close to her ear. "You looking all hot and sexy already almost got me into one fight tonight. I don't need to push my luck."

9

What was he doing bringing Kerry back here? Worse, why did he admit that she looked sexy?

And that was the moment Jesse knew that he had fucked up.

He and Kerry were standing in the residence living room, awkwardly shifting like two kids suddenly thrust together on the gym floor in the middle of a school dance. What else could it be besides awkward? It was two thirty a.m. on a hot-as-hell August night, and he was alone with the woman who, though he wouldn't admit it, yes, shit yes, he had been secretly fantasizing about for the past ten years, and now here she was standing in front of him freshly showered and braless with no place else to go. This was a lot. A whole fucking lot.

Okay, Jes, get a grip, he told himself. At this point he may actually be reverting back to middle school. So what if she was standing here braless? It wasn't like he'd never seen a breast before. He's seen plenty of breasts in his day. Big, small, that just right middle size that fit perfectly when you . . . Jesse paused and mentally kicked himself in the head. A mental dropkick, because nothing less would do.

This was Kerry. Kerry was not a woman who he needed to associate with breasts. Jesse stilled over the stupidity of his statement and looked at her. Her this time—not her body, but her. She looked adorable standing there tired and damp, but still like Kerry, trying to act like she was fine. He saw the strain and wear the night had put on her when she looked at him now, though, with clear tiredness in her big brown eyes. And then he spotted something else as her eyes shifted and she rubbed at her arms.

"Uh, listen," he said, "if you're uncomfortable here, I can take you somewhere else. You want to call Val? Or you can go to a hotel. I can try and get you a room?"

She gave him a skeptical look that edged on insulting.

"In a nice place," he added. "Damn. You over here looking at me like I'm suggesting something that goes by the hour."

She smiled. It was small, but it was still a smile. "I wasn't looking at you like anything," she said. "And why should I be uncomfortable here? This place is like a second home, and you guys are like family. Thanks for bringing me."

She looked around again. "Listen, it's late and I don't want to hold you up. If you just direct me to a blanket, I'll be fine on the couch. You can go to bed or back to doing what you were doing."

The family comment didn't sit quite right, and confusion swirled around Jesse's mind until her meaning clicked. The looking around, her being uncomfortable. He took a step toward her. "And just what do you think I'd have to go back to doing?" he asked.

Kerry raised her chin and looked at him defiantly. "I don't know. It's the middle of the night, so that's your business. I just don't want to be a third wheel and end up messing up your plans."

Jesse growled. "You know, you really can be presumptuous to the point of just past cute, and I think you've reached that point."

She crossed her arms and frowned. Jesse told himself to keep his eyes up where they belonged. He was mad at her anyway.

Kerry shrugged. "I don't know. I mean Erika or anyone could be over. And just how am I being presumptuous? I'm only going by past experiences."

"One freaking woman on one freaking morning."

She shrugged again. "One that I know about."

Jesse stared at her, insulted but also confused by the whole argument. He waved his hand with a flourish. "Well, Mom, would you care to inspect the place? Do a bed check?"

Kerry's glare was cutting. "We both know I'm not your mother," she said, but then her eyes went immediately wide as soon as the words were out of her mouth.

Jesse took another step forward so that they were only inches apart. "Well then, stop acting like it. I've had two in my life already and they are both dead. Trust and believe I'm not taking on anyone else to fill that role."

Kerry closed those wide eyes but still Jesse could see the hurt on her face mixed with anger and some despair, but when she looked back at him he was surprised to see a resignation that pierced him more than her anger ever could. "I'm sorry. I shouldn't have been all up in your business, Jes. It's late and you're being nothing but nice to me."

He sighed. "Erika being here was just a thing that happened." Perfect, he was not only thinking like a middle schooler but sounding like one too. No wonder she was treating him like a kid.

Kerry nodded, then yawned. "Well, I guess things do happen. Just like I happened to get kicked out of my place tonight. Thank you. I'm sorry I'm being such a pain in the ass when what I should be is grateful."

"Don't mention it. And it is late. Come on and let's get Ms. Grateful a place to sleep tonight. The couch won't do, because we both have plenty of work ahead in the morning."

Jesse led her out of the living room and down the hall. For a moment, he paused in front of Mama Joy's room, then a second later thought better of it.

Not there. He couldn't have her sleep there. The thought of putting Kerry in that room, or anyone for that matter, wasn't something he could emotionally deal with. Sure, he and his brothers would have to face it, and probably one day soon, but not now he wouldn't. Not tonight.

He turned right and headed toward his brothers' rooms. On this floor were his and Damian's rooms, along with Mama Joy's, and one flight up was the space shared by Lucas and Noah. Honestly, with the way his ridiculous mind was going, it was probably best to put her up in Lucas and Noah's space. But that was just that. Stupid. He was a grown man and could keep his thoughts and his hands separate, plus Lucas was home way too often to put her up in his room. So Damian's it was. Though he was a stickler on top of having a stick up his ass, his room was the obvious ready choice. It was by far the neatest, and he didn't often sleep there. Right now, it was just an oversized uptown closet for his particular ass. If he didn't like it, too bad. Besides, Jesse reasoned, he probably wouldn't even know about it since by the time he might notice, Kerry would surely be back in her own apartment.

"You can sleep in here," he said, opening Damian's door and flipping the light on in the room that was usually off limits to everyone but his prickly brother. He was instantly assaulted by the heat of the closed-in space and rushed over to crank up the in-window air conditioner. "You don't have to do that for me," Kerry said. "I don't want to put you through any extra trouble or add to your mounting bills."

He shook his head. "Stop with the trouble. It's hot as hell in here. I need you rested and comfortable to be at your best anyway."

Kerry nodded and looked away from him, nothing further to add to his comment.

Feeling the need to fill the silence, Jesse continued, "Sorry, it's been a while since anyone has been in this room, and when he's not here, Damian keeps everything shut tight." He glanced at the bed. It was, as always, made to almost military precision. But the fact that it hadn't been slept on had him worried about dust. Jesse leaned over and gave the linens a big sweep of his hand.

"It's fine, Jes. You don't have to do that," she said, looking around. He knew she was taking in Damian's various sports plaques and trophies that Mama Joy had still kept up and on display for him. As if Damian needed any further motivation to remember his greatness.

Jesse cleared his throat. "You're right. I was just, um, making sure. The sheets should be clean."

"Even if they're not, at this point, I'm too tired to care."

He smiled, then blinked, getting her meaning but not really wanting to leave. He was suddenly glad she was there. Though she wasn't saying much, she made the silence of the house that much less quiet. "Oh yeah, right. Well, I'll leave you, then. The bathroom is down the hall. I'll hang in my room for a while so that you can go first."

She nodded. "Thanks."

"Yeah, thanks. I mean, you don't need to thank me. Just good night or, well, see you in the morning," he said on the way out the door.

He couldn't stay and say more, and he'd already taken things past the point of awkward, he thought as he now stood in the hall outside the room. He knew if he stood there any longer, he just might ask her to sit up with him. To talk to him until he fell asleep. To let him hear her voice and take away this terrible overwhelming feeling of loneliness that was getting old every night.

But just then Damian's door opened, and Jesse jumped. *NERD!!* went screaming through his head.

"You're still here," Kerry said softly.

He looked at her with surprise he had no business feeling. "Oh, um, yeah. I was just going to ask if you had remembered to pack your toothbrush and tell you where the towels are." He went to the linen closet and selected a towel and washcloth for her. It was an old set that had been in the closet for ages, unused by any of his brothers. The guest set. Cream with a pretty rosebud embroidery on the edge.

Jesse handed them to Kerry, and she took them with a small smile. "Thanks. I didn't remember a towel." But then she waved a toothbrush in his face. "But I did remember my toothbrush. At least I was thinking that far."

He nodded. This was getting weird. Things had never been this awkward between the two of them. It was getting into the land of Strangeville. "Well, okay then," he said quickly. "My work here is done." Okay, beyond Strangeville—he was entering Weirdville. Who talked like this?

Kerry raised a brow and started off toward the bathroom. "Good night. Again."

He nodded and waved. "Good night." Fucking waved with a goofy shake of his hand like a full-on rom-com movie dweeb. He looked down to see if perhaps his pants had hiked up to past his belly button and tight around his balls.

Jesse closed his door and said a silent prayer that both sleep and the morning would come quickly, because the sooner Kerry was gone, the better for all involved.

10

Sooo, KERRY THOUGHT. She was taking a shower for the second time in just a few hours, but she was hot and maybe a little bothered and Jesse Strong was just a few feet down the hall sleeping. That wasn't awkward. Much.

Nope, she told herself. It wasn't awkward at all. But it was morning now, and she'd had her more than way past awkward night and then some. Cheap wings, a minor explosion, wet body and pointy nipples on parade included. But today was a new day, and she would not make more of this little sleepover than it was.

After changing into a top that was overly wrinkled, due to the duffel bag throw-in, and last night's leggings—that was what she got for not being as prepared as Mrs. Robins with the go-bag— Kerry let out a calming breath and told herself once again that none of this was a big deal. She was lucky and grateful that Jesse had come to her rescue last night, and today she'd let him know in the most unawkward, easygoing way possible. She'd get coffee going and make a quick breakfast—wait, maybe not on the breakfast. Cooking would just make the situation more awkward. To the point of bordering on desperation, she thought as she went back into Damian's room and once again made sure the bed was perfectly made and nothing was out of place. Her stomach growled. Maybe she'd run to the corner and pick up some breakfast sandwiches. That wasn't weird. It was closer to something that coworkers did, anyway, and nowhere near as intimate as what making breakfast implied.

Grabbing her wristlet, she made her way quietly past Jesse's closed door and down to the next level on the way out the residence entrance.

She was just about to pass the kitchen when she was stopped in her tracks. "You're not going to dip out on me without a word, are you? Now, how is that any way to show gratitude to the guy who put you up last night?"

Huh and what?

There was Jesse already up and over by the stove looking way better than any man ought to in shorts, a tank and an apron that only served to outline the fantastic athletic shape of his body.

He turned her way and smiled, his locs, for a moment, haloed by the early-morning sun coming though the kitchen window. Kerry swallowed, suddenly parched.

"Um, no, I wasn't. I was just going to run out and get some coffee. I thought maybe pick up a couple of sandwiches."

He walked over to her with a grace and smoothness that should be illegal. Who knew, maybe it was in certain counties down South. He took the wristlet from her hand and sat it on the old Formica table.

"No need," he said. "I already have everything ready to go. You just sit and give me a few minutes."

Stunned, Kerry had no choice but to do as he asked. So she sat and watched the cuteness of an early-morning Jesse as he made her breakfast.

"One egg or two?" he asked.

She blinked. He was so adorable with his bare feet, hair all askew and sleep still clouding his slightly puffy eyes.

"One or two?"

She'd take four of him right now. But that was just being greedy. But really one of him wouldn't be enough. With the way he looked she'd wear the one out, so a backup was surely needed.

"Four?" he asked.

"Huh?" she replied.

"You really want four eggs?"

"What? Huh? No, I, um, one egg is fine."

He walked over to her. Came in close. So close that he was practically hovering on top of her. She inhaled. There was that scent. Damn, it was delicious. She'd gotten a hint of it from the body wash that was in the shower, but this was altogether different. This was that wash mixed with him, and together they made magic. He pulled back a bit and put his hand to her forehead. "You're not getting sick, are you? I hope you didn't catch a cold from rushing out after your shower last night."

Kerry caught hold of her senses and pushed his hand away. "I'm fine. Don't worry about me. I just didn't catch what you were asking."

He frowned. "Well, you look a little off."

Now it was Kerry's turn to frown. There was the Jesse she knew and didn't love. Just the version she needed to bring her back to earth.

"I said I'm fine," she said, pushing back from her chair and getting up. She went over to the sink. "Can I do something? I feel useless just sitting while you do all the work."

"You don't have to do anything, but if sitting makes you uncomfortable, get your coffee and pull out some bread for toast. How about that?"

"Fine," she said in a tone she realized was probably a little too businesslike for the likes of this kitchen.

He nodded, then went back toward the stove. Kerry let out a breath before going about making the coffee and fixing toast.

In no time Jesse, after a few pushes of the microwave buttons and a short while in front of the stove, was putting a plate of egg, sausages and toast in front of her. The shocker was the side bowl of grits, smooth and creamy with butter and even some shredded cheese on top.

"Wow, this is a real breakfast," she said.

Jesse sat across from her and grinned. "Were you expecting a fake one?"

She took a bite of the over easy egg and mixed it with the grits. Damn, they didn't even need any more salt or pepper. "No, I wasn't expecting a fake breakfast, but I can admit I also wasn't expecting this."

He mumbled a quick prayer under his breath, then started to eat. After a few bites, he stopped to catch his breath and look at her. "You know, I hope to surprise you and everyone in many ways in the upcoming weeks."

Kerry paused midchew on the sausage in her mouth and stared at him. Though his words were said lightly, almost flippantly, she still caught the underlying seriousness, mixed with a hint of desperation, in his tone.

"I'm sorry, Jes," she said, and meant it. "I didn't mean to doubt you."

He grinned, turning the mood once again. "Just so you know, I can burn in more than one room of a house."

Kerry shook her head as her eyes rolled toward the ceiling. "Trust, I don't doubt you can."

He laughed, then sobered. "So I was thinking about the shop."

She nodded but kept chewing, then took a sip of her coffee and spoke. "Good. I'd be concerned if you weren't."

He got up and went to the sideboard and picked up a tablet, tapping some buttons and then placing it next to her setting.

She looked at him with confusion, but he took another bite of his breakfast and pushed his chin forward. "Look. I was playing around on Pinterest and looking up ideas for the shop. It may look like a lot, but it's all things I think we can do to update the shop for not too much money."

Kerry frowned but couldn't help being intrigued about what he was pinning, since this was Jesse and, honestly, it could be anything—from cakes as in literal to cakes as in asses. But she took another bite of the delicious food, then wiped her hands and picked up the tablet. She smiled. She liked how Jesse's mind worked. The pictures he'd pinned were all modern but still had a hint of tradition. There were images of yarn stored in baker's racks or apothecary cabinets, and there were knitting needles housed in painter's cans and clay flowerpots. Each was unique and, he was right, not all that expensive. There were also some cool furniture pieces: chairs and chaises with woven seats and backs made to look handknit that were cool. Marrying some of these with a fresh coat of paint and rearranging the furniture could really update the shop, but would they be able to do it and would it be enough to create buzz and keep the shop afloat?

She looked at him. "I like these ideas." She grinned at one pin. "As a matter of fact, I have a couple of them on my inspiration board. But do you think we can do it?"

He took the tablet from her and stared at it. "Not all of it. But some. I'll get my brothers to help. At least Lucas and Noah while they're here. Damian may give us trouble, but he'll get on board."

Kerry looked at him.

Jesse shrugged. "Who knows. Maybe he will. If he doesn't, I can't let it stop me."

Kerry smiled against the hint of skepticism that was gnawing at the lower part of her belly. "No, you can't."

The meal was finished, thankfully less awkwardly than it had started, and Kerry got up to clear the plates, but once again Jesse stopped her. "You go on. I got this."

"No," she protested. "I can finish up. It's the least I can do for you letting me stay here."

His eyes grew serious. "Kerry, stop!"

She stilled and looked at him with confusion. "The dishes are the least I can do."

He let out a long breath. "Stop acting like I did you some great favor when you're here and already doing so much for us."

She nodded as warmth swirled up and over her body, blanketing her chest in momentary peace. "I'm not doing anything I don't want to do, Jes," she whispered out.

But he seemed not to hear her and continued talking. "Besides, we're like family, and family is there for one another."

The chill came over her at double the speed the warmth had.

Family. He'd used the same word she had the night before. The word she'd regretted as soon as it was out of her mouth. She stared at him, searching his expression, but he was already picking up plates and going to the sink. "Yeah, like family," she agreed. *Though we're not. Never have been.* But she understood. Jesse needed family, and needed her to fill that space that was suddenly void. The one that gave him comfort and safety. But she knew she couldn't do it. At least not for any real length of time. She'd be okay faking it for a while, but longer than that and she'd come out a version of herself that even she didn't recognize.

She cleared her throat. "Okay, fam—" she started, then stopped when the words felt ridiculous on her tongue. "Tell me where I can find an iron. This top has me looking like I've come out on the wrong end of a bad night, and it's driving me crazy."

He looked at her like she had asked him where she could find the way to Mars, not an iron. Finally, he responded, "I think Mama Joy has an ironing board set up in her room—well, her old room. You want me to get it for you?"

Dammit. Mama Joy's room? Why did she go and ask? "No, you know what, I don't really need it," she said, putting up her hands. He put the plates in the sink and started to walk past her but casually took her hand.

"Come on, Kerry. It's just a room."

But it wasn't just a room, she thought as he rushed to open the door, and together they both looked wide-eyed into the private space that was Mama Joy's.

And just as Jesse had said, there were an iron and ironing board ready and set up in the far corner by the old wardrobe.

Her scent was still there, and the room was the same as it'd been before she tried to make her way to the hospital that Wednesday night, feeling unwell with chest pains. Little did she know she'd never make it back home after dying from a massive heart attack en route. Kerry took in the way the bed was haphazardly made, the sheets thrown up as if Mama Joy had known she should just leave but couldn't quite walk out without some attempt at tidying. Even in her last moments she wanted things just so. Her eyes shifted and she caught sight of Mama Joy's unfinished knitting in the basket by her bedside. The colorful remnants of yarns she recognized as years of old favorites of Mama Joy's. There was petal upon colorful petal stitched together. She knew Mama Joy had planned to make a beautiful winged glory shawl. Now it would never be done. Kerry quickly averted her eyes, but not fast enough.

She turned to Jesse. He didn't look well. His tanned skin was quickly draining of color. Kerry shook her head and pushed him toward the door. "I've got it. I'm good now. Why don't you go and finish up in the kitchen. I'll meet you downstairs soon." But he was already coming into the bedroom. Going to sit on the edge of the bed. As if on autopilot, his hand reached out and he fingered the pretty remnant petals.

Dammit. Why did she go and ask for a stupid iron? "Jesse, are you okay?"

Though he nodded his head yes, she knew he wasn't. How could he be? She didn't know what to do.

He let out a long and ragged breath and looked up at her. "This will never get done now, will it?" he said, referring to the petaled shawl. His eyes were full of water and desperation. Kerry was afraid she might break at any moment; the two of them falling apart wouldn't do either of them any good.

"What am I doing?" he said. "I mean, what was I even thinking assuming I could fill her shoes and take over the shop?"

He blinked back tears that glistened in his eyes and threatened to spill over as he bent down and picked up one of Mama Joy's well-worn slip-on sneakers. He tenderly ran his thumb over the laces, and a tear fell. Kerry choked back a sob, as it felt like her own tears would flow along with his, but she stuffed it back down when she heard his next words.

"I'm such an idiot. I should have listened to Damian. It's not too late, you know? He's right—we can just sell and everyone can start over. It was foolish and selfish of me to think that I could do it. To think this highly of myself was ridiculous in the first place."

"What's selfish is talking like this now. And don't get me going on this thinking-highly talk. Didn't you just tell me in the kitchen you weren't letting anything stop you? Not even Damian?" She didn't mean for her voice to come out as harshly as it did and didn't know it had until his head snapped her way and his eyes narrowed. Kerry tried to soften the blow by sitting by his side and covering his hand with her own. Something else she hadn't quite planned on. But it just felt like the thing to do at the time.

Still, it distracted him enough to stop his tears and get him arguing, which was safer ground as far as she was concerned.

"Can't you tell bullshit when you hear it? And how am I being selfish by being honest? It's more like I'm finally thinking practically." He let out a sigh and looked at her, his eyes taking on their usual softness now, though she sensed a slight bit of that guarded thing he thought he did so well. "Look, I know originally I thought what I was doing was for the best. So much so that you thought it too." He sighed once again and put down the shoe. "But I can't have you put your life on hold like that. Not for me." He stroked her hand, and the unexpected sizzle that zapped up her arm had Kerry instinctively pulling back. His tears, the shoe and the iron were immediately forgotten, fear of her own emotions replacing his.

"You're right," she said, giving him a bit of a shove and getting up, then taking the iron from the ironing board and marching toward the doorway. "Are you so full of yourself that you think I'd put so much of myself aside and give this much of my time and energy just for the likes of you?"

His slight wince let her know that maybe her words were too hard, but she wouldn't feel bad for them. He had nerve, and his ego needed a check.

"Well then, go! I'm telling you that you can go!"

She started down the hall back to Damian's room, then turned back to him, surprised to find him not far behind.

"It wasn't like I needed your permission to stay in the first place. And it's not like I'm staying for you." She let out a breath, not sure in that moment why she really let it get that heated. Kerry lowered her voice. "Look. I'm not staying for you. That part is true. Not just for you. Though, yes, you can use my help, but it's also true that you would be fine or close enough to getting by without me. I'm doing this to help you flourish and because I still believe in the shop. I don't want to see it close. I believe in what Mama Joy built here over all these years. Almost as much as it was for you, this place was like home for me too."

Without her thinking, that damned errant hand came out once again and was now stroking his arm. Damn, he was way too easy to touch. She pulled back. "Didn't you have dishes to finish? And I have a shirt to iron."

11

KERRY DIDN'T HAVE time to wallow in the embarrassment or the emotions of the conversation with Jesse because, just as she was finishing unplugging the iron and slipping into her blouse, Damian showed up.

Deep in thought, she didn't hear him come in over the sound of Jesse washing dishes, or maybe it was the sound of her brain stuck flipping over in hyperdrive about the conversation they'd just had back in Mama Joy's room. It was good she'd gotten him back on track, but it was just barely, at that. And really, he was almost too much to take. Talk about thinking he was all that. She couldn't with Jesse Strong, even if she wanted to at times. She paused midway through pulling on her blouse and thought of how he'd looked at her. For a moment in the midst of his desperation, she thought she had seen a hint of desire, but maybe she was wrong. Maybe she had only imagined it, or wanted to imagine it. But that was the last thing she should want or want to imagine. Shit. Kerry sighed. More likely than not it was just Jesse being Jesse. His usual way. She could call it flirty, but it kind of wasn't. She knew that now. Still, the touch of his hand was so powerful, so electric, she couldn't help but jump back as if shocked, and that shock, that immediate response, it damned well did make her angry. Just as much as his egotistical words.

Kerry looked over at her phone. Crap. Why hadn't she heard back from her landlord yet about the state of her building? Staying here much longer would definitely be detrimental to their relationship and her nerves. And lately her nerves had had enough—Mama Joy, the shop, her place . . . it was just one unnerving moment after another.

"Sorry. If I thought my bedroom would be occupied, I would have knocked first."

Kerry quickly spun around. The arrogant voice at the doorway as she buttoned the last button on her top let her know that there was no respite on the horizon for said nerves.

She glared at Damian, both pissed and embarrassed over having been potentially caught with her pants down. The embarrassment left little room for her to feel any type of way about being in his space. "Seriously, Damian, didn't Jesse tell you I was in here?"

"He didn't," he said with an arrogant smirk. "And, well, it's not like I actually asked him. When I saw him in the kitchen washing dishes, I just assumed he must have been cleaning up after his company from last night. Or maybe she'd either just left or was still in his bedroom. How was I supposed to know the reason for his domesticity would be you, Kerry Girl?"

"I wouldn't quite characterize myself that way, Damian My Boy."

She let out a breath. She didn't quite want to address the whole innuendo of being Jesse's overnight guest, but yes, she still felt she needed to explain things. It wasn't like she could argue with Damian's assumption when it came to Jesse.

"It's no big deal really. Well, maybe it is. I hope it's not. There was an explosion at my place last night and Jesse came to get me. Well, Lucas came first, when the fire department was called. And he let me crash here. Jesse, that is. I hope it's okay that Jesse said I could use your room." She was rambling. Why was she rambling when she'd clearly said it wasn't a big deal?

Surprisingly, immediate concern came to Damian's eyes. He grabbed her by the shoulders and looked up and down her body. "Are you all right? Was there a fire? You didn't get hurt, did you?"

She lifted her arms and pushed his hands down. "I'm fine. As you can see. Thankfully it wasn't as serious as that."

"Yes, she's fine. No need to be putting your paws all over her like that."

The bass in Jesse's tone had both her and Damian spinning toward Jesse's voice.

In a flash Damian was back to his usual cool self, leaving Kerry wondering if the moment of kindness had ever happened and why Jesse was so weird. "You should talk. Paws? That's funny coming from the original bear in the woods. Wasn't it you I found with your hands all over her just the other day?"

Hold up. Kerry could tell he was about to go back to a potentially dangerous place and emergency breaks were in order. "You two plan on growing up anytime this year, or nah?" she said.

"I choose nah," Jesse replied, and Kerry rolled her eyes, connecting for a brief moment with Damian.

He gave her a slight grin, then sobered. "Seriously, what happened?" he asked, but now that he'd assessed that she was fine, he had divided his attention and was going toward the small closet. When he opened it, Kerry wasn't surprised at all to see his suits and dress shirts all perfectly aligned and in color-coordinated order. She hoped he'd find time to help them with organizing the shop half as well, because this closet was a dream.

"I thought you had your own place downtown?" she asked, her mouth working before her brain could stop it. She remembered too late that not even Mama Joy spoke about Damian and his downtown living situation. From what Kerry had gathered, Damian was half-secretive about it, which may or may not have had something to do with his roommate or sometimes bedmate being an older colleague at the financial firm he worked at. But who knew? Certainly not Kerry, and she didn't have business opening her mouth to ask. She was the not-quite-Goldilocks who had slept in his bed without permission last night.

"I do," he said, his words short and clipped, "but I still keep a few things here."

She frowned but nodded anyway, vowing to stop the questions there.

But Jesse took no such vow. "Yet you're so quick to want to sell off your ready-made storage unit."

Way faster than Kerry and maybe even Jesse expected, Damian whirled on him. "Fuck you. You know I don't think of this as a storage unit." Damian stopped suddenly and let out a slow breath as if he'd surprised himself with his outburst.

Jesse stared at him. "I was just messing with you." He shrugged. "Well, sort of. But still. I get it. I know the decisions are not easy for any of us, bro."

"No, they really aren't," Damian said. "So how about you stop acting like it's just about you and think about all of us?"

Kerry caught the thickness in the air that came with the weight of Damian's words.

Jesse ran a sober hand over his face, and when he looked back at Damian, his eyes sparked with mischievousness once again, letting him and her know he refused to go there. "So, what is it then, why you here so early? You get into it with your sugar mama?"

Damian looked at his younger brother like he was about two seconds from beating his ass, but Jesse just laughed. Giving up, Damian turned to Kerry, she guessed refusing to give Jesse any more pieces in their little game of checkers. "I'm through with this one. Now come on, you didn't tell me what happened with your place, Kerry."

Kerry paused, first taking a moment to get her bearings, then glad for the chance to defuse the situation. "I don't have all or any answers really. I think it was something with the building next door. Some sort of explosion, and then I had water gushing from my pipes and was told I had to get out along with the rest of the people in my building. They say it's just a precaution because of the building next door. I should be able to go back today. I'm sorry for invading your space."

Damian frowned, grabbed two suits and three shirts, and put them into a garment bag. "It's no problem," he said. "Not like I was using it."

She wasn't sure that it really wasn't a problem but was glad Damian wasn't too put out over her using his bed.

Kerry went down to the shop right in time to catch Val coming to the door. In impatient Val form, she was both ringing the shop bell and dialing Kerry's cell at the same time. "What are you doing here at this hour?" Kerry said, letting her in. "After last night, I thought you'd be sleeping in. Besides, it's your day off."

Val was done up today in workout gear—tight Lycra that showed off her curves—though Kerry knew she wouldn't be caught dead actually working out in her designer leggings and matching crop top. Working up a sweat would ruin the effect of her suspiciously flawless makeup. Kerry frowned. Val's makeup was flawless. Too flawless for it to have been a good night with Craig, that was for sure. She knew her friend, and if all had gone to plan, she would not be at the shop looking ready to conquer the next conquest at this hour of the day.

Val's brows drew together as she gave Kerry a "Spare me" look. "Girl, it's not even worth the conversation . . . but I'll fill you in later," Val mumbled under her breath, then flipped her frown to a huge smile as Jesse came down the steps followed a few moments later by a stone-faced Damian. One of her perfectly arched brows rose at Kerry, and Kerry gave a "Don't start" look. As if that ever worked on Val.

"Hey, boys. How are both of you on this fine morning?" she said in her best flirty, round-the-way-girl type of way.

"We're good," Jesse replied while Damian stayed silent. "How about you?" He paused. "Did my boy take care of you last night, get you home all right after you both disappeared from the restaurant?"

Val's smile immediately vanished. "Your boy?" She shook her head. "Your boy didn't get me anywhere."

Jesse raised his brow. "I was just making sure he treated you okay." He looked at Val skeptically. "And you treated him okay."

There was a not-too-polite snort from Damian at that.

Val smiled again as she looked from Jesse to Damian, then back at Jesse again. "Oh, come on, I'm sure your friend is fine." She sighed dramatically, then shrugged. "Also, I'm insulted. Why would you think I'd hurt anyone? I'm as gentle as they come. Not that there is or would be anything to worry about when it comes to Craig. Not a thing at all."

Val made a face before turning Damian's way. "This is not something we need to be discussing so early in the morning."

By the way Val smiled at Damian, Kerry could tell that Craig was a distant ten-hour-ago, long-forgotten past.

"Damian," Val started, and Damian looked up at her with annoyance over being directly addressed at all. It was amazing how he pulled off such aloofness. "It's been a minute since I've seen you around. But it looks like life has been treating you well." Her eyes roamed his entire body suggestively and, well, yep, Craig was officially done.

But then Damian blinked and cocked his head to the side, and Val seemed to remember the circumstances as to why he would be in the shop at this hour of the day. She cleared her throat. "I mean treating you well, all things considered. I'm still so very sorry for your loss. Mama Joy is a terrible loss for all of us. I can only imagine what you all are going through." The tone of her voice told Kerry her words were sincere. She could only hope that the guys would recognize that sincerity too.

Shifting her eyes, Kerry saw the harsh scowl Damian was shooting Val's way. What the hell? Val may be a little too open with her words at times, and yeah, a bit crass, but she was still Kerry's friend and she didn't want to see her hurt. Kerry stepped forward when she saw Damian take a small step and open his mouth as if he was about to deliver one of his cutting remarks.

"Val always enjoyed helping out with the kids when Mama Joy would come by to give the children lessons at the center," she said.

"I really did," Val said quickly, her voice laced with an odd desperation that was unlike her usual clapback self.

Kerry looked at Val with confusion.

"I bet you did," Damian shot back, and Val's brows drew together.

Okay. This was dangerous, but at least it was more like her friend. For a moment Kerry thought Val had been kidnapped and her body taken over.

Val gave him a drawn-out up and down that now held little admiration, and her smile could cut granite. "That nasty-assed attitude work for you down on Wall Street, Damian?"

He shrugged, unfazed. "It doesn't not work."

She continued to stare at him, then licked her lips dramatically before shrugging as good as she got. "I bet it does, but it's still not cute. A thank-you would have sufficed."

Damian twisted his lips before finally nodding and relenting. "Thank you." The corner of his lip went up ever so slightly in what could have been a smile but Kerry knew was not.

Val smiled wider now, though, then turned back to Kerry, seeming to forget Damian's snub and going right back to their conversation. "Though, as for help, I don't know how much I really was. You and Mama Joy were never any good at getting these thumbs of mine coordinated. Lord knows you both tried."

Kerry shifted her gaze from Val to Damian, wondering if she'd imagined the exchange but knowing she hadn't. Jeez. Being in the midst of this crew, it was at times hard to keep track. She reminded herself to stay focused and on her toes. Right now that focus was on Val and keeping her in line. "You were worse than some of the kids. Even tried Mama Joy's patience with your impatience. A right gnat you are."

Val laughed. "Yeah, but at least she didn't give up on me." Her voice grew wistful as she looked around the shop. Kerry caught the slight glistening of tears in her eyes. "I thought maybe this summer would be the summer I actually got it."

"You can still get it."

Val blinked and snorted. "So, you're saying you're not giving up. You're gonna teach me?"

Kerry sighed, then smiled at her friend. "Yeah, if I don't have to beat that ass too much. You are a nerve plucker. I may just pass you on to Jesse."

Jesse's eyes went wide, and Val laughed. "Now I am insulted, Jesse Strong. Is this how you plan on running Strong Knits? Because I suspect you're going to have plenty of women coming in for lessons once the word gets out."

"Private lessons? Maybe I need to dust off my needles." Lucas walked through the front door as he made his little declaration, and once again Val's eyes lit up. Kerry couldn't resist smiling. Val was like a kid in a candy store.

"What are you doing here?" Damian asked.

"Good morning to you too," Lucas said, unfazed. Then he turned Kerry's way. "I came to check on Kerry and see how she is after her harrowing night." He put on a show then, flexing biceps that did not need to be flexed. "Complete with FDNY rescue and all."

"I thought you said it was no big deal," Damian said, deadpan.

Kerry laughed. "It wasn't."

"No, it definitely wasn't," Jesse chimed in. "And if I recall, all you were was a government messenger. It was me doing the actual rescuing."

Kerry's eyes shifted between the three of them, not quite knowing what they were really arguing about. Then her phone buzzed with a message, taking her attention from the strange but entertaining morning show.

Her heart dropped. "Shit!"

Like the trained rescuer he was, Lucas was immediately at her side.

"What is it?" he asked, his firm grip at her elbow and forearm.

Kerry looked at him. Then over at Jesse. Her eyes went to Val and she pushed her cell out to her friend.

Val read the text and Kerry saw the corner of her lip quirk up. "The message is from her landlord. Turns out the building next door caused some structural damage to her building, so it is temporarily uninhabitable for the next few weeks."

"It says maybe up to six!" Kerry wailed.

"Yes, maybe up to six," Val said calmly, as if Kerry's life wasn't being completely destroyed by that damned text. "But on the upside, you are allowed to go in and get your things today between ten and one under the supervision of the FDNY"—she made a gesture toward Lucas—"and they are offering temporary apartments during the time you are out of yours."

"Yeah, in either the Bronx or Brooklyn on a first-come, first-served basis. What do you think those odds are, and what will my commute be like getting from the community center to here to wherever me and my bags are staying?" Kerry blinked back tears and the room began to spin.

"Don't worry, hon. It will be fine," Val said.

"Yes, it will be fine," Lucas said. "The damage isn't as bad as this text implies. You may be back in sooner."

Kerry looked at him. "You knew?"

He nodded. "I heard this morning. I was coming over to check on you and tell you that too."

She heard Jesse let out a breath as he walked over her way. He moved to her side and pulled Lucas's hand from her arm. "Here," he said. "Take a seat."

Lucas stared at Jesse for a moment but let Kerry go and took the chair next to her at the table. "I just heard and wanted to see if you knew and also how you were dealing with it. Looks like there's more damage than initially thought from the building next door, and structurally, with the age of your building, it's just not safe for you to go back right now. But don't worry, it shouldn't be for long. Just like the text said."

Kerry let out a long sigh as she rubbed her forehead. She thought of putting her head down on the farmhouse table or, better yet, crawling under it. Thoughts of just how temporary "temporary" would really be and the commute nightmare of traveling from either the Bronx or Brooklyn while doing two part-time jobs was something she didn't relish with the way transit had been performing lately. She let out a slight moan, affording herself that, then straightened her back. Enough of this. What was she doing wallowing? It wasn't like she could—well, she could, but she wouldn't—go to Virginia crying to her mother. Besides, she didn't think she'd be a welcome third wheel there anyway.

"I guess I don't have any choice," she said, getting up from the chair. She looked at the time on her cell. "I need to get going and gather what I can before stopping by the management company to check out whatever this temporary housing is. I don't know how far out they're talking about in either. Off the top of my head I guess I'd pick the Bronx since it's closer to here. Brooklyn is huge, and I could end up in a place closer to Staten Island than Manhattan, with my luck. It would end up with me on the subway at midnight."

"Well then, don't take either," Jesse said, surprising the room.

Kerry pushed her glasses up farther on her nose and looked at Jesse like he'd grown a second head. An alien one, and so much less beautiful then the one he usually sported. "And you propose I do what exactly? This text doesn't give me much of a choice. I see either A or B. There is no C listed." She waved her phone in his face. "Would you care to read it?"

Jesse shook his head. "No, I don't care to read it," he said in a teasing tone that infuriated her that much more. "I got the gist from the recap. But you're wrong; there is an option C. You could stay here."

12

KERRY'S MIND DID a pause-skip thing as her heart sped up while Jesse just continued talking. She must not have heard him right. He hadn't suggested she stay there? Like indefinitely? But there he was still talking, and "indefinitely" is definitely what it was sounding like he was saying.

"You're here helping us out until the shop is up and running, plus you have your work at the community center. That's a lot on you, plus you are still actively interviewing for full-time positions. We're grateful that you're continuing to spare us the time."

Kerry stared at him. "I thought we settled all that gratefulness crap this morning, Jesse."

"Excuse me?" Damian suddenly said. "I hope nothing was settled in my room, because those are twelve-hundred-thread-count sheets!"

Kerry turned on him with a hard look, and Jesse whirled around at the same time. Damian put up his hands to them both. "Okay, I was just joking."

Kerry let out a breath. Sure, he was just joking, but little did he know how close to her own thoughts he had come.

"Just so you are," Jesse said, then turned back to her. "Like I was saying. There is another option. It's ridiculous for you to up-root and go to another borough when everything you need is right here. We've got plenty of beds." He paused, and Kerry heard Val chuckle. Jesse then added, as if he had caught Val's chuckle, and his own words too, "I mean we've got plenty of room—well, a lot of space." She caught the embarrassment in his voice. "What I'm saying is, you won't be putting anyone out."

"What?" Damian balked, chiming in once again from his own personal peanut gallery. "I was joking earlier, but Kerry living here? What are you thinking?"

Kerry turned from Damian back to Jesse, unable to keep the shock from her eyes. Damian wasn't wrong. What could Jesse be thinking? One night was more than enough to push the boundaries of awkwardness between the two of them. Her living there would just be too much. She held up a hand. "Thanks, Jes, but that's really not necessary. Though I don't want to move to an-other apartment—or borough, for that matter," she said, twisting her lip, "I can and will. I'm lucky to have the option. Besides, if it gets late at night"—she turned to Val—"I'm sure I can stay with Val. Or better yet, maybe I can stay with her outright." Kerry's eyes went wide at Val, and she tilted her head a bit, giving her the "Go with me on this" signal. She needed help out of this mess.

But in spectacular craptastic form, Val just looked at her, blinked and then smiled before turning to Jesse. "I think living here is a great idea! Jesse, who knew you would be the knight to save the day? So, you're not just a pretty face after all."

Jesse just grumbled at that, so Val ignored him and turned back to Kerry, who considered adding a growl to Jesse's grumble. "Not that my place isn't always open to you," Val said, "because it is, of course. It's just that with you spending so much time here, working, I know it will be more, um, convenient for all involved. Logically, it's the best choice."

Her pauses and emphasis on certain words made Kerry want to walk over and pinch her. Hard. But since they were in the middle of the shop in front of the guys, she just gave herself a mental note to save the pinching for later.

"It sure is," Lucas said, further surprising Kerry with his agreement. Then he salted the mood by throwing the ball back to Damian. "Isn't that right, Dame? And she can use your room. I would offer her mine, but I'm in and out so much, that might get a little inconvenient." He looked at Kerry with a definite sparkle in his dark eyes. "For you," he added, "not for me. Not at all. Now, thinking things over a little more deeply, Noah still is in and out with his shaky living arrangement and the tour going on. He's got lots up there in that space. So yeah, Damian's room would be best. It's like an oversized walk-in closet anyway."

Damian growled at that one. "Why is it everyone has so much of a problem with the closet? I mean, my room. It's not a freaking closet."

"Of course it isn't," Lucas said. "But still, she can use it, right?"

Damian looked from Lucas to Kerry, and the hard look he gave her made her want to tell him where he could shove his convenient room and color-organized closet and then walk on out of there. But where would she go? What would she do?

For a few tense moments they all stood there in charged silence, the air thick with the anticipation of who would speak next. But the off energy was soon broken when Jesse clapped his hands together and ended the little standoff.

"Perfect," he said. "I'm glad we got that settled." Jesse put his arm around Kerry's shoulder. The gesture was a lot more casual than the mood from that morning but still had the same intense impact that put her heart in a stutter. He gave the top of her shoulder a squeeze at the same time as Val came over and gave her a nudge in her side.

"Now let's go and get the rest of your essentials, roomie," Jesse said. "That way you can get back here and we can get going on this never-ending to-do list."

"Roomie"? Oh hell!

Kerry shook his arm off. "Don't worry about me," she said, quickly backing away. "You've got plenty to keep you busy here, and I can take care of my things myself."

"Well, I'm heading that way," Val said. "I can go with you and give you a hand before I hit the gym."

Kerry looked her way with sharp eyes. As if she was hitting the gym. She knew for a fact that Val's membership had expired five months ago. But unlike her friend, Kerry would not be blowing up her spot, at least not today. Instead she just raised her brow. "I think you may have helped enough. Thanks."

Val grinned. "No need to thank me. You're my girl. That's what friends are for."

Oh really? Right now, she wanted to pop this particular friend one right in her big mouth.

She mentally groaned. Just a month ago she had thought she had a plan, or at least that things were halfway set and stable, but now . . . She sighed. Now it all felt shaky. Mama Joy was gone. Her mom was gone too, though just a few hours away, but still, she was not there, and Kerry was left as the keeper of their small but still valuable apartment. This whole displacement situation just didn't sit right with her. It wasn't that she didn't trust their landlord, but trust and foolishness were two different things when it came to rent-controlled apartments in New York. She couldn't lose their place. She'd seen too many long-standing neighborhood families moved out of their apartments and rents hiked up to triple, sometimes quadruple the rates for less than what she was being moved out for. She had to be sure this was just a temporary thing. For all she knew, she could be gone, and her landlord could end up Airbnb-ing her place and she wouldn't be the wiser.

Kerry shuddered at the thought of Swedish tourists sleeping in her bed, going through her under-sink cabinet and, oh God, her night table. "I can walk with you guys too if you'd like. I was just gonna head to the gym, but I've got time. Maybe I can help find out the status of things for you," Lucas said.

Oh God, no! Lucas seeing what she had in her nightstand drawer. No way!

"You're a regular Fire Scout," Kerry said, then immediately felt bad because he was only trying to help and indeed was helping. She didn't have any reason to give him anything but gratitude.

"You mean Boy Scout? And no, that club wasn't for the likes of me," Lucas retorted.

"I'm sorry. It's just been a long twenty-four hours. I really should be thankful."

"You don't need to be sorry, Kerry Girl, and you don't need to be thankful." Kerry was stilled by the surprising hint of steel in his voice. She looked into his dark eyes and saw how serious he was.

She nodded. "Okay, I won't," she said. "Still, you really don't have to come with us. I don't want to put you out any more than I already have and you can at least let me be thankful for that. Also, I don't have that much to pack, so I can take a car back. Don't worry," she added, taking in his frown. "I've got this." Kerry added a smile that she hoped was reassuring but felt the strain on the ends of it and knew she had failed terribly.

She looked at the three brothers, all so different but, in that way that family is, surprisingly similar. She could see the good in them. And Jesse did have valid points about the commute—compared to staying in an outer borough, she knew it would make her life so much easier, all things considered.

She glanced at him, and he smiled. It came so naturally, almost too naturally, and screw her foolish heart but it thumped, thumped, thumped harder and brighter in her chest as if it were waiting for him to wake it up. She hated her responses to his cues, his gestures, his every little quirk. It was fine when she was a teenager, but dammit, she should be well over it by now.

Jesse wasn't the only man in her life. It wasn't like she'd been crazy enough to think he cared about her or that she should somehow save herself for him. But still, after all this time, he was the only man in her heart, and here she was so many years later hanging on. Still an interloper in this family that wasn't quite hers.

She didn't have the right. They were going through so much with their current state of family upheaval, and now here she was interjecting herself into this already turbulent situation. She looked at Jesse. "I know you don't want to hear it, but I'm sorry for being an intrusion, and thank you."

Jesse sighed, just as Damian suddenly shouted out, "Oh, enough.

Stop apologizing, and cut it with saying 'thank you' already. You sure know how to beat shit into the ground, Kerry Girl."

Heat rose quickly up her neck, straight to her ears. "Excuse me for trying to be polite even during my crisis." Freaking Damian, being an ass. But where was the surprise in that?

He held up his hand. "Shouldn't you get going?" he said. "That text implied it was time sensitive, so you'd better go and get your stuff while you can."

Kerry blinked. Wait, was he really relenting? Like, out loud?

"I suggest you get moving quick," he said, and sealed his declaration of relenting by waving his hand as if shooing away an annoying child. Damian now looked at Jesse. "And you, we need to talk more about your plans and how you intend to get the shop reopened as fast as possible. Because no money coming in means just that—no money coming in. I know you have remodeling plans, but you have to keep them in check. This is not just for you to run away with. We won't be able to keep this space on dreams and wishes. Taxes are due soon, and who knows what else will come up. You need to keep that in mind."

Lucas ran a hand across his forehead while Jesse shook his head and let out a breath. Kerry didn't know if it was in anger or awe over his brother's whacky reversal. Either way it was probably not supposed to be as sexy a gesture as it turned out to be, but still it was a lot to take in.

Lucas spoke, his words bringing Kerry's gaze from Jesse. "You sure you're okay getting your things on your own?"

Kerry blinked, trying to get a handle on herself. "I'm fine," she answered, knowing it was maybe three-quarters of the truth.

His smile was only slightly reassuring. "Good luck, then. Give a shout if you need anything. It looks like my workout is going to be here, refereeing."

"I'm sure she'll be fine," Jesse said sharply, catching a frown from both his brothers.

But Kerry could do nothing but agree. "Yes, I'll be fine," she said, and headed for the door.

"Of course she will," Val said. "She has me!"

Now it was Kerry's turn to dole out the hard glares.

AS THEY HIT the pavement, Kerry fought hard to hold on to her swirling emotions. She looked up Seventh Avenue at the tall NYCHA projects and the clear blue sky that framed the rooftop water towers. It was way too lovely a day for this much turmoil to be going on in her life. Then she turned and looked at Val, no longer able to hold back the words that had been champing to come up. "What the hell was that all about? You were supposed to have my back in there and yet you were practically throwing me to the lions."

"Hmph," Val countered. "If you're lucky, you'll be eaten by dinnertime."

She shot Val a look that said she didn't think she was even close to being funny. "Cut it out with that. I don't need those kinds of complications in my life. It's bad enough with this whole Mama Joy thing and the shop and me trying to figure out my job situation, and now I've got this apartment situation on top of it. What if it goes on indefinitely? I can't afford rent anywhere else— hell, I can barely afford paying what I'm paying there now, which is why I'm looking for other positions."

Val paused in her stride and looked at Kerry. "I thought you were looking for another job because you'd gotten your degree and were ready to move on."

Kerry waved her off, not liking where this was going. Her friend was getting dangerously close to a place she wasn't sure she was mentally or emotionally in the mood to visit. "Yeah, that too. But I do like working with the children at the center, and working at the shop makes me happy too." The shop part she purposely tried to downplay.

"Oh, I'm sure it does." Kerry didn't like the smug look in Val's eyes, but then her friend's eyes softened and she gave Kerry's arm a soothing rub. "Come on. Don't. It won't go on indefinitely. This is just one of those things that happens, and thank goodness it isn't worse. If it was, you could have been hurt in that explosion." She grinned. "And the best part of it all is you have the Harlem Knights, as they are all ready and willing to come to your rescue." She thumbed her fist down the avenue toward Strong Knits. "Listen, there are plenty of worse situations to be in. The way both Jesse and Lucas were rushing to your side . . ." Val fanned herself with a wave of her hand. "Lucas with all that swagger, plus his smile and those firefighter muscles, and Jesse and his too-fine, sexy ass. Even the hard-ass demon Damian himself was swayed to your side. I almost peed myself right there."

Kerry pulled a face. "Ugh. Thank goodness for small miracles."

Val rolled her eyes and shrugged her shoulders. "Well, the fact remains: I don't know what you're complaining about."

"That's it," Kerry countered, "you don't know. I've known those guys practically forever, and sexiness or swagger, it all means nothing. They think of me as nothing more than family. Their Kerry Girl."

"Sure, Jan. You keep telling yourself that. Not one of them looked at you like any sort of girl."

Kerry didn't dare go where Val was headed. "No. You're wrong. Well, maybe not all that wrong. I could have been overstepping with the family talk."

Val looked skeptical but nodded.

"They probably only think of me as at most a very distant cousin, or the tagalong friend of that cousin. Tolerated at family gatherings, but nothing more than that."

"Fine, but we'll see how distant you stay now that you're under the same roof. I mean, you've got Lucas on the one hand and Jesse on the other. And then there is the wild card—smoldering." She fanned herself again, first by her chest, then her crotch area. "Damian. Wait. You're out of hands. Not to mention Noah too. I tell you, favor surely ain't fair."

Kerry couldn't help but laugh at that, and it got stuck in her throat, turning to a cough. She looked up at the clear blue sky again and realized that she hadn't laughed in too long. She missed the feeling. Maybe favor wasn't fair, and maybe she should just take it where she could get it and be grateful.

At her apartment, Val proceeded to pare down Kerry's wardrobe to the barest of necessities—which, in Val's opinion, meant the most provocative clothing she owned. Anything deemed appropriate for Sunday service at Shiloh Baptist was out. Kerry should have felt flattered over all the hand knits she was rolling into her bag, but these were things that she had made without ever planning to actually wear them. At least not out in public. The couple of sleeveless sweaters were fine, but the knitted tank tops with crochet details were pushing it.

"You took the time to make them," Val said. "I don't know

why you're making that face. They're perfect for summer and a waste just taking up space here. Let them do their job by highlighting your assets." At that Val grabbed her own assets and gave them a quick lift.

Assets. Yeah, right. Kerry sighed but let Val continue to roll. She knew arguing over this would be a waste of time she didn't have. Instead, she threw in more essentials and changed the subject.

"So come on and spill it. Tell me what happened with Craig last night?"

Val's eyes rolled up to Kerry's now scarily watermarked ceiling. Maybe it was best she was leaving. That stain looked ominous, and she didn't need her upstairs neighbor's floor falling in on her.

"He was in and out. Literally. That's about it. It was over so fast that I didn't even have time to put effort into giving him directions. Not that he would have heard or taken directions anyway," Val said.

Kerry frowned. "Well, that sucks." Val gave a snort and Kerry couldn't help but laugh. "Still, things looked so promising between the two of you when you left."

Val shrugged. "I thought so too. I mean he seemed so enthusiastic when we were at the table, but damn, he came at me like he did those chicken wings. He was all about eating the middle when all the good stuff was up at the tip. And there he was. Completely ignoring it."

She let out a long sigh, and Kerry grimaced, then remembered her BFF in her night table and dived for it. "Can't leave this here."

Val frowned, then picked up Kerry's multicolored knit skirt. "I don't think you'll be needing it where you're going, my dear."

"Just shut it. You act like you're sending me off to work at the BunnyRanch and not the local yarn shop. This conversation is stupid. And for your information, I'm taking it because I don't trust who will be coming in and out of my apartment under the guise of repairs while I'm gone. You never know what snoops will be up in here touching things."

Val made a face. "Ewww. You're right. Take your vibrator, girl, and keep it safe."

Val picked up Kerry's already short denim shorts and a pair of scissors, looking like she was about to hack off two good inches.

"What are you doing?" Kerry yelled. "Not to mention you're supposed to be helping me get the essentials for work and interviews. I don't need these shorts made into booty shorts."

Val held up the shorts and the scissors. "Who says booty shorts are not essential in this case?"

"You're out of your mind!" Kerry said. "Are you sure you're not still slightly hungover from last night?"

"Cute, but no. I'm perfectly lucid. We're about to go on break at the center and you're about to have a couple of uninterrupted weeks in captivity with those fine-assed men. It's time to shoot your shot, woman. Trust and believe, if you don't, plenty will."

With that declaration, the image of long-legged, heavy-toed Erika came to the forefront of Kerry's mind. Val waved the scissors again. "I see you're getting my meaning."

"I'm not admitting to getting anything," Kerry said, crossing her arms over her chest. Then the memory of Jesse and how good he had looked in the kitchen as he cooked her breakfast edged out the unwelcome image of Erika. "Let's just say I do let you go all Scissorhands on my shorts . . ."

Val grinned dangerously.

"If I do," Kerry continued, "you'd better make them look just as good as Bey's from Beychella, and they had better be just as magical, because I'm not sacrificing my ass or my dignity for anything less."

Val held the shorts up to her head in mock salute. "As you command, Kerry Girl."

13

"WHAT'S UP WITH y'all? Why is everyone looking so tense?"
Noah directed his comment to all of his brothers, but
then he laser-focused on Damian and shook his head and grinned.
He walked over to his brother and patted him on his shoulder.
"You really need to calm the hell down, bro. You're looking like
you're straight ready to square up." He rubbed Damian's shoulder.
"And damn, you're stiff as shit. I told you that you need to add
more stretching to your routine."

Damian shot Noah hard eyes. "I'm not in the mood for a routine from you, pop locker."

Noah snorted, then stepped back.

"He's just mad because I offered up his room."

"Offered? You just gave it away. Why not give away your own?"
Damian said.

"What, with me in it?" Jesse grinned. "You think she'd share?"

"Now is not the time to joke, Jesse," Lucas chimed in.

"Who said I'm joking?" Jesse countered at Lucas's butting in before he turned back to Damian. "Besides, it's not like you didn't agree to it."

"And it's not like it wasn't an emergency," Lucas added.

"It's not like she didn't have other options either. Besides," Damian added, "if I didn't say yes, once again, I'd be the fucking bad guy. Both of you, no, all of you always make me out to be the bad guy."

"Do we?" Lucas said.

"Well, aren't you?" Jesse added.

"Fuck you both," Damian growled.

"Now boys," Noah chimed in, and they all stilled. The eeriness of it felt like a voice from the past. Noah just shook his head and laughed. "Not one of you shitheads say it. Stay on topic and tell me what happened here last night. I just came to get a few things, then I have to leave for more rehearsals, and now we have another person living here. A female person? Looks like I picked the wrong time to sublet."

Jesse shook his head. "It's not like that. And don't go getting any ideas. It's Kerry. She's temporarily displaced and the fancy prince here is acting like giving up his room, the one he doesn't use, is a hardship."

Damian shook his head. "See, the bad guy."

"No, the selfish one. Your room is nothing but a closet. I don't know why we're still having this conversation. All it shows is how petty you are. This is Kerry—the least we can do is extend her help for all she's doing for us."

"I saw how you were helping her this morning. Looking at her like she was fresh crab legs brought out at the buffet. She had you up cooking and washing dishes this morning."

"She didn't!" Noah exclaimed. "Damn. Kerry Girl! Got that good-good!"

Jesse leveled him with a hard look, and he covered his mouth before he turned back to Damian. "I was just being nice. Something you wouldn't know the meaning of."

"Screw you, little freeloader."

"Get in line," Jesse said.

"Just be sure Kerry isn't in that line and stays in the right bed while she's in this house. Because if you screw this up and treat her like you have every other woman you've encountered, you could end up damaging a lot more than just her heart. You could essentially be sinking this business before it gets off the ground."

Jesse shook his head. He was stunned for a moment, but dammit, he couldn't let it show. Not now. Not ever. "Like I said, this argument is stupid and a waste of time. Not that it's any of your business, but I'll say it again: I was just being nice to Kerry. Like Mama Joy would have wanted, mind you. Now how about you go and clear out some space in that oversized closet of yours, maybe a drawer or two, and make her feel welcome."

Damian let out a long breath, and Jesse thought he'd finally gotten through to him when he looked like he was going to turn and head upstairs, but he paused. "Just remember what I said, Jes. Make sure she's not in that line."

Jesse couldn't pause the rage that popped to the surface of his being. "And what if she is?"

Lucas's head snapped around his way. "Wait, she isn't, is she? Don't fuck this up, Jesse. This is Kerry. She's not one of the usual women you run in and out of."

Jesse let out a long sigh, then looked from Lucas to Damian. His eyes went to Noah for a bit of help but couldn't even find any encouragement there. "You know, you all can really be big-league assholes at times without even trying. Like, top scoring. So, you insult me and every woman I've ever been with all in one fell swoop while thinking you're complimenting Kerry. Good job, dicks."

He expected some words from them—if not an apology to him, then at least an admission of poor word choice. But they just stared and left him to think over Kerry, Erika, the girl from the bar who . . . fuck all, once again her name was escaping him. Blue. Dammit, he really needed to stop labeling women by location and get his act together. He really was a fuckup.

But still, it wasn't like he was talking about defiling Kerry. Not that he'd ever defiled a woman in his life. And the way his brothers were looking at him, you'd think that was the case. And you'd think any of them were better than him. What, just because Damian had a steady corporate job, and Lucas was a respected civil servant with hella benefits and shit, and Noah—he looked at Noah . . . Well, at least Noah's star was somewhat on the rise. He was about to go on tour and hadn't been in and out of Mama Joy's for handouts in the past year.

Still, they acted like if, and this was a huge if, he was to get with Kerry it would be a hookup. A one-and-done situation. As if there would be any sort of such thing with the likes of Kerry. They also acted like they had some sort of personal skin in the game when it came to her. The thought of the way Lucas had rushed to her side came to his mind and gave him an uncomfortable tightening in his neck. This was Kerry. Sure, he'd had his thoughts over the years, but they were his. He didn't want to even come close to thinking of any of his brothers thinking of her that way.

"You know what? Let's stop talking about this. It doesn't feel right. This is Kerry, and we're just temporarily helping her out, like she's helping us out. It's no big deal, and we need to stop making it one." He stared at Damian. "You were going to get the room ready. I think you should before she gets back. You don't want her going in there and moving your suits herself."

Damian's brown face lost a hint of its color. Finally, something to get his ass moving. His lips tightened and he nodded. "Fine. I'll move some things," he said, then got even more sober than usual, which for Damian was a feat. "But before I do it's time to get real." He looked to each of his brothers, then focused on Jesse after pulling an envelope out of his back pocket.

"What's that?" Jesse asked.

"It's our asses being handed to us is what it is."

Jesse swallowed, but the lump that had formed in his throat at the official-looking envelope was too thick to go down.

"What is it, Dame?" Lucas asked. "Spit it out. Why are you being so cryptic?"

Damian let out a long breath. "It's proof of a hundred-thousand-dollar home equity loan that Mama Joy took out and which, now that she's dead, is coming due."

Jesse blinked. A hundred thousand? Where would they get a hundred thousand dollars? Her insurance barely covered her burial and the due taxes.

"What are you talking about?" Lucas asked, coming forward and taking the paper out of the envelope. "How do you know about this?"

"I got a call. Now that she's gone all I'm getting is calls as her executor," Damian said.

Jesse stared at him now, and suddenly his just-past-thirty-year-old brother looked much older than his age.

"What does this mean?" Jesse asked. Then he cleared his throat, hating how stupid and small his voice sounded. He should be stronger. This shouldn't scare him.

Damian stared at him at the same time that Noah came over and put a hand on his shoulder. Fuck. Was everything over before it had even started?

Finally Damian spoke. "It means we have only a couple of months to come up with this money or we lose both the shop and the house. I can't sugarcoat this, Jes. She took out the loan because she couldn't fund the suppliers, keep inventory, pay taxes and keep the house running. I wasn't lying when I said this was a losing business."

Jesse felt his world begin to crumble. "So you want to sell."

Damian shook his head. "No, I don't want to sell. I never did. I just don't see a way not to."

Jesse let out a breath. "Time. We still have time, don't we?"

Damian nodded. "We do. Only a short time."

"Okay, give me that. Give us that." He stared at Damian.

Finally Damian nodded. "The rest of the insurance can hold the bank off for a while and take care of part of the loan. I'll look at the books and see where more corners can be cut. But then it's time to really get serious. This is not a game, Jes."

Jesse felt Noah squeeze his shoulder. "You got this, Jes."

"Don't worry. We're not giving up. Not yet. It's not time to throw in the towel," Lucas said.

Jesse wanted to believe them. Wanted to thank them for not giving up and for sticking with him. But this next big blow, it scared him. It made him feel the weight of potentially tanking the shop and losing out on what could have been financial security for all of them. What if it didn't work? Maybe he should tell them to just let go and sell now. If they did, they could split the profits from the house and each move on. How could he expect his brothers to take such a huge chance and bet on a loser like him?

Damian frowned. "Stop it, Jes. It's already been decided. We're doing this. You're doing this. So get out of your head and get your ass in gear to get this shop up and running. Besides, you've already gone and given up my damned room. There's no turning back now."

He turned to head back upstairs to the residence. "I'm heading up so I can make room for Kerry, and when I come back down, let's seriously talk about opening the shop in the interim so that you can get some revenue flowing. If you're going to do this, you need to do it, Jes."

Jesse nodded. "Fine. And you're right." He looked at them all. "Thanks. But if I'm going to do it like that, I'm going to need some help from you all too. Remember, the name on the sign still says 'Strong Knits.' I may be doing the day-to-day running of the shop, but this is our place. Ours. Damian, Lucas, Noah and Jesse's. The Strong brothers."

"Okay, this is getting to be too much even for me, Mini Ma," Noah said, then tossed a ball of wool into a basket across the room. "We need to get going. I'll do what I can between work and rehearsals, but you know I'm only around for the next couple of weeks."

"That should be all we need," Jesse replied. "We understand you have to go."

Noah's eyes clouded.

"Don't do that," Jesse said. "It will be fine and enough," he said reassuringly.

"Yeah, don't worry," Lucas said. "I'll be in and out. I can help a few days a week on my off days. Plus, for now we have Kerry."

They looked to Damian, who turned back from heading upstairs. "I just got this one straight, Noah. I don't have time to pull you in too. Go and do what you were meant to do. It will be fine. We have Kerry, if this one," he said, tilting his head toward Jesse, "keeps his head on straight, so to speak. All should be fine. It will be Jesse with the day-to-day. Plus Kerry, and Lucas when he can, and I'll be keeping a close eye on the finances."

"Not too close, though," Jesse chimed in. "I don't think you need to do that."

Damian looked at him. "Like your favorite security blanket, brother. Like you said, it's the four of us now."

Jesse let out a breath. "Yeah, I guess I did say that, didn't I?"

14

So, THIS ISN'T *awkward at all. Nope. Not. At. All.*

Kerry was unpacking her life for the next few weeks, putting her drawers in a drawer that most likely had recently been holding Damian's drawers. Blah. The circular thinking was a little too close for comfort, and though she could still smell the scent of the cleaning wipes that Damian had used to disinfect, she thought about giving things another quick wipe down.

As she reached into her bag, her hand hit a distinct lump, and she suddenly worried over where to stash her old friend. *Keep it safe,* Val had said. As if anywhere here in this house with Jesse just down the hall was safe. She was going to lose her mind thinking of him and it, and worrying over the sound traveling through the walls. Shit, maybe she should have left it back at her place. But then she'd only worry about the firefighters in her apartment finding it and playing a quick game of toss the vibrator. Kerry shook her head and decided she'd keep it with the rest of her personal feminine products. Not that any of the guys probably cared about peeking in on her life, but if they did, one look at the bag with her extra-long ultra-thin winged pads, plus tampons, and they were sure to not venture further in their explorings. Kerry slammed the drawer shut. This was ridiculous. She was going on twenty-seven and now had to consider these things? Living with boys was stupid.

Going over to the closet, Kerry admired the slim felt-covered hangers Damian had left free for her. He'd allotted twelve inches of space in his closet. With the way his suits were placed, she was almost afraid to let her things touch his perfect lineup. Still, she quickly ran out of space, so there was nothing to it. Damian would just have to deal. She paused—or she would. Either way, Kerry carefully inched over each suit one quarter inch at a time and claimed another two inches. She had a couple of blouses, a pair of cotton and Lycra pants and a skirt that were perfect for interviews that she really didn't want to fold and have to reiron if the opportunity arose.

Everything out and nothing left to do but start her new not-quite-normal, Kerry straightened her back and prepared to head back downstairs. She didn't know what to expect, especially after the odd scene she'd returned to once she'd squared things with her landlord and retrieved her stuff.

She had been able to tell immediately that she'd walked in on a serious scene between the brothers. They all fell silent, and the energy was tense, making Kerry just want to take her bags and bolt. But Noah seemed to recover first and was at her side with a smile and quick looks between himself, Jesse and Damian. "Don't mind these two, Kerry," he said, taking her duffel from her hand and heading for the stairs. "They just like to go at it. And hey, if Damian's bed is as hard as his head, you can always use mine. I'll be on tour, so it's safe." He grinned. "And even if I'm not."

She gave his arm a smack, though she knew he was only kidding. "Thanks, but no thanks. I'm sure it will be fine."

"Yeah, I'm sure it will be, jokester," Damian said. "Besides, there is hardly any privacy up there with you and Lucas and that open space."

"There is that," Lucas said. "Not that I wouldn't enjoy the company."

"I bet you would. You hate being alone," Noah said. "You're probably missing me like crazy now."

"Yeah, don't count on it. Who's missing who? You're the one who moved out so quick."

"I moved for work. It was just much easier."

"We all moved for work," Damian added. "But here we are now."

Kerry looked to Jesse. He was oddly quiet and, more strangely, seriously taking in the exchange between his brothers.

"I'm sure Damian's room will be just fine," she said, then looked over at Damian. "Thanks again."

"Yeah, sure," he responded. Then nodded. "Listen. I've got to go. But I made some space for you. It should be, um, enough."

She raised a brow but smiled and nodded. "More than enough." What was going on here? It felt weird, but not like their normal weird, and not like it was just about her. Kerry felt like there was a puzzle piece that someone was unfairly holding away from her.

Damian turned to Jesse. "We'll talk more later once I look into exactly where we stand. In the meantime, I guess we're clear and you just proceed."

To that Jesse didn't respond but only nodded, which gave Kerry even more unease. What the hell had happened while she was packing at her place? But Damian just left, and with him gone

Jesse tried to do a quick cover, finally smiling at Kerry and walking over to take her bags.

"I've got them," she said, stopping him. She gave hard looks to each of those who remained as she picked up her suitcase and threw it across her body. "I'm going to unpack. You guys just continue what you were doing."

When Kerry made it back down to the shop, though, it was quiet. Noah and Lucas were not in the main room, and only Jesse was left. He was taking yarns down from a display that had been on one of the top shelves for the past six months.

"Are you sure this will be okay?" she asked.

"What?" he responded, pausing where he was on the small ladder to turn her way. She walked toward him to give him a hand. "You don't think I should take these down now? I figured I might as well get moving. We've got a lot to do. Damian is right about getting money in here fast."

She shook her head and took an armful of yarns. "No. I'm not talking about that." At the moment the display of warm tweeds was not on her mind, though she knew it should be. "Taking these down is fine," she said. "As a matter of fact, it's long overdue. But I'm talking about me moving into Damian's room. Even though it's temporary, I don't want to make you or your brothers uncomfortable. I hate the idea of intruding on your life, and I feel like it was still pretty tense when I got back."

She hated the fact that she couldn't shake her sketchy feeling from that morning, and she hated more that she couldn't shake her feelings over coming in to see Erika leaving the other morning. How many mornings like that would she have to endure with a smile while she was living there? Hopefully not many, because with just the one she thought she might have reached her limit.

Jesse handed her more yarn as his eyes hinted at sparking. "You're not intruding on my life at all. And I thought we'd cleared this up."

"Yeah, but it didn't seem that way when I came back this afternoon."

He let out an agitated breath. "What you saw this afternoon was just posturing, on all our parts. I would have thought you'd be used to it by now."

It was Kerry's turn to frown. She would have thought so too, and for the most part she was used to it. She'd seen enough of it over the years of being in and out of this shop and in and out of their lives. But now, without Mama Joy, it somehow seemed different. She had been the mediator and the ultimate ender of all their squabbles. Without her, every situation seemed that much bigger, at least in Kerry's mind, and to her it felt like the brothers' relationships were teetering on the edges of their existence.

She couldn't bear it if she was the thing that took them over the edge.

"My brothers have no reason to be uncomfortable," he said as he stepped down from the ladder. She took a step back, but he was still really close. So close she had to look up at him. "And even if they are, I don't care. You're here and that's that. I'm fine with it, so they should be too." He cocked his head to the side, peering at her more closely. "Why? Are you not comfortable with being here?" There was a quick flash in his eyes and his lips quirked up. "Any particular reason why you shouldn't be?"

Kerry stared at him. What was he playing at now? One minute hot, the next cold. "No, Jes. I'm fine with it. There's nothing for me to be uncomfortable about."

His smile widened and he stepped back, letting out a sigh that was followed by a distinct flush of embarrassment to his tanned cheeks. "Good," he said, the relief evident in his voice. "We can move on now, right?"

"Let's. Please." *Dear Lord, please.* She wouldn't—no, couldn't let him know he was getting to her. Kerry did her best to smile as she put the yarns in her hand on the table, arranging and rearranging them by color and then by texture. She hoped they could move on. He seemed to be.

Jesse tapped her on the top of her head.

"What's with that?" she said, rubbing at her head. "We're not in high school."

He frowned. "Well, then stop overthinking like you're studying for the SATs. Your living here is not that serious. And you could do with getting over yourself a little too, missy. Not everything is about you."

Kerry blinked. Not about her? So she was right—she had walked in on something else. Which meant she needed to get over her own shit, and quick. What she had said to Val earlier was true. He didn't think of her as anything more than a distant family member, so distant that she'd be lucky if he even tried her potato salad if offered at the Strong family barbecue.

"I am over myself," she said. "I mean, I don't know what you're talking about. When was I ever into myself?"

Jesse laughed.

"Either way, I'm not thinking about my living situation. But what's the problem? Is it anything I can help with?"

His smile quickly disappeared. "You're doing more than enough. I couldn't ask for more."

Kerry didn't like the sound of that, but something in his voice let her know she'd pushed enough for one day.

"Fine. And I got Damian's message loud and clear. We need to get the business up and running as quickly as we can. Is taking these things down and doing your planned renovations even still possible?"

Jesse looked around. His eyes were full of determination, but now she also saw something else she couldn't quite place. Fear? Uncertainty? Desperation? Maybe a bit of all of that. "It has to be," Jesse said. "I'm going to make sure it all works out." He gave her a wobbly smile and her heart did a little half tilt. "I'm not worried about it, Kerry, and you shouldn't be either. We'll give this place the face-lift it needs and get the shop open quickly. Plus, with you here giving me a crash course to get me in shape, we've got this."

Kerry let her eyes go to where his had gone as she fingered the tweed yarn. "Do you really want to go that far? It would go so much faster if we just reopened as is. You all don't have a lot of money to spare."

He reached out and touched the yarn too. It was intimate, the gentle way his fingers trailed over the threads. Kerry could practically feel his fingers caressing her own skin. She swallowed, pulling her hand away and lacing her fingers, interlocking them with those of her other hand.

"We can't afford it and we can't not afford it. Now is the time to pull out all the stops. We only have one chance at this." The fear and desperation in his voice was clear now.

Kerry reached over and patted his hand.

He looked at her coolly as he pulled his hand away. The look was not like one she was used to, and neither was his tone. "We have to at least give the place some sort of meaningful change and modernization. We need to move the furniture around, paint. Give the windows a face-lift. Perhaps new signage. Do something to let people know that, although it's not completely changed, there is something new here."

Something new. Jesse's words, even his in-the-moment cool demeanor, resonated with Kerry. He was right. Hell, she'd known he was right when she'd overheard him back when she was helping Errol with his tangled project. She looked around the shop again. Lighter paint in strategic spots would bring out the beauty of Mama Joy's dark woods, giving the shop a much-needed brightness. Bringing in some of the ideas from his Pinterest boards could certainly help modernize the place, and updating the windows could do a lot for street traffic.

"You're right, I know. But still, we should be careful. You wouldn't want to alienate any of the older, long-standing customers."

"Don't worry, we won't. Besides, I've got you to be sure of that."

Kerry's brows tightened. "What is that supposed to mean? Are you trying to imply I'm some sort of fuddy-duddy?"

Jesse's lips quirked as he looked her up and down. Dammit if she wasn't suddenly self-conscious about her overly ironed top and practically to-the-knee shorts. It was as if the shorts that Val had chopped were calling her name, but just as fast as she heard their call, she let the sound fade away. She'd never be able to pull them off. And even if she could, the effect would be wasted on Jesse. Better to save them for a night out with Val. Surely, she wouldn't go home alone wearing those. But that thought caused her to pull up short too.

Whose home would she go to? Right now, she couldn't even take a guy back to her own place, and there was no way she'd be pulling one through here, not in Damian's room. She grinned; the thought of Jesse having the type of run-in that she'd had with

Erika did hold a certain amount of appeal. She twisted her lip. It was all wasted thinking. Wasted and silly.

She stopped Jesse with a challenging glare. "Well?"

"Of course I'm not calling you old," he finally said after two beats too long. "I'm just saying your sweet charm will be sure to keep the seasoned set coming through."

She let out a groan. "Whatever, dude. I got your point." She turned, annoyed, but glad he was showing his ass and helping put the kibosh on the prickly feelings she was having. "Since you started, let's continue with taking down the old yarns. Back up on the ladder with you," she ordered as she set the tweeds aside. "Let's move it. There's only so much time left today."

"Ker, I didn't—" he started. She looked at him, waiting for his next words, but he stopped. "You're right," he said, seemingly switching gears and heading back up the ladder. "There's only so much time left. Can you spot me and catch the yarns as I toss them down?"

15

DESPITE ALL ITS weird awkwardness, it was still a good day. Plans for the shop were hashed out and firmed up. At least Kerry felt they kind of were. Jesse seemed confident, and that was enough for her to at least feel a moderate amount of relief, though she couldn't shake the feeling that something was still off. But if they followed their schedule and had the help of the other brothers, they should be about ready to successfully fully reopen within a couple of weeks, if not sooner. Sure, that would probably not satisfy Damian, but nothing probably ever would. This way he'd at least be moderately appeased with what she hoped was steady progress. Kerry, for one, would back Jesse up. At least for now.

He'd convinced her—they were either in it to win it or they were out. "Mama Joy would be proud," Kerry said as she picked up another box of sorted yarn to move it to the storage area. When Jesse didn't respond, she thought maybe he hadn't heard her. She stepped around to see him and noticed the hard set of his jaw. "Okay, note to self. Don't bring up Mama Joy."

Jesse's pupils seemed to dilate as they focused on her. "No," he said softly. "Of course you can bring her up. I'd just rather you didn't go on with me on all that 'she would be proud' bullshit though."

Where the hell had that come from?

She watched as he stalked over to the large counter and reached to pick up the remote. In seconds the shop was filled with the sounds of the local R&B station. They were playing an old nineties jam that was still in high rotation. There was smacking, flipping and rubbing down, and Kerry was getting some serious deflection vibes from the way Jesse was nodding his head as if he was suddenly all into the old groove.

Kerry rolled her eyes, then marched over and picked up the remote and flipped the switch to another station. But when a more contemporary song came on with lyrics about working and spinning on it, Kerry opted to change it back. She lowered the volume. "Fine, but you could turn it down a bit. I got your message loud and clear. I'll temper my words, or better yet, I won't talk at all." She started to walk away, but his hand on the top of her arm pulled her back. She swung around to him, looking him hard in his eyes.

"That's not it. You can say what you want, Kerry. It's me. I just don't know how well I can receive it, and I don't want to hurt you by acting like an ass and lashing out in the wrong way."

Kinda like you just did. Kerry bit at her lip as she looked at him more closely. She could see that now. He really didn't want to act like an ass, as he said—at least not all the time. And he really was hanging by a thread. Struggling at every turn with trying to find the right words to say, and even worse, the ones to hold back on. And she did the same. If it was hard for her, then how much harder must it be for him? His emotions must be totally on edge, and here she was constantly underfoot. She knew what it was like being afraid that whatever you said would surely come out wrong and so, in the end, opting for the simplest and the shortest thing.

"I understand," Kerry said.

Jesse nodded. "I know you do. And I'm sorry about that. I wish you didn't."

Just then Kerry's stomach growled. Loudly.

"Well, if that isn't necessary comic relief," Jesse said.

"And at my expense," Kerry mumbled. "Who would have thought it."

He reached out and gave her arm a nudge. "Since when have we ever been embarrassed around each other, roomie?"

"Since when have we not?" Kerry blurted out before her mind could stop the words.

Jesse looked at her in shock before his eyes went soft and he smiled. "Have you always been this silly? We'll be getting closer over these next few weeks that you're here. I'm sure we'll get to know each other a lot more intimately than a stomach growl as time goes on."

She side-eyed him, and he laughed, more of his typical easygoing self back.

"Chill it out a little, Ms. Dirty Mind." He shook his head, then came closer to her. Looked her in the eyes with a playful grin. "Jeez. Now I see why you were embarrassed. Kerrryyy! I wonder if Ma Joy ever had any hint of just what types of thoughts were going on behind those innocent big brown eyes."

"You chill! I was referring to the thought of you and getting intimate with your bodily functions. I hope you can remember that there is a woman staying with you and put the toilet seat down when you go. I don't want to hit water if I have to go in the middle of the night."

He leaned back up and tilted his head. "Don't worry. My ma taught me well enough about that."

She nodded and turned away, but her stomach growled again.

"I'll be back," Jesse said, starting for the door.

"Where are you going?"

"You're obviously hungry. I'm going to the bodega and picking us up some sandwiches."

She put up her hands and shook her head. "You don't have to feed me, Jesse. I don't want to put you out."

He let out a frustrated breath. "And I'm supposed to concentrate over the racket of your stomach." He smiled. "Relax. I could eat too. Chopped cheese is okay? Chips and a soda?"

Kerry nodded. "Fine. With extra hot sauce."

She wouldn't argue with him anymore. If he wanted to feed her, she'd let him. Besides, at the moment she needed her appetite satiated, and more so she needed Jesse Strong out of her immediate space so she could take a much-needed deep breath.

JESSE TOOK A deep breath. Though it was warm, the late afternoon air, thick with the weight of summer in New York, was just what he needed to clear his head. Was he really made to be cooped up inside a shop all day? Would the stuffiness of it all, the tediousness of a sure 'nuff more than nine-to-five stifle the life out of him? He froze as he realized he was doing what he'd always done whenever what felt like a scary and, who knew, possibly promising opportunity came before him. He was making excuses and planning his escape.

It was his way. He was good at it. The only person who'd never let him run, who'd somehow been able to hold on to him when everyone else considered him a lost cause—his mother, his first foster families, the group home—was Mama Joy. And now here he was trying to run from the opportunity she had left him. No, with the bank loan and his brothers going all in with him, it wasn't an opportunity but a responsibility that she'd left him.

He slowed his steps further and looked back toward the shop, now noticing the trash next to the cans off to the side, and frowned. He'd have to clear that up. Mama Joy would never let there be trash in front of the shop. Not ever.

The image of her sweeping and clearing carelessly thrown trash from the sidewalk when it should have been something he did for her burned through his memory. He could no longer make excuses. Just like he could no longer lie to himself by saying it was his fear of the shop that had him on the run. No, it was the woman who was currently inside the shop: Kerry, with her serious demeanor but at the same time equally soft heart. She scared the shit out of him. Her looks, the way she stared. He knew she wanted him. Worse than that, he knew she cared for him more than he ever did or would deserve being cared for. Still, the fact remained that he needed her. Needed her for the shop and needed her for his soul right now.

She hated it when he said she would be the driving force that kept the old customers coming in, but it was true, and not in the way she'd taken it.

The older women came because of the kinship they'd felt with Mama Joy. During the times that Jesse had been in the shop, in and out, sometimes sitting in the back during a class or just hanging in the loft, he loved seeing the women as they came in and their immediate transformations when they entered the shop's welcoming atmosphere.

He would watch as it seemed like a little of the weight of the world—not all of it, mind you, but just a bit—was lifted from their shoulders as they browsed the yarns or talked about a pattern with Mama Joy. For that small stretch of time they were almost carefree. Mama Joy had a gift, and that same gift was in Kerry too.

And he couldn't lie to himself about Kerry any longer either. He thought of her inside the shop now, angry, agitated, hungry and possibly a little hurt by his mixed signals. He was a first-class jerk for confusing her, though. A-plus on that one. If there were degrees for screwing over women and fucking up their minds and hearts, then he'd have a doctorate for sure. But he didn't know what else to do when it came to Kerry. Jesse let out a sigh as he got to the bodega door and walked inside. His eyes met the slightly judging gaze of Mickey, the black-and-white cat that guarded the establishment from his perch on a high spot over the laundry detergents and floor cleaners. He gave Mickey a nod and got dust in response. *I feel you, Mick,* he thought.

He waved to Santi, who was on the register, and went to the back to place his order with Ray, who was on the grill. Jesse fought to clear his mind of Kerry as he looked around the shop. He grabbed a two-liter soda for the two of them to share, put it back and went for a sixteen-ounce for her instead and a beer for himself. Then the image of her tossing all those beer cans and Erika came to his mind, and he put the beer back, guilt rising up his throat. "Shit, I might as well just get myself a juice box, acting like this," he mumbled to himself.

"What was that, Jesse Strong?"

Jesse turned and looked down at Sister Purnell, one of the shop's regulars and Mama Joy's longtime knitting circle friends.

The petite older woman with the barely lined caramel skin was currently looking up at him like she was ready to take off her flip-flop and hit him with it. It was clear that she'd heard what he'd said, which was just perfect. She was probably thinking, "Is that how Joy raised you to talk?"

"Um, it was nothing, Sister Purnell. Thanks so much for the food you dropped off. It was delicious. You were too generous. All you ladies were," he said by way of trying to cover his getting caught cussing in public by the old lady.

Sister Purnell looked him up and down sternly, then waved her hand. "It was nothing," she finally said. "What else should I do? Joy was my friend; practically family. Of course I'm gonna look out for her boys." She cleared her throat loudly, then frowned deeper. "You gonna pick a drink or just stand there letting all the cold air out of that icebox?"

Jesse was tempted to curse again, but thankfully he held it back, or he just might have gotten a flip-flop to the head. He opted for the two liter and closed the fridge.

Sister Purnell nodded, then reached up for some rice mix on a high shelf. Jesse instantly grabbed it for her. She finally cracked a smile. "Thanks, dear." She looked at him closer, and he fought to not crack under her inspection as the hairs on the back of his neck started to rise. "You're all right. I can see that," she finally declared.

Jesse blinked as he tried to let the woman's words wash over him. How could she say that when he felt anything but all right? What gave her the right? Just because she called herself saved and fancied herself some sort of prophetess. She was prophesying up the wrong tree today. Jesse cleared his throat. "If you say so. I'd better get going. My sandwiches are probably up."

He was about to walk away when her words stopped him before he got past the ramen noodles. "Dinner for two?" Sister Purnell's voice was as innocent as it could be for such a loaded comment.

Jesse turned.

"I wouldn't go so far as that, Sister Purnell. It's just dinner—nothing more."

She smiled wider, and Jesse hated the sharp look behind that smile. "Well, you keep behaving, Jesse. We'll be by to check on you, and tell Kerry I said hi. I'm glad to hear the whole uproar at her building wasn't too serious and she's landed in a safe place."

Jesse nodded and mustered up a weak smile as he hightailed it to the counter.

Jesse couldn't pay for his sandwiches and get back to the shop fast enough. He was all right, a safe space and they would come to check on him? A vision of Sister Purnell and the Old Knitting Gang busting in on him, needles and hooks at the ready if he dared defile Kerry, had him practically sweating. And here he had thought having her in the shop to bring in the sweet old ladies was a good idea.

16

IF TIMING WASN'T a total bitch, he didn't know what was. He had perfect, or at least in his mind it was perfect, chopped cheese just waiting on them—lettuce, tomato, mayo, ketchup, oil and vinegar— but his sandwiches would be ruined if he didn't defuse this situation before his eyes and do it quickly.

"I told her you were out and we aren't officially opened for business yet," Kerry said, jutting her chin toward a stone-faced Erika as Jesse hit the vestibule of Strong Knits.

Upon noticing he'd come up, Erika turned around toward him. She smiled but he still caught the hard edge of tension she'd been sporting around her lips a moment before. Just how long had she been here, and what had these two been talking about during that time?

Erika held up a small bag and waved it at him. "And I told her I wasn't here on business—look, I brought refreshments."

"I bet you did," Kerry mumbled.

Jesse held tight to his smile. That was surprising.

Still, he didn't have time, and he thought he had been clear with Erika when she'd left the other morning. Why was she back here now? "I understand, Erika, but now is not a good time. Kerry and I still have a lot of work to do."

Erika looked down at the bags in his hands, the soda, chips and sandwiches easily visible through the cheap plastic of the deli bags. "Work?" she questioned, her eyes going from the bags and back up to him. "Looks to me like the two of you are settling in for a nice evening." She eyed Jesse, then let her glance slide over to Kerry. The look she gave her before her gaze went back to Jesse could be described as dismissive at best. He felt his blood start to heat. "Come on. Enough with the work. It's quitting time. I'm sure your assistant here would understand."

"Kerry is not my assistant."

"No," Kerry chimed up. She reached out her hand past Erika toward the bags in Jesse's hand. "Not his assistant at all. But I am hungry." She looked at Jesse as she lifted the bags from his fingers. "I'll let you take care of this while I set up the food upstairs. It's getting late and I am ready to eat."

She didn't look twice at Erika as she took the bags and peeked in, giving the sandwiches a sniff. "Oh, they smell terrific," she said, her smile bright and her brown eyes sparkling behind her glasses. "And you got me honey barbecue chips. My favorite!" She was laying it on thick as hell, which spoke to what must have been going on before he'd gotten there.

"I know," Jesse said, knowing he was further exasperating the situation, but he'd thought he'd been clear with Erika when he'd seen her off. Besides, he didn't like her stance over Kerry, or the way she was talking as well as just so happening to show up at the shop lately. It all felt off and, he didn't know, slightly predatory. Like she was pouncing on his feelings of not wanting to be alone.

He hated feeling like he may have let his guard down that much and shown himself to be so vulnerable, especially to someone like her, who clearly didn't have any true feelings for him.

Kerry looked from him to Erika, then cleared her throat. "Well, I'll head upstairs and get this set up."

Erika's exhalation of breath was practically enough to knock down a less formidable person, but Kerry only walked away without a backward glance. He could almost describe her exit as savage, but he never thought he'd describe anything Kerry did with such a word. She was always so sweet, calm and steady. No, "savage" was not a word he'd use for her.

Before Kerry was completely out of earshot, Erika turned back to him. "Your assistant really is uppity in her opinion of herself."

He frowned. "'Uppity'? Hmm. What a strange word to use. But if you say so, she just may be." He smiled, looking back into the shop toward where Kerry had gone, then returned his attention to Erika, more serious now. "And I told you, she's not my assistant."

Erika crossed her arms over her ample chest. The bag with the bottle of whatever she'd brought to ease them both into a sexual trance rustled as she did so. "Well, if she's not your assistant, then what's her position?"

He smiled, suddenly thinking of multiple positions he'd happily like to see Kerry in, some professional and some personal, all probably not feasible if he had any hope of keeping her as his friend. He felt Erika's gaze intensify even further, practically boring through him. Why he had fallen for her easygoing, friends-with-benefits, no-strings-attached line was beyond him.

Yeah, he knew she wasn't seeing him exclusively. It wasn't like Erika hid that fact. But she was pressing him on his relationship with Kerry like she was ready to change that. Her thinning lips and narrowed eyes showed a side of her that he was embarrassed to say he was never interested in seeing. They were both sleeping with other people and exclusivity was never their deal, but yeah, he knew he probably should have seen the signs with Erika and maybe should have been stronger with warding her off when she was getting too close. "I don't think you're in a position to ask that question," Jesse said. Erika's eyes hardened further, and he got the distinct feeling his answer could bring on more problems than solutions—not for him, but possibly for Kerry. He let out a sigh. "She's my coworker and longtime friend, but that isn't any business of yours."

Erika stared at him for a few beats. He could practically hear the clicking of the wheels of calculation turning behind her eyes before she blinked and smiled. "Okay, I get it. You're busy, and she's helping you out." She reached out her hand and brought it around to the back of his neck. She rubbed at it, the action meant to be sensual but, right now, feeling like a vise threatening to turn into a tight clamp. "I just came because I thought you might need some relaxation. You don't want to work too hard. You know what they say about 'all work' and all that."

Jesse ducked his head and removed himself from her grip. "Right now, all work is what it is for me. Listen, thanks, but maybe next time a text first?"

She fixed her mouth into a pout. It had worked the other night but wouldn't tonight. "I did text," she said. "You didn't answer."

Jesse looked at her. His eyes softened and an apology was on the tip of his lips. Erika licked her lips and suddenly for some reason his mind went to his chopped cheese with the works waiting for him inside. He was damned hungry. He tilted his head. "Maybe next time you wait until you get an answer."

———— ‿ ————

KERRY WASN'T WAITING. Screw that. The sandwich was hot, and she was hungry. Hungry and angry. Hangry. She didn't know if she wanted more to take a bite out of the chopped cheese, Jesse or Erika. She shook her head as she sat down, took a breath and looked at her plated sandwich. Definitely not Erika. She was a full-on annoyance but not worth Kerry putting her back into getting stressed over. Besides, for all Erika's hard looks and flexing like she was the shit, it was easy to see she was just insecure and trying her best to get Jesse's attention.

Kerry picked up her sandwich and took a healthy bite. It was good, as usual, with the perfect ratio of cheese to meat, and Jesse hadn't messed up on her toppings and the hot sauce was perfect. But still it didn't taste quite right. She looked over at the empty seat opposite, looked at his still-wrapped sandwich on the white plate with the floral border and thought of Jesse downstairs dealing with a clearly irate Erika.

Kerry had seen different versions of the same story told many ways over the years. Erika was just a new package. Jesse was a man who loved women but didn't love holding on to them. He wooed them fast and easy with his good looks and easygoing smile, and just as fast and just as easy, for him at least, he let them go. Attachment was not his thing. He'd given up a little of his time. But never his heart. She'd seen it since junior high. The girls who would come through looking for him under the guise of being interested in knitting and the shop. They'd have all sorts of flattering words for Mama Joy, and some would even go so far as to spend their precious allowances or hard-earned part-time money on a skein, but the conversation would always find its way to "Oh, and how is Jesse?" "You're his mom, right?" "Can you tell him Sandra, Yolanda, Tisha or whoever stopped by?"

The saddest of all were the girls who actually returned. The ones who used their yarn and actually made something for Jesse. Kerry often wondered what he did with all the hats and scarves woven with the tears of the brokenhearted. And Erika was no different. Here she was showing up at his door when one look at him and it was clear that she was on her way to the back of the line. Kerry frowned. Only difference with Erika the Toe Taylor was that her gift, packaged in tight Lycra with a side of 80-proof courage, wasn't as sweet and innocent as a handknitted scarf.

She worried about Jesse drowning his feelings in alcohol instead of facing them head-on. She knew she couldn't force her thoughts on him or even get him to talk. But still, thinking of him just screwing and getting drunk . . . that couldn't be the way either.

She took another bite and thought of pushing the sandwich aside when he appeared in the kitchen doorframe.

Kerry looked at him, and despite herself, her lips tightened, and she picked up her phone, because yeah, she suddenly had something urgent to check. Now who was the game player? She heard Jesse snort and looked up.

He was walking toward her with a half smile, but she could see the tension in his shoulders. *Don't comment. It's not your business. Don't comment.* "So you got rid of your company?" she said. *Fuck. What happened to not commenting?*

He nodded and sat. "I did. Sorry about that. I hope she didn't give you too hard a time. I didn't expect her to show up like that. I thought the other morning would be the last time." He started to unwrap his sandwich, then paused, scratching his ear. Was he waiting for her to say something? What was she supposed to say to that?

Kerry picked up her sandwich and stared at him. "So I gathered. But I don't think she's on the same page. I also don't think she's one to get the hint so easily. She'll be back." She took a bite of her sandwich, then a sip of her drink.

He nodded. "Yeah, I think you're right. It's probably her just being clingy. She thinks we're hooking up, so I guess that threw her off."

Her soda got caught in her throat and she coughed. "Thinks? Her morning-after look said hookup all the way." Kerry sighed and forced the sweet liquid down with a hard swallow. "You really are a lot, Jesse Strong. But I hope you set her right. I know I was a little cheeky downstairs, but of course she knows nothing is going on between us."

Jesse shrugged. Just shrugged.

"WTF with the shrug, Jes?"

He smiled and reached for her plate. "Come on. It's way too tense and quiet in here. Let's go eat in the living room. The game is on and I want to watch."

Kerry frowned. "What if I don't want to watch the game?"

He shrugged again. "Then we'll trade off on times. You let me check the score and I'll let you be in charge of the remote." Kerry raised her brow. It did seem fair. Now it was her turn to shrug. "Okay, fine. But you're going to tell me what happened with the rest of that conversation."

She followed him into the living room, carrying their drinks and placing them on coasters on the coffee table while he set up TV trays. The fact that Mama Joy had actual TV trays spoke to the woman's constant preparedness and ingenuity. Kerry could imagine her setting up the boys in there to watch TV and eat on special occasions but wanting them to not ruin the furniture, which was an old style but still in good condition, a testament to how well she'd kept her home even with four rambunctious boys growing up there.

She sat awkwardly, her hands clenched to the edge of the tray as Jesse flipped on the TV. He turned and looked at her. "Would you just relax and eat? These sandwiches have gotten cold enough. I thought you were hungry."

"And whose fault was that?" Kerry said, looking over at him.

Jesse rolled his eyes. "Okay, fine. You got me there. But hopefully it's all taken care of."

Kerry took a bite of her sandwich and gave him a skeptical look.

"Don't give me that look. And I was just teasing back in the kitchen. I told Erika we're coworkers and friends. Though I did let her know it wasn't really her business what we were."

Kerry frowned. "Don't you think that was a little harsh?"

He bit into his sandwich and looked at her. "I didn't like the tone she used with you. The assistant comment annoyed me."

"It wasn't a big deal," Kerry said.

He nodded. "Maybe, but I still didn't like it."

Kerry grabbed a chip, suddenly wanting to fill her mouth with another flavor. She watched as Jesse ate and focused on the baseball game on the TV. He grimaced as the Yankees pitcher threw yet another low and outside ball to the batter.

"I know what you're saying," he suddenly blurted out. "But I am focused on work here. Besides, we made good progress today. I know you have to work tomorrow at the center. But I'll continue. I have my checklist. We should be good."

Kerry nodded. "Sure. We should be."

There was a loud crack from the TV, and his attention was pulled forward. "You know," he said, "maybe we should add a TV down in the shop."

"What? Like in a barbershop?"

Jesse's expression hardened. "No, I don't mean like in a barbershop, funny girl. I just think it's an easy and not all that expensive way to make a change."

"But people come to the shop for a retreat. For an escape from their norm. How would having a TV help that?"

He shrugged. "I don't know. Maybe we could show knitting videos."

She blinked. It wasn't like his idea was bad; it was just that she'd never seen a yarn shop with a TV. Though with Jesse's penchant for avoiding boredom and how he seemed to hate silence, she had a feeling that if she didn't agree to this, he'd end up watching TV on his phone during any of his off times anyway. "Who knows," she finally said. "Maybe it could work."

"Of course it will work," he said with no small amount of finality. "It's all going to work." The last part seemed like more of a confirmation for himself than for her.

Kerry went to get another bite of her sandwich and realized it was gone. How did the time eating with him go by like that? He smiled at her. Shit. That's how. She made a move to get up and take her trash into the kitchen when Jesse put out a hand to stop her. "You sit. I've got it." He handed her the remote. "Here. Maybe find us something on Netflix if you're up to it. I promised you the remote."

"But—your game?" Kerry said, looking at the remote as if it were some sort of loaded weapon. Did he say Netflix? Was he using this to imply "Netflix and chill"?

Jesse pushed it into her hand, and she wrapped her fingers around the hard plastic.

"This game is all but over anyway. It's no use watching when I already know the outcome." He picked up their trash and disappeared into the kitchen.

Kerry let his words echo through her head as she scrolled through the Netflix menu. No use watching when he already knew the outcome. She couldn't agree more. She finally put down the remote and headed off to Damian's room. She'd do some knitting in there and watch something on her laptop. It was better that way. If she was chilling with Netflix, she'd do it her usual way . . . alone. Doing it on the couch next to Jesse was way too dangerous for her and her shaky hormones.

She passed Jesse on his way back to the living room and stretched in the most obviously-trying-to-be-nonchalant-and-failing way possible. "You know what, I'm a little tired. It has been a long day. I think I'm going to head off to bed."

Jesse looked at her with concern in his eyes. "You sure? It's still kind of early. Are you all right?"

Seriously? He was falling for this? Kerry nodded and gave him a smile. "I'm fine. Just tired. It's been a lot for one weekend, and with work tomorrow and the kids, I need to get a little rest."

She could see the slight disappointment as it fluttered across Jesse's face, but he covered it quickly. "Okay, then. Rest well. I'll stay up and hang out. Let me know if the TV is too loud for you."

She held her hand up. "I'm sure it will be fine," she said as she headed off to her—no, Damian's room, she reminded herself. "Good night."

"Let me know if you need anything," he yelled behind her.

She turned and nodded.

"In the bathroom or anything."

Kerry nodded again. "I'm good, Jes."

"You're good?"

She laughed this time before turning to Damian's door. She stood there, not quite ready to end the moment. "And so are you," Kerry mumbled as she stepped through the doorway and looked back at Jesse once more before closing the door behind herself.

17

KERRY SHOULDN'T HAVE been surprised to find Jesse not in the kitchen but already in the shop the next morning with his feet up on the farmhouse table knitting away. She had planned on leaving early through the residence entrance, getting a coffee and roll on her way to her morning job at the community center, but when she heard a shuffle and saw that the light was on she turned to head down the stairs to the shop.

As she stepped closer, she marveled at the quickness of Jesse's long, thick fingers and the fine, even quality of the stitches on his circular needles. He looked up at her with half-tired but still very sexy eyes. "Good morning," he said, his voice thick and slightly gruff from lack of overnight use.

"Morning," she said.

"What are you doing up so early?" she asked, then pointed to the almost-done hat on his needles. "Or did you even go to bed last night?"

He put the work in progress down and took a sip from the cup of coffee that was next to him. "I slept a little. Though not well."

Good. Though she didn't voice it out loud, she took some satisfaction in knowing she wasn't the only person in the house not sleeping well. "Well, it looks like you were making good use of your time." She stared at him again after taking in the cute little multicolored rolled-brim hat. "This little beauty going to anyone special?" she asked.

"No," he said, stretching and pulling his tee across his muscles in a manner that was way too provocative so early in the morning for her not to be affected. Kerry swallowed.

"I was thinking of doing a bunch of them with some of our odd yarns. And we could do a display. Maybe hang them with clothespins so that we can sell them. The yarn is doing no good just sitting in the half-off basket. This way we can recoup the cost and hopefully bring new customers into the store."

Kerry smiled. "I love that thinking. What a great idea!"

He blushed cutely before his expression clouded over. "It's not such a big idea. And I wish it were enough, but at least it's something." He shrugged. "I've seen versions of it done all over the Internet."

Kerry gave him a hard look. "So what, you've seen it on the Internet? Ours will be unique to us. It's not like their hats will be our hats. Don't be such a downer."

He made a face. "Our hats?"

"Well, you'll need a bunch to make a decent display. And with fall coming soon enough, you'll want to get it up. I can help you out. Maybe do some fingerless gloves too."

He grinned. "Have time for a cup of coffee before you head to the center? I picked up a bagel, or we have buttered rolls from the corner store. But only if you have the time."

Kerry walked over to the basket that held the yarns they had been stumped over what to do with yesterday. Her mind was already starting to click with excitement over how cute their new display would be.

"Kerry?" he asked, pulling her attention his way. "The coffee? Do you have time?"

She nodded but was already itching to get to work. "Oh yes, I have the time."

HARD AS IT was to leave her new project behind, the community center called, and it was, for now at least, a steady paycheck.

Val practically scared the pee out of Kerry by unexpectedly greeting her at the door when she went to open it in the morning, treating Kerry more like must-see programming instead of her good friend and coworker. With Val's overly friendly smile and super-nosy demeanor, for a minute Kerry thought she may have landed down in front of a Park Avenue doorman instead of her uptown homegirl. But there her friend was, causing Kerry to jump in surprise and pull out her earbuds as the door opened magically before Kerry could even grasp the handle.

"You scared the hell out of me," Kerry said.

Val gave Kerry a quick up and down, then frowned and handed her one of the cups of coffee she was balancing. "Thanks," Kerry said, taking the cup and a fast sip. She hadn't gotten to finish her cup back at the shop, instead getting caught up with Jesse in talk about the hats and fingerless gloves, with the time for sipping and chewing flying by faster than she'd anticipated. Though it was already hot out, the warm liquid was still welcome in the coolness of the center.

Working, low-income parents couldn't afford to send their kids to pricey summer camps, and if your utilities weren't included in your rent, running the AC all day just wasn't an option. Besides, who had the cash for ACs in each room when the novel idea of central air was a thing for the private houses of the burbs? The best you got around here was room to room, which meant most of the fam spending most of the day camping out in one room once the temps got past 80.

Usually taking to opposite extremes of being chilly and then overly hot, Kerry welcomed both the warmth and the air-conditioning this morning. She had awakened with the expected doubts she'd gone to bed with and had a restless night's sleep, but after seeing Jesse this morning and hearing more of his ideas, she could admit to being slightly more hopeful about being able to get through this time with him and come out with both the shop thriving and their friendship, if you could call it that, still intact.

Kerry looked at Val and caught the fact that she was still frowning. "What's with the face?" she said. "I said thanks for the coffee."

Val did a quick finger point, roaming her manicured nails in the air around Kerry's body and indicating her cropped pants, cap-sleeve top and knit vest. "Really? How did those pants and that shapeless top get in your bag? I don't remember putting them in there."

"So this is why you were at the door, to not only scare me but also do a uniform check? Are you going to start doing that with the kids too? Tell me, Teach, was I was supposed to wear my booty shorts to work today?"

Val made a face. "No, but you could have done a bit of cinching. Don't you remember what I said about shooting your shot?"

Kerry started down the hall toward the art room. "And who am I shooting it with? Class 3B?"

"Ha ha, very funny," Val answered. "But know I'll be stopping by the shop and spot-checking. I mean it. You need to come out of that shell of yours and get your swerve on."

"I swerve plenty. Thanks."

Val stopped walking and stared at her. "Woman, please. You ain't swerved in damned near a year."

"It hasn't been that long."

"Maybe not, but you can't count the past mistakes you've been with as anywhere close to a good swerve." Kerry tilted her head as the thankfully now-faint memories of Paul and Brice before him filtered through her brain. Ugh, seemed she was barely any better than her mother when it came to partners. Another reason she should firmly and forcefully not listen to her heart and for sure not her body when it came to matters with Jesse. Better to stay safe and stay in her lane. Swerving was for drunks. And she didn't need any more DUIs on her record.

"So from the looks of your outfit," Val continued as they started back down the hall, "and the fact that you're here on time, I can assume you got to bed nice and early and alone last night?"

Kerry gave her a look. "I guess I can say the same about you."

Val laughed. "Okay, I get your point. Still, I didn't even text you last night because I was hoping you'd not waste any time and dive in feetfirst and be too busy to answer."

They walked into the classroom and Kerry stored her things. There were only a few minutes before the first kids would arrive. She'd already heard the early ones in the cafeteria, enjoying the free breakfast service. "Well, the early to bed part was right. I was pooped out after the weekend." She smiled. "But I am excited about all Jesse's plans for the shop."

Val looked immediately bored. "Good for you."

Kerry laughed. "Sorry this story isn't going the way you'd hoped."

Her friend shrugged. "Well, you could have called me. You knew I'd be wondering."

"What are we, thirteen?"

Val made a face. "And what's wrong with that? If you can't be thirteen with me then who *can* you be thirteen with?"

She had a point. Val was just about the only person she could let her hair down with. Yes, Val was judgy and pushy, and she couldn't give a crap about yarn and knitting, but her friend always had her back, and she had for years. That counted for something. She knew Val had her best, if not misguided, interests at heart.

Val sighed. "I guess it's only me who's stuck in the teen hormonal stage as a full-grown woman, because if I was under that roof, I'd be going crazy."

"So why are you so hell-bent on torturing me if that's how you feel?" Kerry asked.

Val looked at her guiltily. "I don't know. I guess I figured one of us should have the time of her life. You've been around all those fine-assed men for all those years—it's about time you tasted that forbidden fruit. Take one for the team."

Kerry rolled her eyes. "Seriously, this is ridiculous, and none of their fruit is all that forbidden. Trust me. Each one of them has gotten around plenty. Hell, there was one woman I had to practically pull out Mama Joy's all-straw broom yesterday to chase her off the porch. Luckily Jesse came back in time before things got heated, and he got rid of her himself."

Val paused from where she was sorting supplies for the day. "Wait, he got rid of her? Are you telling me Jesse turned away another woman for you?"

"No, of course not for me," Kerry said. "It was just that he'd brought us chopped cheese and the sandwiches were getting cold."

Val grinned. "He bought you dinner?"

"Chopped cheese is hardly dinner."

"You ate, heifer, didn't you?"

"Yes, I ate."

"Was it your last meal for the night?"

Kerry frowned. "Yeah, it was."

"Did you pay? Did he ask you for sandwich money?"

Kerry didn't like where this was going at all. "No, I didn't pay, and no, he didn't ask me for money, but—" She was cut off when Val raised a hand to her face.

"Well then, he bought you dinner. That's it, you and the cheap pretty bastard had a dinner date, and he dumped a surefire booty call to make it happen."

Kerry was left blinking and stunned to temporary silence over Val's logic as she watched the kids pile in for their morning lesson.

Most were happy and bubbly, but it was Errol's slightly off demeanor that pulled her attention to full alert. She greeted each child but watched him especially as they worked on their summer reading murals. Thanks to Emily and her diligence, the kids had made their reading goals, and many had surpassed them, so they had lots of materials to pick from for their murals. But Kerry could see that Errol wasn't himself, less talkative with both the girls and the boys. Even his answers to her were polite but shorter than normal when she'd asked why he'd chosen his book and subject, Benjamin Banneker. She wondered what was wrong but didn't want to press him after he assured her all was fine.

Just as they were finishing their second class, their often-missing director, Linda Perkins, walked by with Mr. Watkins and another man. He was youngish. Early thirties. Brown skin, low-cut hair, broad shoulders and dark, deep-set eyes that seemed to see everything all at once. He had full lips that he held in a serious set, but as he passed the art room and looked in, he nodded at Kerry and Val, and those loose, stern lips transformed into something worldly once he broke into a smile. His whole face did, becoming bright and open and almost angelic. For a moment Kerry thought Val would legit swoon right there, but thankfully Linda Perkins was there to break the potential swoonation.

"Valencia, Kerry, this is Mr. Webb. He'll be shadowing me this next week," Linda started, her voice clipped, her words coming out tight as if she was holding something back.

Mr. Webb smiled and held out his hand. "Please call me Gabriel." His voice was rumbly and deep.

And upon hearing it, Imara turned and jumped from her seat. "Daddy! You're here!"

Both Kerry and Val went wide-eyed as Gabriel Webb's smile went even more cinematic and lethal and he accepted Imara's hug around his waist, giving her a big squeeze in return. What star had this one fallen from? "I told you I would be."

"Yeah, I know you did, but I still didn't think you really would," she said with a huge smile. "I'm glad." It was then that Kerry saw the similarities. They had the same deep-set eyes, chestnut coloring and bright smiles. She looked to Imara's dad's left hand. Nope. No ring, though. Not that it told the whole story, but still it was interesting.

He looked from Kerry to Val, then back down at Imara. "You want to introduce me to your teachers?" he said.

She grinned. "Sure. This is Miss Val. She teaches us art and she's a great singer and dancer. She's also good with puzzles too.

And hair braiding! She's fixed me up a few times when grandma was busy or running late," the young girl said in a lower tone.

Linda's face went slightly twisted but Val just smiled at Gabriel. It was suspiciously shy, bordering on coy. "It was nothing," she said softly.

"Well, it seems like it was something big to Imara."

Val shrugged, which was so uncharacteristically not her, since she was usually front and center ready to take her praise, or better yet she'd have something to say to this dad, giving him tips on hair and how to get it done.

Imara turned toward Kerry. "Miss Kerry is really good at lots of things. She's great with color and really great with yarn. She can crochet and even knit. Can you believe that? She's the one who works at the yarn shop I told you about."

"Is she now?" he said with a voice full of wonder, though the bit of information didn't call for so much wonderment. Kerry had to give it to Imara, she'd be a wiz at matchmaking and making introductions. The little girl was a natural.

Just then Alison came in. Today she was wearing farmer's overalls and had her hair done up in box braids. She'd gelled her edges down to Instagram perfection and had a bright pink bandana topping off the look. Imara looked at her with wide eyes and waved a hand. "And that's Mizz Ali. She likes to be called Mizz Ali." She turned and went back to her seat, intros over.

Linda looked at Alison and blinked. She gave her a quick introduction to Gabriel Webb but kept it about as short as little Imara's and left. Her displeasure over Alison's appearance was clear. They didn't have much of a dress code at the center, it being casual and a summer season, but Alison did take things to the limit when it

came to professionalism and her position. But what did it matter?
She had her position, and that was the bottom line.

But the question remained—what was Gabriel Webb, Imara's
father, doing there, and why was he shadowing Linda? When they
left, Kerry, Val and Alison looked at each other.

"I hear he and the mother are over. Been over. He used to work
out of town, but he's back because the mother was a bit of a train
wreck," Alison whispered in a voice that wasn't near whispery
enough.

Kerry looked around the classroom. "You mind shutting it,
please?" Thankfully Imara was on the other side of the class, but
still, she didn't need the teachers talking about her home life like
this.

"Oh yes, sure, you're right," Alison said. She began to walk out
of the class, but turned back toward Kerry and Val. "One more
thing though."

"What is it, Fanny Farmer?" Val said, clearly done with her.

Alison laughed. "I call dibs!" And she practically ran out of the
classroom, the kids all looking after her.

Val sucked in a breath. "The hell she does," Val said through
clenched teeth.

Kerry looked at Val, whose brown cheeks were purpling. "Hold
on, girl. You don't know that man, and remember, you're at work."
Kerry barely held back on her laughter.

Val glared at her. "The man doesn't matter. He was just okay.
It's the principle of it all. And I won't be on the clock after three,
now, will I?"

"Lord help our lil Fanny Farmer! She'd better watch out."

18

COMING BACK INTO the shop that afternoon, Kerry was surprised to see that it wasn't technically closed. Yes, the sign on the door was flipped to the closed position, but Mrs. Hamilton, Ms. Diaz, Ms. June, Ms. Cherry and Sister Purnell were all there and gathered around the table knitting away as if it was their normal Monday Old Knitting Gang circle and Mama Joy would come out of the kitchen and join them at any moment. Kerry greeted each of them with smiles and hugs, and looked at Jesse with questioning eyes when he surprised her by walking out from the kitchen area with a tray of mugs.

He gave Kerry a smile and an easy shrug, but his look of panic was clearly evident. And she thought she picked up on an edge of relief.

They weren't due to open again for at least another week or two. What were these women doing here, knitting and crocheting among the half-cleared shelves and chaos as if it was a normal day?

"Oh, stop with the looks, you two," Mrs. Hamilton said. "We know we're being intrusive—taking liberties comes with age and all. Stop acting like it's so big a deal and get comfortable." She gave Kerry a wide smile then, softening her expression and making her already round face that much rounder. "I was about to head over to B's place," she said, talking about Ms. June, who was often referred to as Junie B. Her full name, Kerry had yet to catch in all the years she'd known her. Mrs. Hamilton continued, "When I passed by here and saw that Jesse wasn't doing much of anything but shifting boxes back and forth."

Jesse raised a finger. "Um, I was doing a little more than that, Mrs. Hamilton."

She raised her brow at him. "Were you now, dear?"

He tilted his head. "Okay, maybe not that much more."

She turned back to Kerry as if he'd hardly spoken. Jesse would learn quickly that he'd gotten off lightly with that little exchange. "And," she said exaggeratedly, "when I asked Jesse what he was up to, he said he was making plans for some sort of big reopening." She made a *pfft* sound. "Making plans. Well, I figured while he was making plans, we could still have our usual circle here. B's place is the only spot big enough to hold us all, but her elevators are iffy at best, and you know Elena can't do stairs."

"That's the truth. My arthritis stays working on me," Ms. Diaz said. She was a petite older women who, though she said she couldn't do stairs, Kerry had seen elbow and just about tackle more formidable women for the best whiting at the fish market. Their excuse was dubious at best and if questioned on cross-examination would easily crumble. Not that she—or Jesse, from the looks of him—was up to questioning this crew.

"Plus, I brought my carrot cake," Ms. June added with a wide grin, as if that would make the intrusion all better.

Kerry looked down at the carrot cake. Maybe it kind of would.

As far as placations went, a person could do worse than Ms. June's carrot cake. Her baking was out of this world. She actually sold her cakes by the slice to some of the local businesses and made some decent extra money on the side. Kerry swallowed, suddenly hungry.

"We won't stay in your way long," Ms. June continued.

"It's no bother at all," Kerry said, and Jesse coughed. She shot him a look.

"No, you're not in the way at all. You ladies make yourselves comfortable," he added as he handed the cups around.

"Thank you, and we will, dear," Mrs. Hamilton said as her eyes shifted between her friends. "Besides, we were thinking that although you're closed and renovating"—she looked around at the boxes on the floor—"as it is, we thought it would still be good for folks to see some things going on in the shop every once in a while. Let the hawks know you may be down but you're definitely not out. Don't want the vultures to start circling."

"What, have you been talking to my brother?" Jesse mumbled.

There was a chuckle at that from Ms. Cherry. She paused in her knitting. "No, but that doesn't mean we haven't heard things. About vultures and all."

Kerry was going in on the carrot cake but now gave full attention to Ms. Cherry. What was really going on here?

Jesse suddenly looked more serious. Ms. Cherry smiled. "Don't look so worried, Jesse. I'm sure you and your brothers can handle a little bank loan. You'll be just fine." Ms. Cherry was a tall woman with chestnut brown skin and closely cropped, dyed honey-blond hair. As a retired corrections officer, she came off at first brush as abrasive, but always surprised with her unexpected sweetness. Her tone was no nonsense, and when she spoke one was inclined to believe her. But what was this about a loan, and why did the OKG know about it and Kerry did not? Kerry frowned and was about to ask when Ms. Cherry turned to her, switching away from the loan subject altogether. "So, what is this we hear about you staying here?" she asked suddenly.

And with that sweet came a bit of spice.

Kerry paused in her chewing. Dang it. Just when the cake was getting good too. She swallowed. "I, um, ran into a problem at my place."

Ms. Cherry nodded. "We heard." She took a sip of her coffee. Black with extra sugar. "You stay on that landlord of yours. I don't trust that management company."

"Or any company, for that matter," Ms. June chimed in.

"Why should I?" Ms. Cherry said. "I haven't found one yet that can be trusted. Bunch of thieving bastards. The lot of them if you ask me." She picked up the cute little knitted hedgehog she was finishing off and scrunched her nose up at it. She sucked her teeth, then gave it a smile. Kerry shook her head. That was Ms. Cherry. The queen of contradictions. The little hedgehog would end up in a Christmas gift bag this season along with a pair of the crochet slippers that the women would all make for their annual Angel Tree drive for some of the children whose parents were incarcerated. Kerry usually helped too and knew she would once again, now hoping she'd be able to knit faster to make up for Mama Joy's allotted pieces. It was surprisingly sad how the number of requested gifts never seemed to go down each year, only up, and even though Ms. Cherry had been retired for the past five years, she hadn't slowed in her mission of bringing awareness to this cause.

But still Kerry wanted to go back to the subject of the loan.

"So," Ms. Diaz said. "You two been keeping busy here?" Seriously, could they go back to the subject of the loan?

Kerry looked to Jesse, and he cleared his throat. "We have. Ma'am."

Really? That was his answer? Was he really not going to say anything about the store's debt? She shot him a glare.

He indicated the boxes strewed around the space. "As you can see, the place is in a bit of disarray, but I don't expect it to be like this for long. I'll have it set to rights pretty quick." He looked to Kerry for help, and everyone turned her way.

She let out a breath. Fine, she'd play along. "Yes, we should be up and running in no time. Jesse has some great ideas."

They all nodded politely, or as politely as they could while quietly judging, but Sister Purnell frowned. "I hope you don't plan on changing too much. Joy had a right nice flow in here. It was perfect as it was."

"Oh no, don't worry," Kerry said, "it won't change all that much. Just some updates. Jesse has a great eye. You'll love it."

Sister Purnell gave her a hard look. "And what about you?"

Kerry paused. "What about me?"

"What sort of ideas do you have? A young woman like you. Last I remember you were interviewing and still looking for something permanent over there at the center. I hear things may be shifting in that direction."

Kerry frowned. "Really? I, um, hadn't heard that." Damn this Old Knitting Gang. But if Sister Purnell had heard something, there had to be something brewing. She wouldn't go dropping a bit of news without anything to back it up. Besides, Linda had been in the office today, and she had still been there when Kerry left, in addition to Imara's father showing up. Maybe she ought to dress up a bit when she went in tomorrow.

"I'm just saying. It's great you're helping out here, and Joy would be terribly grateful, but you know she and your mama were thrilled about you finally getting that degree," Sister Purnell said.

"Not to mention you're not getting any younger," Mrs. Hamilton said. "Don't you think it's time to really get out there in the world? You're not going to find any marriageable men holed up here in this shop."

Kerry shook her head and laughed. "Mrs. Hamilton, it's not like I'm on the shelf or anywhere near over the hill. Besides, who's looking for marriage? You don't have to worry about me in that area."

Kerry glanced over at Jesse. His face had gone dark, his eyes deepening in coloring along with his expression as he looked at her. She felt her brows pull tight. But then he blinked and smiled at her as he picked up the hat he'd been working on that morning. She noticed it was nearly done. "That's what I keep telling her," he said. "But she knows what a hopeless case I am and thankfully insists on helping me out." He smiled at the women as he took a seat at the head of the table and started to knit. But Kerry could see the tension in his shoulders. She noticed how he threw his yarn. None of his movements were as easygoing or nearly as smooth as they had been that morning before she'd left for work. He looked at her once again. "You can rest assured, ladies, that as soon as we're on our feet, I'll be sure to send our Kerry Girl packing and out into the world where she belongs."

JESSE COULDN'T GET the words of the Old Knitting Gang out of his mind that night. He did his best to smile, be congenial and polite, do all the things that Mama Joy would have wanted. As he moved more boxes to the back of the storage area, he hummed to himself and tried his best to drown out their voices. Not do his old negative self-talk. He could practically hear Mama Joy in his ear shouting over his shoulder. "Come on, Jes, you gonna let the words define you, or are you going to define yourself?" She'd drilled that into him again and again over the years, so much so that he'd almost gotten this close to believing her. Maybe if she'd held on just a little bit longer, he would have.

He put the box down and looked around the storage area that was quickly becoming its own problem. Maybe if he'd held on to her a little longer, he'd have actually started to live the words. But it was too late now. The fact remained that Kerry did have a chance to live the words and he was holding her back.

The Old Lady Gang didn't happen there by chance today. Jesse had no doubt they'd planned to come there after his encounter with Sister Purnell at the bodega. No, he didn't doubt they did have some concern for him. And that concern was serious. The fact that they knew about the loan was a blow. How they knew was anybody's guess. Did Mama Joy tell them, or was it that their neighborhood spy net was more organized than he thought?

The worst of it though was the way they bomb-dropped it right in front of Kerry. He saw her face and hated seeing the hurt in her eyes as she put the pieces together. Maybe he should have told her about the loan right away, but why burden her with more than he already had? It wasn't fair as it was. That much was clear. Just as it was clear the way the Old Knitting Gang was closing ranks and putting up a pretty solid line of defense around Kerry to make sure she had some line of protection in the midst of the lion's den.

They were right though—Kerry needed to think about her future beyond the shop. Settling down, and settling down with someone worth settling down with. A corporate type, not a fuck-'em-and-leave-'em, no-ambition screwup, can't-be-relied-on type like him.

He let out a sigh. It was better to not think about it. Or at the least drink and forget about it. But how could he do that when all that was in his mind and his space was her? Like right now she was there. Just upstairs cleaning up and preparing to go to the residence, where she would be just down the hall from him for the night. All night.

Jesse's phone buzzed. Pulling it out of his pocket, he looked down and saw he was right.

You gonna be long down there? WE NEED TO TALK.

Shit. She wasn't one to give up easily. He put the phone back in his pocket.

The idea of drinking and forgetting now held that much more appeal. His phone vibrated again, and this time it was Ziggy. He and Craig were at Club Dionysus and calling him out.

20 at the door but Big Mike is on it so we're good.

Jesse stared at the message. A comped cover was tempting, and he did want to go out. Plus, the idea of an evening at home with Kerry so near seemed like more than he could handle.

How's the energy? He texted as he walked back into the main room of the shop and flipped the overhead lights off. When he did so, the back-kitchen light stayed on and he suddenly heard the sound of Kerry humming in the kitchen as she washed the leftover cups from earlier.

His phone buzzed. It's a Monday but there are a few prospects here.

Kerry came out of the kitchen then. He couldn't quite make out her features fully, backlit as she was by the kitchen light, but still his heart did a flip when she looked at him and smiled, her even teeth glowing. Eyes shining even through her glasses.

He looked back at his phone and typed.

Nah I'm good. I'll pass.

She must have caught his expression because her smile quickly faded. "You okay?" she asked.

"I'm fine." Of course, he wasn't, but he wouldn't tell her that. She'd been shouldering enough of his burden for him. It was time for him to pull his own weight. Besides, just like the women had not-too-stealthily expressed, he didn't want to do anything that would make her feel like she needed to hang around here any longer than necessary. Once she had her apartment back, even if he still needed her in the shop, he didn't want her to feel any qualms about leaving.

She shifted her feet and bit at her bottom lip. Jesse felt a pull tighten in his groin.

"Well," she started. "I'm going to head up. Make something to eat. Are you hungry?"

Jesse shook his head. "I'm good for now. You go on up. I'm going to do a little more around here, but I'll be up soon."

He saw Kerry hesitate but still felt relief when she didn't question him further but headed upstairs. She had sent that text. Maybe she'd changed her mind? He let out a breath and leaned against the kitchen doorjamb. Like a silly kid, he looked up the stairs and wondered how long it would be before she finished eating and headed to bed herself. Just that thought gave him the same pull once again. Shit. He turned, flipped off the kitchen light and picked up his knitting, and then took the side stairs that led to the loft.

Up here in the shadowed light looking down on the shop and the street beyond, there was still a buzz of summer-in-the-city evening activity; everything looked almost peaceful. It was almost as if he could pretend the last few weeks hadn't happened and his life was still his own. Normal. And he was still him. Loved.

He watched as a young couple passed, and the woman, who seemed to be in her early twenties, paused, pulling her guy's arm, making him stop to look at the display of yarns still in the window. He could faintly see her expression, alight as she pointed to the little ice-cream cone display. She said something to her man, then he rubbed at her belly and laughed. Jesse smiled. From up here his life almost seemed calm, with the sounds of the street beyond, the cars, the people passing full of hope and possibilities. But could he ever be what they needed?

Jesse turned and flipped on the old record player, and the clear but still haunting voice of Marvin Gaye rang out. He sat down and began to knit. The hat he'd started last night was nearly done. He was just decreasing now; soon he'd close. Jesse let out a long breath, then quickly sucked it back in when he saw orange toes come up beside him.

Orange toes, brown ankles, shapely calves and the most delicious-looking thighs made Jesse suddenly ravenous.

Kerry had changed into gym shorts and a T-shirt, and the whole thing had a sexy effect on her body. She was both sporty innocent and over-the-top hot in a way that had him thinking maybe he wouldn't be getting up from his current position anytime soon.

"What are you doing here?"

"I thought you were coming up?" There was a question at the end of her comment though no question was posed. She shifted, and he was entranced by the subtle movements of her body. Jesse forced his eyes up. "But you didn't, so I came to check on you," Kerry finally said. She looked from him to the record player, then back at him again. "You turned on music and everything, and didn't even invite me to the party. No fair!"

"I wouldn't quite call it a party."

Kerry looked through the shelf and the collection of LPs, chose one and picked up the needle and changed the record. Al Green's voice now came through. The soul singer was vibrant and full of energy, talking about how he was tired of being alone. *True that,* Jesse thought as Kerry shook her hips and swung her braids, instantly mesmerizing him. "Now it's a party," she said.

Jesse turned away from her, looking back down at his knitting. Kerry paused, seemingly hesitant at first before sitting down beside him, her body flush against his. He felt his heart start to race as he swallowed down on a lump in his throat. Maybe it was better when she was up and dancing. Subtly he tried to inch away, but playfully she scooted closer. "You're not getting away from me that easy, Jesse Strong," she said. "Besides, I told you I wanted to talk—did you think I'd forgotten?"

He sighed. "I hoped you had."

She smiled. "You hoped wrong. You know me better than that. Now spill it. What was all that about a loan?"

He looked down but she shifted and reached out, her hand gentle but still firm as she turned his face toward hers. "I asked you that since I'm here and giving of my time—I think I deserve an answer."

He stared at her. Hard. "That's just it. You're giving enough. You don't need this weight too."

She glared at him. "Are you actively trying to piss me off?"

He raised a brow. "I could say the same about you."

She made a move as if to get up and he panicked, grabbing her wrist and pulling her back down. When she frowned at him, he put both hands up. "I'm sorry. I didn't mean to grab you like that. But please don't go. Could you just sit here with me a little longer?"

She sighed and looked at him, her eyes going soft and round. But she didn't speak; she only leaned back and sat next to him once more.

He started to knit again. "Yes, there's a loan." His voice was hoarser than normal so he cleared his throat. "I'm sorry I didn't tell you about it." Dammit. It still didn't sound quite right even to his own ears.

She stayed silent. But he felt her tense next to him.

"We—well, Damian just found out about it, so I don't know how the OKGs know. It would seem that Mama Joy took out a home equity loan to keep the shop afloat and used the house as collateral."

He heard her suck in a breath. "Oh no! I'm so sorry. I wish she'd have told me. I could have helped her cut corners with inventory, and I'd have stopped taking a salary and gotten another job."

Jesse looked at her. "See, that right there is why I didn't tell you. And probably why she didn't. You don't always have to sacrifice yourself for others, Kerry. Just like you're doing now. Though I—I mean we need you so much, we know what it's doing to you, and it's not fair."

She groaned. "Shit on that, Jes, nothing in life is fair. If it was, she would still be here, we'd be in the black and none of us would have gone through any of the things we've gone through in this life. Hell, if life was fair, we'd have never met. Screw fair!"

She put her head back and let out a low, ragged breath before shocking him and leaning her head on his shoulder. "It's going to work out. It has to. Downward spirals can't last forever."

Jesse afforded himself a half smile and continued to knit. "No, maybe they can't."

She shifted then. Shimmied a bit and turned, reaching for something on the shelf above them, he guessed. Hopefully she was satisfied now that they'd had the conversation about the loan. Jesse let out his own sigh of relief but then gripped his needles almost to the point of breaking them when he looked her way. She was twisted around and contorted in the most provocative way. She let out a frustrated groan as she arched her back, showing off the cutest round behind, before she finally sat down again with a grin and a skein of yarn. Jesse felt like he might burst.

"I love this yarn," she said. "I think it would make a cute hat and gloves, don't you?"

He could only nod as she scooted closer to him still and pulled out the yarn and began to slowly wind it around her left pointer and middle fingers to make her own yarn ball.

"You know we can just put that on the yarn winder and be done in less than five minutes," Jesse said, his voice probably coming out harsher than the subject of winding yarn warranted.

Kerry shrugged. "Yeah, but what else are we doing right now?

You're finishing off your hat, we've got nice music. I might as well wind this ball."

Jesse let out a breath. Might as well. There were worse and better ways he could be spending his night. But right now he couldn't think of anywhere else he wanted to be. Or anything else he wanted to do. But she shifted once more to get more comfortable on the floor and against the wardrobe, and her hip and thigh rubbed against his, and in that moment the words stopped in the middle of his throat. He leaned his head back and, once again, his fingers began the methodical work of going in and out of the loops certainly, yarn creating stitches that decreased one by one, closing the hole on the top of his little striped hat. *Not that, Jes. Don't think of that.*

This was a new scene for them. Kerry and him. Over the years, they had been up in this little nook, seated in this position, more times than he could count, only the roles were usually reversed. He was the one coming over to bother Kerry while she was quietly knitting away. He looked over at her. She seemed so content as she did the simple act of just circling the yarn around her fingers over and over again. He watched as she drew her fingers out of the center and her little yarn ball got bigger and bigger, bit by bit.

She had beautiful hands. He'd always thought so. A rich brown, they were practically unlined and always looked so soft to him, almost delicate the way her long fingers tapered to neat oval-shaped nails. She made a habit of styling her nails in the simplest way. Usually the polish was either clear or pale pink. Sometimes she'd even step out in a lilac. When she was feeling bold, she would go with bright and multicolored nails, but it was always some version of something soft and her nails always stayed understated, never too long—definitely never long enough to get in the way of her knitting.

As if sensing he was looking at her, she turned to him, her face nearer to his than he had expected, or maybe he got closer to her. He thought she might move back, but no, she just smiled. "What's got you so interested over here?"

He shook his head. "What?" he asked. "I, um, was just thinking about something." Then he nudged his head at her yarn ball. "You're really fast at that, huh?" Fast at that? How is that any sort of conversation?

Kerry's brows drew together and she shrugged. "I guess. It's just something to do. Better than sitting here in silence doing nothing."

Doing nothing? What was that about? What could she be hinting at? "It wasn't like I was doing nothing," Jesse said, holding up his now completed hat.

Kerry's smile was huge and bright. She took the hat from his hands and held it up to the light as if she was holding some sort of winning trophy instead of a small knitted cap. "It's so cute," she exclaimed.

She was so cute. Too damn cute.

Jesse reached out and wrapped his hand around the hat, closing it into a fist. "It's okay. It's just a hat; it's not that big a deal. Nothing to get all excited about."

She stared at him. Challenging him with her eyes. Or maybe he was just searching. Hoping for a challenge or, better yet, an invitation.

Then he caught it. The moment her lips pulsed, opened slightly and closed again. She wanted to say something. Had that look like she wanted to say it badly. But she didn't; he saw the moment when she shut down and retreated. She leaned back farther against the wall. Jesse looked at her and she swallowed. "You know I hope you didn't take what Sister Purnell and the rest of her crew were saying today to heart," she suddenly said. She swallowed again. This time her hip wasn't touching his. No, there was now about a half-inch gap between the two of them.

That half inch might as well have been three feet, or maybe a mile, the way it felt in the moment. He cleared his throat. Best to be nonchalant right now. "Of course I didn't—why would I? It's not like they weren't saying anything I didn't already know."

She whirled on him. "What do you mean something you didn't already know?"

"What are you getting all riled up for?" Jeez, that was unexpected. "I'm just talking about the fact that they are right and it's best that you move on from here as quickly as possible. Get on with your life. Everybody knows that. There are better things for you out in the world than this place. More opportunities, better jobs, better people, better men." The final word hung in the air and hung so long that he had to turn back away from her and look forward again.

"I'm so fucking tired of this."

Jesse turned back to her. He was shocked. Kerry wasn't one to curse, or to show her emotions so clearly either. He stared at her. Her head was back and she was breathing heavily, chest rising and falling as if there was a beast about to pop out at any moment. She turned his way and pierced him with her sharp gaze. "I'm sick of everyone thinking they know what's good for me. Of thinking they even know me, for that matter. I thought I made it clear before that I'd be making the decisions when it came to my life and when, where and who I move on to. I don't need my mother, the women of the neighborhood or even you and your brothers telling me what's good for me, Jesse Strong. If you haven't noticed, I'm a grown-assed woman. Now, if the problem is me being here, and you truly don't want me here, just say so. I do have other places I can go."

She started to get up, forgetting the yarn ball that was still coiled in her lap. With her movement, the ball rolled and started to unravel as it headed for the stairs. She and Jesse both dived for it in unison, the words for the moment forgotten, all eyes on the yarn. Jesse made it first, grabbing the ball as he flipped over and held it up, grinning at her. "Got it!"

But she was coming toward him; down and over him she went. Her body over his. Soft and lush with a sweet *oomph!* She hit him hard and he went instantly just as hard. Her glasses went askew, and he laughed as she reached up and righted them. "This is not the first time you've knocked me down up here, you know."

"Yeah, but this time it wasn't my fault."

She nodded. "True. I'll give you that one, but only partly." She reached up and tweaked his nose. "If you hadn't pissed me off, I wouldn't have dropped my yarn in the first place." He nipped at her finger.

"That's on you, miss. I didn't do anything wrong. Blame the Old Knitting Gang."

She looked up at him more seriously now, and he realized that they were actually having this conversation with him on his back and her on top of him. "I blame you," she said, "for actually taking their words to heart and echoing them back to me."

He swallowed, feeling himself getting even harder now that he realized the extent of their predicament. "Maybe we should have this conversation . . . sitting up."

"Maybe I'm fine right where I am."

He looked up at the ceiling, then back at her. She was over him, her face, her lips, her everything impossibly close.

"Are you talking about fine staying in this house, or fine where you are right now, this moment?"

Kerry smiled. That damned sunshine smile, the one that never failed to open his heart and make his brain all muddled. Sure, he knew it was nighttime, but there was a part of him you couldn't convince it was ten past dawn. Surely the sun was rising, and the day was clear. "Right now, maybe I'm talking about all of it," she said as she leaned down and brushed her lips against his.

Jesse felt his heart slam against the wall of his chest as everything in him and every part of him seemed to move forward at once to meet her. She kissed him with eager, unexpected abandon that set everything ablaze, pressing her lips to his, at first cool then suddenly warm. When she ran her tongue lightly across the crease of his lips, he opened his mouth readily and tasted her sweetness for the first time, just about weeping with the pleasure of it. His lips tingled in time with his dick and he pulled her in tighter toward him. She moaned, the sound a low hum of satisfaction like she'd been wanting it for just as long as he had. The realization of that and the ramifications of it stilled him. Jesse froze, pulling back slightly.

Breathing hard, he pushed back on her shoulders, tilting her up from his chest with slight pressure. The action brought her top half up, but her bottom half unfortunately pressed dangerously tighter to his own. Dammit, that wasn't what he was going for. She grinned, not for a moment looking like their Kerry Girl but instead like the Kerry he'd dreamed of many nights over but never dared to mention.

"We need to stop," Jesse said. "We both know with my track record how this will end."

She smiled at him and wiggled once again. "Of course we do," she said, then leaned in and ran her tongue across his lips once again. She licked up to his jawline, then kissed and kissed and kissed again until she reached his earlobe. "It's a good thing I won't be staying here long enough to ruin you completely." Then she nipped at his ear and came back to his lips and kissed him long and hard enough to curl his toes in his sneakers. His fucking toes! There was music. Strings, a guitar, horns. Wait. That was the record. Jesse stilled. Dammit, the record had stopped already. Shit, this was all Kerry.

All thought escaped Jesse as he grabbed at Kerry and flipped her over. The yarn ball that was between the two of them slipped out and now rolled down the steps for real as he kissed her lips, her neck and headed down toward her breasts. She brought one leg up and wrapped it around his. He moaned and she purred. God, she truly was a dream. The most amazing dream. Of his life. He kissed her deeper. Maybe that was it. This was a dream. He was still asleep and any moment he'd wake up and the day would begin, life would be mundane, and he'd just have to deal with it.

Oh well, he'd deal with that when he had to. Right now, he was going to enjoy this terrific fucking dream. He kissed Kerry harder and enjoyed the velvety stroke of her tongue along with the silky feel of her thighs, and that's when he heard it.

"Yo! Jes! Kerry! Either of you down there?" Kerry stilled below him. Her eyes wide, she clamped a hand over her mouth, fighting to hold back on her laugh.

Shit, Lucas! In the name of Saint Phantom Anti-Cockblocker, go the fuck away.

Jesse silently cursed his brother. As a matter of fact, he cursed all his brothers. Why did those bastards have the world's worst timing? He looked down at Kerry and could tell she was now thinking extra hard. She was about to say something, but he put a finger to her lips.

"Yeah, we're here in the loft. Just finishing cleaning up. We'll be right there!" he yelled. Then he let out a breath.

He heard the pause in Lucas's step and hoped he'd gotten away with sounding convincing.

"Oh," Lucas said. "Okay. You need some help? I'm off duty so I came to help out tomorrow. Need me to help you clean up?"

"No, we're good," Kerry yelled. "I made some pasta if you're hungry. Why don't you get some? It's in the kitchen."

"Yeah, um, sure. I'll do that," Lucas said. "Thanks, Kerry. See you upstairs."

They each let out long breaths and looked at each other over the sound of Lucas's retreating steps and the now-awkward silence with the record no longer playing, it having ended at least ten minutes before. Jesse got up and removed the needle, flipping the record player off. He reached down and pulled Kerry up.

They looked at each other and he wiped the corners of his mouth, then bent to pick up his hat. He saw the string of her yarn. The ball had rolled out of sight. Jesse shook his head. "I'll go get that for you." He turned, and she pulled him back toward her. She leaned up and kissed him again. Everything in him told him to pull away. Told him to listen to the voices in his head that said this wasn't right. That he wasn't right. Not she. But he. But in that moment, he couldn't. All he could do was fall in and kiss her once more. Enjoy the sweet taste of her. The gift that she was giving. The undeserved grace. And be thankful for it.

She ended the kiss and pulled back, which was all the better, because for the life of him he couldn't. Kerry looked up at him. "I meant what I said. No one else is making this decision for me. I

know what this is, Jesse. What and who we both are. So stop worrying. Stay out of your head. And mine. I'm only here temporarily.
What's going on right now, whatever this is, is just between us.
You don't have to feel judged, and neither do I. No one has to
know. I'll be home soon, and we'll be back to just what we've always been. You'll be you and I'll be Kerry Girl."

Then she let him go and started downstairs, leaving him to re-
trieve her unwound yarn ball.

19

COMING INTO THE shop that afternoon and seeing the brothers hard at work transforming the shop with new bright-white paint was a sight to behold. Kerry could already see hints of how much lighter things would be with the fresh white. It made the darker woods that much more striking and the colorful yarns pop like little fireworks.

Kerry had to force the thought that a girl could get used to this from her mind. Just as she had to push down on the physical urge to go in, throw her things down and rush into Jesse's arms like some heroine at the end of a nineties rom-com or, better yet, a late-eighties porn. Grind up against him and take him up to his room and do all sorts of things not ready for the innocent—well, let's face it—not-so-innocent eyes of his brothers. She'd kissed him. Kissed Jesse Strong. And now didn't know how to consider life before kissing Jesse Strong.

Kerry eyed the old farmhouse table that had seen so many loving, sweet knitting circles, looked at Jesse in his tank with his locs twisted up on his head just enough to show off his muscular shoulders to perfection; her eyes seemed to naturally go from his shoulders, to his waist, to his hips, to the table. Lordy. "Oh, you're here, Kerry," Lucas said. "Good, we can use the extra hands."

She blinked and looked into the staring eyes of Jesse. He tilted his head and she could tell he was trying not to laugh while giving her a look of "Could you not!" plus "I know exactly what you're thinking, you naughty girl. That is not what that table is used for!"

Kerry turned Lucas's way. "Sure, just give me a minute to change," she said brightly, hoping there wasn't too much exuberance in her voice. Lucas's furrowed brow and nod told her there definitely was. When she had gone back upstairs last night, Lucas hadn't let on like he'd suspected anything, so everything had seemed normal, but still he was looking between her and Jesse now like he was their dad about to give them the talk. Their hot Korean dad, but their dad nonetheless.

Noah was there today too, tall and lanky, wearing old sweats and a sleeveless tee. He had the small ladder in his hand and Lucas had a roller. Jesse was now shifting a paint tarp. The effect of them dressed down, working hard and loaded up on good looks and testosterone was dangerous and very hot. Suddenly, she got an idea when she noticed how Noah and Lucas looked with the shelves behind them, the old displays ready to be transformed. She took out her phone and started snapping some photos.

"What are you doing?" Jesse said. "I thought you were going to change and help us."

She looked at him. "I am, but you guys keep working. I'm just going to take a few pictures first to get the work in progress. Who knows—we can have them for posterity, or use them for something later?" Jesse and Lucas frowned but Noah smiled. "Good idea, Kerry," he said. "We can use the photos for promo."

"Who says?" Lucas suddenly said, which surprised Kerry. "I said no to the FDNY calendar, and there's no way I'm doing this."

"You said what?" Noah said. "Are you crazy? Why would you say no to that? Do you know how much ass you could have gotten from doing that calendar?"

Kerry coughed and he looked over at her. "Oh, no offense, Kerry." Then he looked back at his brother. "Okay, ass aside. You maybe could have found your dream woman."

She laughed. "From that calendar, I think not. Though still you would have been perfect for it. Just like you all are perfect in these pics." She turned her phone his way and he shrugged, not at all impressed over how good he looked, paintbrush in hand, muscles rippling. Kerry shook her head and took some pics of Noah and Jesse. She laughed when the two of them hammed it up. "Well, at least one of you is humble. I think these are great, and once we're done, we'll take more of you with the yarns. You never know. I think it will be a great way to drum up business." She paused. "As a matter of fact." She took a group shot of the three of them as they worked, with the bins of colorful yarns visible on the side and the old wooden "Strong Knits" sign in the background. "You like?" she asked.

"It's fine. Why?" Jesse said.

"What better time than now to start marketing?"

She hit a few buttons on her phone and yelled, "Voilà! Our first story!"

"What?" Jesse asked.

"Our IG story," Kerry said. "I hashtagged it #RealMenKnit. I also made us a Twitter account."

Jesse moaned. "Shit, Kerry, what did you do?"

"Calm down. It will be fine. I just let the world—well, so far, our zero followers—know that we'll be having a grand reopening soon, so they should look out for us. And don't you love our hashtag? You guys are perfect for it." She grinned.

Lucas shook his head. "Kerry, I already said how I felt about the calendar."

Kerry turned to him. "Lucas. This shop is not the calendar. And you know we have to do everything we can to get people in here quickly or we're not going to make it."

He continued to frown, but Noah raised his hand. "I'm in!"

"Perfect." Kerry said. She gave Jesse a long look. "Come on. You know it's a great idea. Lucas, you know it too."

Noah nudged at his brother's side and Lucas gave him a hard shove back and looked at Kerry. "Fine, but I'm not taking my shirt off."

She nodded. "No problem. And we'll cross that bridge when we come to it."

She looked at Jesse then and winked. He gave her a grimace as she made her way upstairs to change and come back to help with the painting. She figured she'd pushed enough for the moment and would get more promo pics on the sly later. With that crew and hashtag, who knew, #RealMenKnit just might go viral.

Kerry changed into a pair of shorts and an old knit tank that Val had thrown in her bag. She didn't see any other opportunity to wear the improperly blocked tank. She put a sports cami underneath and hoped most of the flaws weren't too obvious. Anyway, what did it matter? They were working. It wasn't like she was being judged. She piled her twists high on her head, then wrapped them up in a print scarf to further protect them from dust and potential paint splatters. She slipped on a pair of old flip-flops and a little extra courage to go along with the whole ensemble.

"You've got this," she told herself before heading back downstairs. This wouldn't be weird at all. She'd made it through last night and today. Well, she and Jesse had, without too much awkwardness. Sure, she didn't get a bit of sleep and they didn't talk at all about the moment in the loft nook last night, but they'd made it through. She didn't know if Lucas or Noah would be staying over tonight and how they would handle things, or if Jesse planned on staying silent and continuing to pretend like nothing happened. She made a face as she remembered how she had tossed and turned last night. She had even contemplated reaching for her BFF, hidden away in Damian's second drawer. But the thought of the potential noise and being in Damian's bed had quickly ruled the idea out.

Kerry let out a breath. It was fine. She'd made a declaration last night and she was sticking to it. What she'd started, she was finishing. Somehow. And there was no way she was letting Jesse and his ridiculous fear of who knew what stop her—no, stop them both—from the potential of what could be a terrific orgasm.

ONE LOOK AT Kerry when she made it back down to the shop and the paint roller practically slipped out of Jesse's hand. What the hell was she wearing and why had she made it her mission to actively try and destroy him?

"Um, little brother. You want to watch what you're doing there. You're gonna get paint on the floor," Noah said.

Jesse blinked. Shit. Noah was right, and the soft salmon color on his roller was currently dripping from the sponge to his hand and ready to hit the floor. Jesse quickly shifted and put the roller over the paint tin. Crap. This was twice. No, three times. It was official, the woman was definitely out to kill him. Those shorts and the way they hugged her hips, not to mention what that top, if you could call that twisted pile of yarn a top, did to her breasts. The whole effect was just not fair. Thankfully Noah's voice had penetrated his not-ready-for-the-afternoon thoughts, and he had pulled the paint roller up in time for there to not be a disaster on the floor. Also thankfully Jesse turned away from Kerry in time to not get fully erect and completely embarrass himself in front of her and his brothers.

Too late though. He looked at Noah and one glance at his smug-assed smirk let him know he'd been found out. He shot Noah a hard glare that turned totally glacial a moment later when Noah called Kerry over to steady the ladder for him. That little shithead. As if he needed the ladder steadied. "What do you need the ladder steadied for?" Jesse said. "You were fine with it a minute ago."

"Oh, it's no problem," Kerry said, walking over to Noah, who sported a shit-eating grin that perfectly fit the shithead.

Jesse let out a deep breath and went back to finishing his accent wall. He wouldn't get riled up. Nope. Wasn't going to do it. He knew when he was being played. He'd seen this game too many times to not know every move. She was probably mad because after Lucas broke them up last night, and thankfully so, he didn't pursue her further, and this morning he'd stayed in his room until she was nearly out the door already for work at the center.

Sure, it may have been just a little cowardly, but right now he figured he just needed to bide his time and keep his distance, and then they could both come out of it all unscathed. No matter what she said, she wasn't as strong as she let on. Jesse let his eyes slide over to where she was now no longer helping Noah but over with Lucas painting trim. They were laughing together, light and easy. She bent down to put a little more paint on her brush, and when she came up again, some dribbled on her thigh. Lucas quickly bent and wiped it off with a towel. Kerry laughed and, in that moment, looked lighter and more carefree than he'd seen her in a long while.

Jesse turned away, fighting hard to ignore the prickles of anger as they covered his neck. He swiped at the wall. Taking his frustration out on it. Finishing the second coat quickly. "I'm running out," he suddenly said to no one in particular but the group in general.

Kerry looked at him, her eyes wide. "Where are you going? We still have a lot to do."

"I'll be right back."

The words came out sharp, and she frowned at him. "Fine, just don't go getting lost. Remember, you're the one who came up with this whole idea of painting."

He looked at her. "Oh, I remember everything."

She laughed at him, the sound light, musical and totally unbothered. "Good for you and your impeccable memory."

Jesse turned to head for the door but was stopped by the sound of Noah's voice. "Hey, can you pick me up a coconut water while you're out?"

"And a beer for me," Lucas added.

Jesse shrugged and let out a sigh. "Why not. You all take what you want anyway."

20

THE SHOP WAS in pretty good shape, though Kerry and Jesse were so very not. Since they had kissed, Jesse had been nothing but weird, doing his best to avoid and sidestep her. And when he did encounter her, he went overboard. He either treated her like they were in an eggshell-walking, sketchy-boss-with-subordinate, full-of-too-much-sexual-tension-but-scared-as-shit-of-HR thing, or like he was a newfound kinda-hot-but-still-awkward-and-weird jealous boyfriend whenever one of his brothers showed her any attention. He was enough to make her head spin. It all seemed to boil down to him not wanting to be near her. Could it be he really did regret their kiss? Every time she'd gotten within two feet of him, he'd backed away like he was allergic to her or something. It was damned infuriating.

He was damned infuriating!

Fine, if that was how he wanted to play it. *Cool*, Kerry thought as she headed into work at the center. She could wait. Maybe not for long, but she could wait. It wasn't like she'd not held out for him this long. Kerry stopped short then and shook her head. How ridiculous was he? No, how ridiculous was she? Waiting, holding on, putting her life on hold while Jesse controlled all the moves. How long was she going to do this? She was no longer Kerry Girl but Kerry. Not his girl but a woman with wants and needs. If he wasn't ready to be the man, to get his head out of his ass and fulfill them, then she surely needed to get her head out of her own ass and do it herself.

Nodding, she let out a breath and gave a small fist pump to gear herself up. Now she just hoped Jesse didn't show his ass and could put on a professional face in front of the kids today. If avoiding her was his thing, fine. They would do it that way. At least she'd gotten him to agree to living up to the commitment that Mama Joy had previously made with the center to have the kids come in for an outing. They had so few chances to get out, with funding being cut left and right, but the shop was so close, and this was something the kids usually enjoyed. She was glad to still be able to do it.

After his little storm-out while painting, Jesse had returned a short while later with the requested beverages for his brothers and even a drink for her. They finished the painting and were sharing a pizza when Damian showed up just late enough to not get dirty. Kerry got them to take a few more posed pictures with some yarns once they'd cleaned up.

But things got awkward again when Noah threw her on Jesse's lap and they all were posing for a selfie. She tried to scoot up and over when she saw how uncomfortable he seemed. But once she inched over closer to Lucas, Jesse pulled her in tighter, making things hella more obvious instead of keeping their secret like she was sure he'd planned. She couldn't get her head around the man, but then again, that wasn't her main objective right now, now was it?

"You got some, didn't you?"

Kerry gasped and her eyes went wide as she looked around to make sure nobody had heard what Val had said.

"Could you not, Ms. Big Mouth! And the answer is no."

"Dammit," Val hissed. "Do I have to go over there and throw you in somebody's bed?"

"No, you do not," Kerry said, "and I can find a way to a bed just fine by myself, thank you." Wait. She couldn't believe she was actually having this conversation. Like seriously entertaining it. What had happened to her over the past week?

Val looked at her seriously. "How do you know this? What's your plan, and are you getting close?" Her eyes took on a serious glint, and Kerry fully expected her to pull out her bullet planner to start taking strategy notes at any moment.

But she knew her friend, so she went along with it. She looked back and forth around the classroom, then went to the door and peeked out to be sure no one was in the hall. Kerry came back in. They had a few moments before the kids would be in, so she pulled up a chair next to Val's.

"I don't have a set plan, but let's just say things are in motion."

Val's brows shot up. "Things? In motion? Please tell me we're talking dicks and tongues, because if we're not, I'm going to make you eat paste right here and right now."

Kerry tightened her lips but nodded.

Val pumped her fists in the air. "Yes!" She looked at the clock on the back wall and sat back down, realizing they didn't have much time. "Now, tell me which one? Jesse? Lucas? Noah? Damian?"

Kerry frowned at her.

"Lord, could it be all of them, or more than one? You lucky wench!"

"Are you crazy?!" Kerry yelled.

Val took a breath, then smoothed her hair and fanned herself. "Sorry, I got ahead of myself. Of course it's Jesse. It's always been Jesse for you."

Kerry frowned deeper. She didn't like the sound of that. Always been Jesse for her. That didn't bode well with her one-and-done plan. She blew out a long breath of air. "It's not like that," she said, and waved a hand in the air. "We did end up making out in the loft the other night. But we were interrupted when Lucas came home, and now Jesse's acting all weird. I think he's scared to take things further. Doesn't want to mess up our friendship or some such nonsense."

Val's brows drew together, and she was quiet. Quieter than Kerry was comfortable with. Finally, Kerry gave her shoulder a shake. "What's up? Why are you silent now?"

Val shrugged, then smiled. "No reason."

Kerry stayed quiet, readying herself to greet the kids, but Val's voice stopped her. "It's just that Jesse really isn't the type to not take things all the way. I mean, his track record is pretty much get in and get out. Or get in and in and in again. But he's definitely not one to hesitate, not once the horse is out of the gate."

"And your point is?"

Val shrugged. "I don't have one, really. I'm just thinking that this is interesting and maybe wondering, what could be different about his feelings for you that he wants to take things slow?"

Kerry was about to tell Val she was wasting her time and totally overthinking it, but the kids came in, saving her from saying words she knew she might have to eat later anyway.

KERRY KNEW IT would be hard on the kids being in the shop without Mama Joy, so she was grateful for the fact that they still had a small group to make the trip today.

Each of the children had gotten permission from their parents, who all knew of Mama Joy's passing away, so there would be no angry letters sent to the center later. At least Kerry hoped so. You still never knew. But she'd tried her best with due diligence to avoid surprises. She didn't want to disappoint the kids who already had projects in the works and were looking forward to the outing. There were nine girls and three boys on this field trip, including Errol, who had once again made a tangle of his scarf. He had his brown paper bag clenched too tightly in his hand. He was clearly excited to head to the shop, but oddly still showing some of his old suppression.

On their way out, Imara Webb's father, Gabriel, had stopped by the class and asked where the shop was, saying he might stop by to pick up his daughter. With him shadowing Linda and the rumors that he might take over her job, Kerry couldn't do more than give the address and welcome him.

"That's odd," Val said.

"You think?" Kerry said, and shrugged. "He more than likely just wants to pick Imara up on their way home, like he said. Why are you reading more into it?"

Val frowned after Gabriel's retreating form. "You know me, I side-eye first."

Kerry laughed. "It didn't look like you were side-eyeing when you were just smiling in his face."

Val shook her head. "I wasn't smiling. That's what you call good old-fashioned 'sucking up for job security.' Word on the street is that ol' Linda is out, and if she is out, then who knows what other shake-ups could be in store around here. I don't want to leave this job." Kerry caught the worry in her voice. It wasn't just about a job or financial security for Val. She'd lost a lot in her life, and though she always acted carefree and like the life of the party, she was a lot more fragile than she let on. She really did care for the center and the kids it served. Val was often the first to arrive and one of the last to leave, making sure any late stragglers were picked up and being the first to know when there was a problem with one of the kids.

Kerry reached out and patted her friend's hand. "Don't worry. Everything will be fine here. Your place is secure. All you do for this place won't be overlooked." At that point, they both heard Alison singing loudly as she walked past on the way to her office. "Well, not for much longer," Kerry added.

THEY ARRIVED AT the shop, and Kerry was momentarily stunned at Jesse's meticulous preparation. He'd followed her directions to a T and then gone above and beyond. The places for the kids were set with easy-to-knit yarns for them to choose from for new projects, plus easy-to-follow instructions for a beginner scarf or a more advanced infinity scarf. There were sets of size eight straight and circular needles for the kids to choose from. All in all, she could not have been more impressed.

She'd only planned on the simple scarf and was going to give the children only two yarn choices. She loved that he'd gone further into their stock to find these yarns. But she was perplexed by the mini tree with lovely birch branches that was also in the middle of the table.

"I thought we'd work a yarn tree today," Jesse went on to explain. He took out his tablet and proceeded to show the kids photos of small trees made into colorful creations by being wrapped in yarn. The kids where mesmerized. Kerry didn't know if was the pretty photos or Jesse's expert explanation and delivery. The man definitely had a way with words, and she could see that the years of watching Mama Joy interact with children had not been wasted. He was a natural.

"Do you think we can make ours look as pretty as those? What if we mess up?" Mercedes Reid asked.

Jesse smiled at her and shook his head. "Don't worry, you can't make a mistake," he explained to the children. "No matter what you choose, I'm sure it will turn out beautifully."

"Even if I put this pink with this green?" Maya Parker asked him.

"Especially if you put that pink with that green. As a matter of fact, I think it should be put on that left branch. It would look great there. Have Ms. Val help you. She's not the best knitter, but this is a project that even she can do." Jesse teased Val as he explained his decorated tree idea, which he planned to use for a window display.

The kids did a beautiful job decorating the little yarn tree, and Kerry knew it would look great in the shop. She decided to snap a few photos for potential promo and to commemorate the moment for the kids. She made a note to ask the parents later for permission to post it.

Jesse's eye was terrific, as was the natural way his mind worked. As she watched him sitting casually between Errol and Sylvie Bowls, she wondered why he had taken so long to come around to this side of the business. He was showing them an easier way to hold their yarn, and the kids were laughing and chatting happily. The relaxed atmosphere reminded her of how it used to be with Mama Joy when she'd taught the kids in the shop, and in that moment, Kerry had such an intense feeling of hope that it was almost palpable. It also low-key scared the hell out of her.

Imara tapped her, pulling her attention away from staring at Jesse.

"Are my stitches okay, Miss Kerry?" she asked. "I think I messed up," she added with frustration.

Kerry looked down at her and smiled, seeing the dropped stitch that ran down three rows. "It's just a dropped stitch. Nothing that can't be fixed. Don't worry."

She reached for a crochet hook and sat next to Imara to show her how to pull up the stitch. Just then the chime on the door sounded, and all eyes turned that way. Jesse stood. "Can I help you?" he said, partially blocking the view of the kids from the tall man's view. "I'm sorry, but we're having a private class this afternoon. You're welcome to come back when we reopen."

"Daddy!"

Jesse turned and looked from Imara to Kerry, who nodded, then watched his stance relax. It was amazing how quickly he went from the Tooth Fairy to the Rock, then back to the Tooth Fairy again. She stood. "Jesse, this is Gabriel Webb, Imara's dad."

Jesse shook his hand. "Nice to meet you."

Gabriel looked around the shop. "Nice place you have here."

His tone seemed to have the slightest bit of judgment, but no, she had to be imagining that.

Jesse nodded. "Thanks." He looked toward the kids, who were smiling with delight. "We like it."

"We sure do, Daddy," Imara said. "And look." She held up the piece of knitting Kerry had handed back to her. "Look at my scarf. I made a mistake, but Miss Kerry fixed it. Isn't she great? She can do anything. Just like Grandma. Maybe even more than Grandma."

Kerry didn't fail to catch the raised brows that were exchanged between Jesse and Val at that point.

Gabriel walked over and looked at his daughter's knitting. He smiled and looked over at Kerry. "It's beautiful, baby, and you're right. Miss Kerry can do anything."

Val walked by just then and nudged Kerry in her side, mumbling in her ear, "And there I was thinking my hair braiding was some big whoop."

Kerry fought to hold back her laugh, and they finished off the outing without too much further incident. Jesse wasn't quite as relaxed as he had been before Gabriel Webb had arrived, but he didn't show his tension to the kids, and they all had a great time, leaving with their projects in fresh ziplock bags ready to be continued at home.

The only snag came when they were walking the kids back to the center for the official dismissal. They were just leaving the shop and out on the street in front when a couple of the neighborhood boys decided to go in on Errol.

Kerry knew these boys. They were sometimers who dropped by the center but didn't participate in the formal everyday program. Still, the center didn't turn anyone away. If they wanted to come as drop-ins, they could. Though in her opinion, stricter regulations were in order.

When her class left the sanctuary of the shop, the other boys, who, if they had been at the center, would have currently been in music or math class, were walking by, each holding either a juice or an ice pop. They zeroed in on Errol. "How'd your knitting go, Errol?" one of them said.

"You make a tea towel or maybe a bib or something?"

Errol immediately looked embarrassed but just kept walking, looking straight ahead.

The fact that they zeroed in on him and not the other boys was odd. But then she noticed how the other boys huddled together and walked over to the side, making themselves small and out of the way, almost invisible.

Kerry saw how tightly Errol held on to his little knitting bag, how he still tried to hold his head high, but she could also see the fear in his eyes.

Gabriel was just about to say something when Kerry heard Jesse's voice over the boy's laughter. "You boys interested in a lesson?"

Their laughter died as they caught sight of Jesse in the doorway of Strong Knits. He was twirling a knitting needle between his fingers like a drumstick while staring at the boys in a no-nonsense manner.

He gave them a nod. "How's your grandmama, Troy? Tell her I said thanks for the pie. Better yet, I'll tell her myself the next time she stops in. Did you like the jumper she made for you?"

"Jumper?" the boy next to Troy yelled.

"He means a sweater!" he tried to quickly explain. "It's British."

Troy looked back at Jesse then and Jesse stared back. The kid quickly sized up the situation and shook his head no, saying his grandmother was fine. He tapped his friend twice on the shoulder and they made tracks across the avenue.

Kerry gave Jesse a smile but could feel the change in energy from poor Errol.

"Don't worry about those boys," she said.

He smiled bravely. "Oh, I don't, Miss Kerry. It's not a big deal." But still, he took his knitting and shifted it tightly into a smaller fist, making it practically invisible for the rest of the walk back to the center.

"SO, WHAT WAS up with the new little *That's So Raven* and the broke-down Blair Underwood?"

Kerry was back at the shop. She had picked up some oxtails, rice and cabbage from the local Jamaican take-out place. She and Jesse had just finished dinner and were now knitting on the living room couch upstairs in the residence.

She was tired after the busy day with the kids and walking back and forth to the community center. So a quiet evening making stitches was pretty much all that was on her mind right now. She guessed Jesse had other plans.

"Huh?" Kerry asked, slightly annoyed to be pulled from her project. It wasn't complicated, but of course he was talking to her right when she was on a row that required counting. She put her finger in place and made a mental note of where she was while searching for a stitch marker in the bag next to her.

"You know, the little girl with the cute braids but so much chatter and her daaaad." He said in a long, exaggerated way, suddenly sounding like a tween girl. Kerry would have laughed if he wasn't being so frustratingly immature.

She put her knitting down. They had at least had a decent afternoon and were settling in for a nice evening, and here he came with the stupid. "Her daaaad." Oh hell, she was doing it. How was it Jesse could so easily bring out the brat in her? She sighed. "Could you be more immature? You're talking about a student of mine and Gabriel, her father. He's also," she said, frowning and picking up her knitting again, "shadowing Linda at the center. The story is that he may be the center's new director."

Jesse paused in his knitting. "So your boss."

She put her knitting down again.

"My director."

Jesse frowned. "Now, how is that different from your boss?"

Kerry's eyes shifted left to right. "Well, it isn't, but it's also not confirmed, so this conversation is useless."

"How is it useless?" he asked. "The guy is influential, not to mention clearly interested in you."

Kerry sucked in a breath, and Jesse quickly held up his hand. "Whatever, but he's been shadowing your director, and interested or not he's keeping some sort of eye on you."

"Maybe he's keeping an eye on Val."

"That's practically the same thing, you two are so close. The fact remains that he was here today along with his little Raven Baxter, who could not stop going on about the program and how much of an inspiration you are."

Kerry felt her face start to heat up. "I wouldn't go that far, and her name is Imara, not Raven. You sound like a child." She went back to knitting her hat.

She watched Jesse pick up his knitting. He'd finished three hats already, and she had some catching up to do. She started to knit faster.

"You're right. That was childish. And you sure have a way of winning over your bosses," she heard him mumble.

The nerve. Kerry looked over at him, ready to hand him a new one, then stilled. Did he say *bosses*? She took in his picture-perfect profile as he seemingly concentrated on the task before him, slipping the yarn in and out of the neat little holes to create the pretty little ribbed hat that would keep some lucky kid warm this winter. He should have been at ease, but his jaw was locked tight, his full lips just as tight. It was quiet in the house; well, semiquiet. The TV was on with the baseball game playing. But clearly neither of them was focused on it. Lucas was back on duty, and for the first time it registered with Kerry that they were once again truly alone.

She put her needles down and eased closer to his side, placing her hands over his.

Jesse looked over at her. "What are you doing? You should be knitting. We need as many of these as possible if we're going to make a decent display."

She gently pushed his knitting aside, taking it from his hands, hiking up her long gauzy skirt as she slid one knee over the top of his waist, straddling him. The feeling of his jean shorts against her inner thighs as her skirt came up was rough and welcome as she moved over him.

Jesse put his hands to her shoulders, though, as she came forward to kiss him. "What are you doing? We have work to do."

"What did you mean I have a way with winning over my bosses?" she answered. "I thought you weren't my boss."

"What are you going on about, Kerry? This is not the time for playing around."

She kissed his ear, then looked him in the eye. "Who's playing? I want to get this straight. When I called you boss, you said that you weren't my boss and not to call you that. Now you're saying I sure have a way of winning over my bosses." She leaned in and kissed his jaw. "Which is it?"

"Which is what?"

"Are you my boss or not?"

"What does it matter?" He looked her in the eye. "For the record, I'm not, and who says you're winning me over?"

Kerry looked down between them and shifted her hips, rubbing against his already hard erection. "Something says I am."

He let out a groan before pulling her in closer. This was delicious. Jesse pulled her in closer still, no longer resisting but grabbing her with both hands by her ass cheeks and bringing her as close to him as possible. Their lips came together with an intense pressure and he kissed her like he'd been as hungry for her as she'd been for him these past two days.

She sank deeper into his lap as she drank him in. Letting herself enjoy him with all her senses. She savored the taste of him, the sensual, rhythmic stroke of his tongue as it captured her and playfully battled for dominance. He ran his hand over her shoulder, down her arm and up her side. Everywhere he touched seemed to burn with delight. Kerry twisted her hands in his long locs, loving the soft feel of them. The sweet coconut scent. She wound them around her fist and tugged, leaning up on him and coming down, kissing him deeper. Not wanting this moment to ever end.

Sure, she knew it might be a mistake, but there was no way she was admitting that. Not with the way her heart was thumping and her blood was boiling and her body was tingling. This was everything she had ever dreamed of and more. He was everything and more.

If it was a mistake, she'd deal with that later. If there would be heartbreak, she'd deal with that later. Right now, there was only pleasure. Hers and his. And she was seeing this through. Completely and fully.

JESSE WAS GOING to enjoy this. That was if he could last. He was rock hard and felt like his heart was pumping so hard and fast that it might hop up and end up in either his or Kerry's throat at this rate. He needed to calm down. Kerry must think he was a sweaty mess, going on like he was some kid just out of high school, or a freshman frat recruit, at best.

Jesse willed his heart to calm down and hoped his hard-on would hold out on top of it. Maybe he should look at the TV. The game was on. That sort of thing was supposed to be a surefire hard-on extender. Not that he ever needed anything to last with any other women. With all the other women he'd been with he'd never had trouble lasting during sex. He'd lasted as long as he wanted. And when he was ready for it to be over, boom, he called it and it was done. But with Kerry, he thought as his hands stroked her sides, came across her trim waist, felt around her soft, pillowy hips and tasted her peach lips, with her he felt completely out of control. He didn't think he'd last three more minutes into this kiss, let alone thirty seconds actually inside her.

But God, he sure wanted to try. Jesse breathed in deep and let his tongue stroke hers. She let out a moan, and Jesse opened his eyes. She was so pretty. So damned pretty that he froze, seeing the look of erotic abandon as her eyes fluttered closed behind her glasses, the beautiful blush of purple coming through on her cheeks and across her collarbone. Her lips were swollen and puffy, making his throb to kiss hers again.

He could destroy her. He could so very easily take all this beauty, and could ruin it. He knew this. And that would in the end destroy him.

Kerry moaned once again, then opened her eyes and stared at him. She tipped that no-longer-innocent tongue out and licked her top lip, causing his dick to respond in time, then she gave him a one-quarter sweet, three-quarters wicked smile.

Jesse smiled back but couldn't quite meet her eyes. This wasn't right. It was better to keep what they had where it was and his fantasies about a future of even thirty seconds with Kerry where they belonged.

Kerry tugged at his hair, this time nowhere near as sensually as she had earlier. She looked at him with stern eyes.

"Ouch! Gentle, Ker," he said. "I'd like to keep my hair follicles, thank you."

"Don't you dare, Jesse Strong. If you go and get all up in your head now and leave me to finish off myself, I'm kicking your ass."

Jesse froze. The thought of Kerry finishing herself off put his mind in a tilt. He felt his mouth drop open and it took a moment to remember to close it. "Wait a minute. Nice girls like you don't do things like finish themselves off."

She shifted on him again as she pulled back, seriously testing his limits of control.

"Whoever said I was a nice girl, and how would you know what nice girls do and don't do?"

Jesse frowned and looked at her. Well, she had a point there. A couple, at that. Kerry leaned in again, this time bringing her tongue out and licking long but gently at the tendon along the side of his neck. She came up and whispered in his ear. "And wannabe bad boys like you should know it's not polite to leave girls like me hanging. So come on and finish what you started."

Jesse would have laughed over the cuteness of it all if he wasn't so hard. He wrapped his hands firmly around her ass cheeks and waist, and hefted them both from the couch, heading down the hall. "All right then, Nice Girl, but remember, you asked for this."

Her laughter was the best "yes" he'd ever heard. "Oh, I'll remember all right. Trust and believe it's something I'm sure neither of us will forget."

21

"YES. YES . . . YES . . . yes . . ."

The low and whispered yesses were by far the best Kerry had ever heard or dreamed of in her life, and the fact that she was hearing them from the lips of Jesse Strong was almost mind-boggling. He'd carried her first to his bedroom and paused outside the door, but then looked her in the eye and shook his head.

"Um, it's kind of a mess in there. I wasn't quite prepared for a guest."

She gave him an "Oh really" look and he tapped her on her behind.

"Don't you start, now," he said, and headed toward Damian's room.

Once there, though, it seemed like all Kerry's bravado of moments before faded as Jesse lowered her to the bed, more gently than she had expected, and began to kiss her with more tenderness than she ever thought possible. He kissed her neck, her shoulders, then went down, lifting her top slowly while fluttering kisses on each bit of exposed skin he encountered. The feeling of his warm lips mixed with the sensation of the cool sheets at her back was driving her out of her mind.

When Jesse finally got to her breasts and lightly kissed her nipples through her bra, he tipped out his tongue, wetting the fabric. Her nipples peaked and hardened, and the flesh between her thighs responded in kind, causing her to squeeze her legs tighter together. Kerry felt it, the moment when his smile spread across his face, and she brought her head up. "Don't get all smug now."

Jesse looked up at her and shook his head. "Believe me, there is nothing smug about the way I'm feeling. This is just pure unadulterated joy right here. And I plan on swimming in it."

She laughed but the laughter died in her throat as Jesse leaned up and pulled his T-shirt up over his head, flinging it to the floor. Kerry fought to catch her breath. Jesse grinned. "Good. Now you know a little bit of my suffering."

Kerry covered her face as she felt the heat creep up. Jesse reached out and pulled her hands away, kissing each fingertip as he did so, causing electric tingles to go from their tips throughout her body. "Your hands are so beautiful," he said, his voice low and more serious than she had expected.

Kerry felt her brows draw together. "My hands? That's unexpected." She pulled her hand from his and waved it across her body. "I mean, there is a whole lot more here to admire."

He grinned and pulled her hand back into his but leaned forward and kissed her lips before pulling back. "I know and totally agree. I plan to properly admire all of it, woman. But I have admired your hands for a long time, so I just thought I'd let you know that." He kissed the tops again, then let his tongue tip out, the pink tip teasing her index finger, causing her to clench tight between her thighs.

"I love watching you knit. Watching the way your fingers move. So smoothly, with such confidence. It always mesmerizes me. You make so many cute things. Hats, scarves, gloves . . ." His voice trailed off, but she could tell there was more he wanted to say. He kissed the tip of her finger again, then leaned in and gave it a tiny suck, the sensation giving her an even harder pull between her legs. Kerry sucked in a breath.

"I always wanted to receive one of those cute knitted gifts from you." He paused, and for a moment he looked embarrassed. "You know, I was always jealous. Every holiday you always gave something handmade to the others but not to me."

Kerry stilled. Had he really noticed that? She couldn't believe he'd noticed that. She pulled her hand away and looked at him. "I didn't," she said. "I mean, I would always make something for Mama Joy and maybe a hat or two for your brothers, but that was no big deal."

He shrugged and poked his lip out, looking every bit like the cute thirteen-year-old she'd fallen for a million years ago.

"Besides," Kerry added, "how can you say that when somewhere in this house is probably a box full of your handmade discards?"

"What are you talking about?" Jesse asked, sitting up and looking more interested.

Kerry bit her lip and shook her head. "It's nothing." She waved her fingers in front of his face. "Continue with what you were doing."

It was Jesse's turn to shake his head. "Oh no, ma'am. You're not doing that. What were you going to say? No holding back on your words when we're both hot and horny for each other. The least we can do in this state is be honest."

Kerry looked at him wide-eyed. Honest while horny? Kerry swallowed before she spoke. "I just always felt I never needed to add the hard fruits of my labor and my love to the pile of gifts you've received and tossed aside from so many girls over the years." He stared at her with confusion in his pretty green eyes, so she continued. "I'd seen that drama played out way too many times to want a part in it."

Jesse was quiet for a moment but finally, after a few beats, seemed to understand the meaning of her words. He tilted his head, then nodded. "I get you. I was a jerk when it came to girls."

Kerry raised a brow.

Jesse sighed. "Cut a naked man some slack, please. But I'm talking about you here. You and me. We were never them. When it comes to you, well, still, a man can dream."

Kerry nodded. "True. Just like a woman can wonder why we're having this conversation while we're both half-naked when there are so many better things we could be doing."

She leaned up and put her hand to his chest. Feeling his heartbeat under her palm, loving the life out of it. She kissed him and he returned her passion in kind, taking the kiss deeper, then finally going lower, his hands lifting her skirt and pulling down her panties as she raised her hips. Once again, Jesse paused. "Shit."

She lifted her head. "What now?"

He laughed. "I should have stopped by my room," he said, an apology in his voice. "Just give me fifteen seconds."

She laughed. "Okay, but I'm counting in my head."

Thankfully he only needed ten and was back before she barely got the rest of her clothes off herself. "Shoot, I wanted to do that," he said when he saw that she was already under the covers. Naked with a smile.

"Don't worry, there's plenty left for you to do."

He grinned and threw the condoms he'd brought in onto the nightstand and took off his shorts and tank. "Don't worry, Kerry Girl. I plan on doing it all."

22

"DAMMIT. ON MY good sheets too?" Damian sounded like he was ready to call 911 over the unwelcome sight that had invaded his bed.

Jesse groaned and sucked in a breath. God, Kerry smelled sweet, even first thing in the morning. He pulled her in closer toward him, and she moaned. How could she be sleeping through this? But then again, they had gone more than a few rounds last night.

Damian growled. "Did you hear me? I said those are my good sheets."

Jesse sat up, careful to keep Kerry covered while making a gesture for Damian to keep it down. "Would you stop being so dramatic," he whispered. "If these were your good sheets, you would have taken them with you to your place. They are your moderately good sheets at best, you stingy bum." He looked into Damian's angry eyes.

"They are my good sheets," Damian countered, "and now they are ruined with your, well—" He made a face as he looked from Jesse to Kerry's covered form.

Jesse reached to cover her further, and she shifted, her hips moving provocatively and his dick jumping as if being signaled by the call of a bell.

"Freaking crap," Damian said. "Just throw away the whole damned bed."

Kerry groaned and sat up, clutching the sheet to her naked chest. She reached over to the nightstand for her glasses and Jesse dived to be sure her ass stayed covered. It was bad enough that Damian was standing there. There was no way he was getting a look at Kerry's naked body. No. Fucking. Way.

She put her glasses on, then looked back and forth between the two of them. "Seriously, isn't it a little early to be having this conversation? And why are you arguing over sheets anyway?" She leveled her comment at Damian, who was staring at her now openmouthed. If he drooled, Jesse swore he was going to punch him.

"Don't worry, I'll replace them," she said. "Now, what are you doing here so early in the morning, and why are you barging into my room? I mean, technically it is my room, at least for right now. So, do you mind . . . ?" She made a shooing GTFO gesture with her hand just when both Lucas and Noah appeared in the doorway.

"What is going . . . ?" Noah started, and fell silent when he saw the two of them on the bed. His smile went wide, but Jesse immediately noticed Lucas's frown.

"This is getting ridiculous," Jesse said. "What are you all doing here and why are you all in Kerry's doorway?"

"Kerry, you're the one who told us to come to work this morning," Lucas said.

"Oh, yeah. Sorry. I forgot about that," she said. "But not in my bedroom."

Noah laughed. "Yeah, that's Jesse's job."

"Go downstairs now, brother, before I beat your ass," Jesse said.

Noah laughed, then looked at Kerry. She was glaring at Noah with deadly intent, not realizing she looked sexy as hell wrapped in the sheet with sleep in her eyes. Her lips were still swollen from all their kissing last night.

Noah sobered. "It's not you I'm afraid of right now. It's the new master of the house over there." He put up his hands. "Don't worry, Kerry, I'm leaving. I'll, um, get the coffee started. Is there anything else you want? Eggs, bacon, juice? You, um, want to keep your strength up."

"Go. Now," she said to them all, and finally Jesse and Kerry were alone once again.

Jesse immediately leaned in and kissed Kerry on her bare shoulder. "I'm so sorry about that. My brothers are the worst. They shouldn't have done that and made you feel uncomfortable. I'm going to individually and collectively kick their asses."

Kerry shook her head, then looked at him with eyes more serious than he had expected. There was no trace of the soft, sensual eyes from last night, and he was instantly missing them. "Don't worry about what Noah said or about what happened between us last night."

Jesse frowned. What was she talking about, don't worry? Who was worried?

"I am definitely not the master and don't think of myself as any sort of mistress of this house. What happened between us was lovely, but I know what it was. It changes nothing. I won't hold you back, and I won't cling to you."

He blinked, her words not quite registering.

"Don't you want me?"

Kerry looked at him and smiled. "What do you mean, don't I want you?" She reached out and touched his chest, then leaned forward and kissed him. When she pulled back, she licked at her lips. "If what we did last night is any indication, then of course I want you." Then she patted his thigh and grinned. "Now come on. Let's get going, because if we're up here for any longer, I'm afraid your brothers will be back."

Jesse watched as Kerry got up, slipped into a robe and headed out and down the hall to the shower. When she was gone, he slammed his head back against the headboard. Hard. She didn't want him. No, she wanted him, but not the real him. She knew the real him. The piece-of-shit, no-good, can't-be-depended-on, lacking him. And she had decided he was only good for a temporary fuck and she'd get that and move on. Jesse nodded his head. He couldn't blame her. Kerry was no dummy.

She'd been in his life long enough to know the ropes, and if he were her, he'd do the same. He got up from the bed with heavy legs and an even heavier heart. He pulled on his boxers and proceeded to strip the bed, taking Damian's moderately good sheets with him. Oh well, the way he saw it, he had maybe a few good weeks with her left. He might as well do what he could to make the best of them before she said goodbye forever.

KERRY TURNED ON the shower, looked around as if she was a spy on a covert mission and then quickly hit the button on her cell, dialing up Val. It was still early and Val was probably asleep, but she'd forgive her once she knew what the call was about.

"This had better be good," came Val's groggy and deadly sounding greeting.

"I did it," Kerry whispered. "I mean, we did it?"

"Well then, explain to me why either A) you are not still doing it or B) not sleeping it off?" Val said, clearly annoyed over the wake-up—but come on, she should be shouting over *it*.

"For the record," Kerry said, starting in on her explanation, "I was sleeping it off—I mean, me and Jesse were still sleeping, but got woken up and caught by first Damian and then Lucas and Noah. Hell, the whole crew of them caught me practically naked in the bed."

That news finally woke Val up. "You lucky freaking duck!" her friend yelled in her ear, causing her to wince. "What is this life you're living? Who wakes up like this? Did you flash them? I know you didn't, but I sure would have! Just a little bit to see who reacted how. You didn't flash them, did you?"

Kerry sighed but couldn't help smiling. "Of course I didn't."

"I knew it. But shit, a girl can dream. Damn! So what are you doing now? Where are your four Harlem knights?"

"I'm in the bathroom. Jesse went to get dressed and the others are downstairs. I stupidly asked them to come over this morning to help out and take some more promo photos, but now I just want to get out of here and hide. It was all so awkward. Damian and Lucas looked horrified. Noah was practically ready to marry me off and start calling me sister-in-law. I'm sure that must have scared Jesse to death."

"Why would it scare him?" Val asked.

"Why would it not?" Kerry said. "The last thing he wants is a woman clinging to him, and I'd be the worst possible one. It was hard enough getting him to sleep with me. I know he wanted to, but getting him past the whole not-wanting-to-hurt-me, good-girl, settle-down thoughts he had about me were hard."

Val was quiet.

"Are you still there?" Kerry finally asked. "Did you doze back off?"

"I'm here. Just thinking. Are you sure he's having the thoughts you think he is?"

"Why are you asking me that? Of course. I know him."

"Okay, if you say so," Val said, then brightened her tone. "Do you need me to come over there today? Handle a little crowd control with all those men? I have a hair appointment at ten, but I could come over when I'm done?"

"No thanks," Kerry said, now more stuck in her head on Val's words. "I'll be fine. I can handle them."

"I'm sure you can," Val said, then hung up.

THE MORNING WAS awkward as hell, and Jesse could feel the eyes of his brothers on his and Kerry's every move. Still, they got a lot of the finishing touches done on the shop and even agreed on the TV idea and where it should be put without too much of an argument.

After color-coordinating the fall sets of wools and cottons in the bins where they would best be shown off with the new wall colors, Kerry took more promotional photos of them, hashtagging to her heart's content, and then they decided on where to put the new yarn tree.

"Ma Joy would love this," Lucas said as he anchored the tree securely to be sure it wouldn't fall if knocked into by a passing customer. "This was a great idea, Jesse."

Jesse was surprised by the compliment. "It wasn't much."

"No, he's right, she would love it. And it turned out beautifully."

Jesse turned around when he heard Kerry sniff. She was blinking. "Are you okay?" he asked.

She wiped quickly at a tear before it could fall. "I'm fine. I'm getting hungry, how about you all? I'm going to head up and make some sandwiches. I'll let you know when they are ready."

As soon as Kerry hit the top of the landing, all three of his brothers pounced on him quick as flash.

"What the fuck did you and your randy ass do?" Damian yelled before looking around and lowering his voice to a hiss. "I mean, seriously, with Kerry."

"Our Kerry!" Lucas added.

Jesse's head swiveled Lucas's way. "How is she our Kerry? You all saw her—she was sleeping with me last night."

"Yeah, but in my bed," Damian said. "On my good sheets."

"Once again, fuck you and those cheap-assed sheets. You know those sheets are from TJ Maxx at best, so stop going on about it."

"Fuck you right back. Don't put down the Maxx!" Damian countered.

"Are we really on the damned sheets right now?" Lucas said. "We need to talk about Kerry and what you plan on doing about her."

"Also we need to talk about how you'd better not mess shit up before we get this shop up and running." Damian said. "Don't forget how much we need Kerry. Now you owe us for the loan *and* my fucking sheets. Shit, I should charge you for the whole damned bed."

"Could you not right now, Dame? Just for a minute?"

"I could *not* if you could have kept it in your pants. This is serious. Yes, the improvements are looking good and we've paid off a little with the insurance, but we still need thousands. The opening has to be huge. We need buzz. Our reputation is going to be everything. In the end, this is a yarn shop, not your personal fiber-arts Tinder."

"It's not going to be looked at that way," Jesse said.

"Oh really? Have you seen some of the comments we're getting on social media?"

"I have, and they're positive. We're starting to get some traction, and it's great. People are even checking for your ass."

"Yeah, that's great. And lots of woman are talking about you. Namely some of your past conquests."

Jesse sighed. "Everyone has a past. Some skeletons in their closet."

"Okay, Bones, you go with that. Just don't let it bury all of us."

Lucas groaned now and Jesse turned his way. "What is it? I know you're dying to get your dig in."

"It's not a dig," Lucas said. "I just want to know what you intend to do with her."

Jesse looked at Lucas. His normally pretty easygoing brother looked like he was ready to fight him. Shit, what was really going on here? "What are you so worried about her for? Talking intentions and all that. Why?" Jesse asked, instantly putting his guard up.

"Of course you know why," Lucas said.

"No, I don't. And what's with the 'of course'?"

Lucas seemed like he was fighting for control of his breath and searching for the right words. "Kerry is not like the other girls you've been with."

"And how would you know that?" Jesse shot back. "Were you there last night? No. Maybe she's exactly like the others I've been with."

"Watch it, Jesse." This warning came from Damian. What the hell had he gone and done? Jesse paused, remembering Kerry's words from this morning. Damian was right. He'd better watch it. Kerry was worth more than his snide rebuttals. He let out a long sigh. "No, she's actually better. Kerry knows me for who I truly am."

Lucas sighed while Damian grumbled.

"That's great," Noah said.

Jesse looked at Noah, his smile, he knew, weak at best. "Yeah, it is. I'm lucky. She knows me and still wanted to fuck me, no strings attached. See, she's under no illusions like any of the other women that I've been with that I'm truly worth a damn to love or invest something as precious as her heart in. So you all don't have to close ranks and get all up in arms over our Kerry Girl. She's a smart and strong woman. She's going to be just fine. Now help me out and let's get the last of this yarn unboxed."

GOD, HE HATED his brothers. Hated them just as much as he loved them. Why did they have to go and be so right, right fucking now? Was it too much for him to have a moment of normal happiness in his life?

Of course he knew that Kerry wasn't his forever, no matter how much he wished she were. How much he wanted to fight for her to be. But shit, couldn't he at least get some time to play pretend? Mama Joy was gone and he was alone. Didn't he deserve that?

They were all gone and Jesse had closed up the shop, their reno work finished for the day, nothing else to be done, and with Kerry gone to work at the center he honestly didn't feel like staying in. Damian's words stung, and Lucas's judgment burned. As Jesse walked the avenue, though, he couldn't let go of what Damian had said about Kerry's hashtag. He knew he had to check. Turning and heading toward the park between the projects and behind the fire-house, he leaned against the back of a bench and pulled out his phone.

Most of the posts had lots more likes than he had anticipated, and there were lots of comments from people looking forward to the opening. Each of the posts with photos of them brought lots of likes. Kerry was smart and a great photographer as well as a mar-keter. His brothers were photogenic, so why not use them? But as usual, Damian was right. There were some comments, way too many to just brush off, talking about him being a noncommittal dog. Whew. Blunt much? He could take the "dog," but the "non-committal" might lead to what people would think about the business.

Jesse frowned. The post with the most traction was one with an old picture of Mama Joy with him and his brothers when they were young. He knew the picture. It was from their kitchen, and the comments were full of complimentary things about Mama Joy and how much she was missed and how many great things she'd done for the community.

Kerry had captioned it, "Come on out to the grand reopening and make Strong Knits stronger than ever!" He let out a long breath, then looked up the street. The hour was getting late and the sun was shifting, preparing to make its exit, though you wouldn't know it from the bustling Harlem block. Stronger than ever, huh?

He knew then he needed to do more to repair his reputation if that would ever be true. First stop: Bird's and Blue. He flipped to the contacts in his phone. Next was Remmy's Florist and Devon, and he'd work his way further uptown from there.

23

THE PAST WEEK and a half had been stressful—hell, the past few weeks had been the most emotionally draining of his life, and his life had been nothing if not an emotional roller coaster—but this was it. The time was finally here. Today was the day. The official Strong Knits reopening day. Scary and exciting, but mostly scary, without the assurance of Mama Joy at their backs. Jesse told himself to put those fears on the back burner, as Mama Joy used to say, where they could simmer down or boil out. But either way, today was still the day.

He had Noah help him pull the old iron bench from out back and put it in front of the shop, and after flipping the front door sign from closed to officially open, Jesse took a seat in the warm August sun, hoping for everything but expecting nothing.

Damian said he'd let some woman he knew from the local paper know about the reopening and she might come by to interview them, but it was only a firm maybe. He could only hope. With the loan coming due, it was make-or-break time, and Jesse knew they could use any additional media attention they could get. As long as it was positive, that is. Dammit, Damian was right about that. Though the store looked great and Kerry had taught him how to run it, he knew he still needed the community behind him and to stop the negative comments online.

His "Sorry I was a shithead" tour was going about as well as could be expected. Most of the women he'd apologized to for ghosting were pretty much over him. The hostile ones acted skeptical but were still receptive to news about the shop's reopening. Yeah, it might have gotten a little sketch with one or two, but he'd made it clear that he was focusing on getting the family business up and running. That seemed to be enough to quiet things down online and in his DMs.

Still, Jesse had to admit he felt hollow. Though Kerry had made her feelings clear and he'd gone along with it, Jesse wanted to be able to say he was taken. Because the fact was he was. Taken, that is. Whether she knew it or not, Kerry had taken his heart, and there was no way, right now at least, that he could even consider anyone else by his side. Not that his feelings on the matter mattered.

He'd woken that morning with Kerry in his bed. Over the past two weeks, Kerry had taken to using Damian's room more in line with the way Damian had, like an expanded closet, and she spent her nights with Jesse.

She'd worked with him at the shop during their soft opening, showing him the ropes. Mostly they'd knitted, their little hat display now proudly hung in the window. Kerry had finished four sets of coordinated mittens, which he'd never figured out how she'd finished so fast. They'd knit, then make love almost every night and make plans for the shop, but somehow in those plans, Kerry never used the words "we" or "us." It was always "you" and "your brothers," creating a clear distance and a space for her to make her exit. He guessed he should be grateful for that, but his heart couldn't let him be.

"I can't believe you beat me downstairs this morning," Kerry said, coming out of the shop and sitting beside him. Her smile came soft and open, her eyes sparkling, and his heart thumped harder. Shit. How was it her smile always did that to him? It was brighter than the freaking sun that was rising over the East Side tenements. "You could have slept more," she said. "You didn't sleep so well last night."

He frowned. She was referring to the nightmare he'd had last night. He'd thought he was done with them, but obviously he wasn't. This was the second time he'd embarrassingly woken with a start, shaky and sweaty. Even worse, he'd woken Kerry up too, and she'd seen his state.

He knew why, of course, but admitting it sucked so hard. It was because she'd leave him soon, and he hated it, but better to let her go sooner rather than later. It would end up the same anyway. Why draw out the pain? And the dream, it was the same as his old one of years ago. Him coming back into that room and his mother, always his mother, walking out. And away from him forever. Too bad the reality was so very different. A walkout could somehow be better. It wouldn't hurt so much if she'd left him under her own power, by her own choice. But that wasn't how it was. No, his mother hadn't walked out but checked out, the drugs finally taking her and her warm-as-sunshine smile away from him in an overdose when he was six.

She'd always told him she loved him, more than anything, she said. But still, it wasn't more than that. He knew he was wrong. Mama Joy taught him he was wrong. That she had no choice and she did love him, but that kid, he still didn't know.

Kerry smiled again, and it didn't fail to both mend and shatter his heart all at the same time. He felt guilty for the way he'd handled things last night. Owed her an apology. She'd tried to soothe him. Tried to get him to talk, but he shut down. Told her it was nothing, and when he'd seen the look of hurt in her eyes, had soothed her in the only way he knew how without words, but was that enough?

It was for him. Almost. The way she'd tightly wrapped her legs around him. Her hands had threaded through his hair, her eyes searching his for answers. And he'd almost given them. Almost given in. He had been so close. So close to an "I love you," but it had been stuck. Stuck in her searching eyes and his cowardly throat as instead he'd only kissed her and taken, and, as usual, she'd given.

Jesse opened his mouth to say something just as Noah walked up, saving him. Seeing his brother reminded him of another good-bye soon to come. He'd be leaving for his tour and had been staying at home the past few nights, having given up his sublet in Brooklyn. "You two were awfully quiet last night," Noah teased. "Don't go turning into old married folks on me, now."

Jesse looked at Kerry. "Don't worry. No chance in that," he said.

Noah shot him a look. "What are you talking about? Don't eff it up, little brother. There are plenty who would like to make an old married one out of this one. Kerry is lucky I'm about to go on the road."

"Yeah, right," Kerry said. "The whole lot of you are nothing but big teases." Kerry looked up the block in time to see Lucas. "And here comes another one."

Lucas smiled at her and took her into a hug, kissing her cheek.

Tease for sure. He gave Noah a dab and only nodded Jesse's way, which was fine by him. Jesse didn't want to hear another one of his speeches or get another judgmental look, which was all he'd been getting since the day he and Kerry had been found out. It was as if Lucas really thought she was *their Kerry*, as he said.

Screw that.

Like Kerry had made perfectly clear to him, she belonged to no one, and just like he had to figure it out, his brother had to also.

Damian came walking up the block carrying balloons, looking like that Shadow dude from *American Gods* mixed with that deadly damned *It* clown.

"Thanks, but it's not my birthday?" Jesse said.

Damian rolled his eyes. "What's a grand opening without balloons? We have to let people know in any way possible that we're here, right? Might as well shout it out. Can't let you jerks say I'm not doing my part."

Kerry took the balloons with a smile and a nudge to his side. "And who would dare say that? Thanks, Damian. I think they're lovely. We should put them on the edge of the bench and in front of the door."

As they tied the balloons, Jesse looked at her in her pretty skirt and multicolor knit tank, her brown skin glowing with a soft shimmer.

"Now come on in. I made pancakes. Hopefully we'll be crazy busy today so let's eat while we can," Kerry said.

And she was right. They were busy, with folks lining up to come in even before they were officially open. Starting with the Old Knitting Gang, who showed up and brought with them not only potluck for the party, including Ms. June's carrot cake, but thankfully, some extra folks from the neighborhood, including a few elderly men who may have had less of an interest in knitting than in some twisted hookup. But they also had nimble fingers and deep pockets, so Jesse was grateful to have them.

Strong Knits reopened to brisk business. Jesse put his looming fear aside as he and his brothers posed for photos with the well-wishers from the neighborhood, Lucas telling the OKG jokingly that the photos were free, but it would be a five-dollar charge for each muscle feel-up.

Suddenly there was Ms. Cherry, though, silencing the increasing raucous group. "I'll do you one better, Lucas Strong," she said. "How about one thousand dollars for a hug?"

Lucas was momentarily dumbfounded, his eyes going wide as he looked at a straight-faced Ms. Cherry, who only shot him back a raised brow.

"You're not outdoing me, Cherry," Mrs. Hamilton jumped in, yelling. "I got a grand on sweet Noah here." She put her arms out to Noah, who gladly slid forward. "Come here, baby, and don't worry, I'll slip you a little something extra for your trip," she added when she gave his bicep an extra squeeze.

"Stop being cheap now and bring out the big bucks and the big guns," Ms. June said then and cocked a finger at Damian, who dropped his fork down on his plate midchew. He shrugged, putting his plate aside and coming over to give the woman a huge bear hug.

Jesse shook his head. "We can't take this kind of money from you. It's too much."

"You can and then some," Sister Purnell said, reaching into her bra, because of course her cross-body floral purse wouldn't do in this case, and pulling out a wad of bills. She stuffed the bills into Jesse's hand.

"Why can't you?" Mrs. Hamilton said. "Don't block our blessing by trying to refuse, Jesse."

"That's right," Ms. Cherry chimed in. "Blocking is not an option in this case, and if you have a problem with it, then consider it our club rental fee or call us silent angel investors." She blinked quickly, and suddenly the lump in Jesse's throat was too large to ignore. "Joy was like a sister to us," she said. "And that means you boys are family, and we take care of family."

Jesse swallowed at the memory of Mama Joy laughing and sharing with these women over the years as he sailed in and out of the shop with a quick quip and hardly a backward glance. What he wouldn't give now to be able to go back to just one of those days. To take time to stop and sit and knit with them. To see his mama happy and smiling with her friends once more. He didn't deserve this, like he didn't deserve her. But then he blinked and there was Kerry. She was smiling and looked happy. That smile, these women, this money. It was hope. Could this actually be working out? God, he was scared to think so.

"That's right," Sister Purnell said. "Now you boys just keep doing what you do, and Jesse, you've got this." She turned to Damian then and gave him a sharp look. "And you stop worrying so much about loans and all that. When it's meant to work and it's for you, then it's for you. One day you're gonna learn."

Damian nodded down at the small woman, knowing when he was beat. "Yes, ma'am."

Sister then put out a little box she'd made for additional donations in the middle of the farmhouse table and told everyone to give like their heart led them.

Somebody turned on the music and Strong Knits was officially for real-real now open for business once again.

Kerry didn't think things could get any more emotional. That donation from the OKG had just about taken her out. She took a breath and looked around. Seeing the shop so full of people and thriving took her back, and looking at Jesse now, so comfortable and in the place where she knew he belonged, and where she was starting to think he knew he belonged too, gave her hope. Gave her hope, but at the same time, ripped her apart with the stark realization that it was time for her to move on.

Val entered the shop then along with some students who'd come from the center, and Kerry's emotion meter went clear over to tilt level.

Val had the kids do a presentation, reading thank-you notes to Mama Joy, and after each child read their note, they attached it to the little yarn tree with a safety pin. When all was said and done, the tree looked more beautiful than the one at Rockefeller Center, and more full of love.

As they were decorating the tree, Ms. Cherry started to sing and before long there wasn't a dry eye in the house. There was a sense of closure and new beginnings that they hadn't had at Mama Joy's funeral, and it took all Kerry had to not burst into uncontrollable tears and fall into Jesse's arms or take the path of least resistance and run out the door.

Seeing his moment, Noah stepped in, his smile bright as he admonished the crowd for their tears. Sounding every bit like a little Mama Joy, he told them, "Drink up, stitch well," and then he looked at his brothers when he said, "Love hard and live in the moment, not in the past." He ended his little speech by promising to come home quickly and not to be too big a big shot once he became a huge international star while on the road.

Everyone laughed, and Kerry knew Jesse and all his brothers

were having a hard time keeping it together. Real men didn't just knit. They cried their eyes out too. Though they may not come out and say it, she knew they'd be counting down the days until Noah was back home, and they'd be running up international phone charges left and right in the meantime. Family was like that, and they were all they had.

Kerry and Jesse locked eyes again, and she blinked fast while wiping away her tears. He was striding toward her, but suddenly stopped when Gabriel Webb came up to her, handing her a tissue. She saw the exact moment Jesse's jealousy reared. As if he should be mad, whether as her boss, old friend, first crush or current bedmate.

Kerry wiped at her eyes, thanked Gabriel and looked around the party. It was like that damned old DMX meme up in there with all of Jesse's exes packed into the place. There was Brenda, Latisha, Linda and Felisha. Plus dammit if there weren't at least three Kims, and she bet Jesse had hooked up with all of them. This opening launch party was like old home week for him. And of course there was Erika too. No, Jesse didn't have a leg to stand on in the jealousy department.

Kerry closed her eyes against the cavalcade of women. It was a lot to take. But thankfully she didn't have to take it. They weren't serious. She was just another on his list of names. She'd known this going in and she would damn sure know it going out. Plus, it was better this way. This was what she'd wanted from the start and it was better being hit with the reality of it square-on now.

She gave Gabriel as much of a smile as she could muster so as not to make the party mood awkward but still watched Jesse as he now turned his attention to Errol Miller. Her forced smile faltered as she saw the intense look of sadness in Errol's eyes. He was longingly looking around the shop, but she could see his mind was a long way off.

JESSE TURNED AWAY from the scene between Fake Blair and Kerry, and caught sight of Errol Miller. The boy had been unusually quiet, and he'd been on Jesse's mind since the incident with the neighborhood kids. He walked Errol's way. "How are you, E? How's that scarf coming?"

Errol only shrugged, his silence mirroring his sullen expression. Finally, he spoke. "It's fine, I guess."

Jesse frowned. "You guess? Convincing."

"Yeah, I guess."

"Okay then. Well, know you're welcome here anytime for tips or when you're ready for another project. We have tons of extra yarn."

Errol nodded. "Thanks, but I don't think I'll have much time. School's about to start and I'll probably be doing basketball once that happens."

Jesse looked at him. "Wow. That was about the worst endorsement for intramural sports ever, but okay," he said jokingly, but Errol didn't crack a smile.

Jesse sobered. "Sorry. I get it and it's cool. Just know the offer is always open." Errol was about to walk away, but Jesse stopped him with his voice.

"You know, I played ball too. Basketball and baseball. I was better at baseball though. I knitted while hanging in the dugout to pass the time while waiting for my turn at bat. I still hate waiting."

Errol looked at him now with more than a little skepticism.

"No, really," Jesse said, "it's true. And I took more than my fair share of crap for it." He grinned. "Ugh, the fights. I had plenty, but they stopped quick enough. Coach and Mama Joy weren't having it from me or anyone else. Plus, you've seen my brothers. And it's okay. I always made them eat their words with each triple or home run I hit."

Errol finally cracked a smile.

"Working with yarn helped me with my game. My focus and concentration, you know? I wasn't the best student, so I needed that. It sort of kept me centered, if that makes sense."

Errol was quiet. "It does," he finally said.

"Hey, it's great for hand-eye coordination," Jesse added. He liked talking to Errol. He could see the struggle the boy was going through, and he didn't want him to give up on something he clearly enjoyed.

"As if you ever had any trouble with your hand-eye coordination."

Jesse let out a breath and watched as Errol's eyes traveled up Erika's long body.

Jesse gave her a look. "Seriously? That's your greeting?"

"What?" she said. "I was talking about basketball."

Just then Val came over. "What up? Erika, are you talking about what an expert ball handler you are?" she said, with a smile that could cut through steel.

Kerry walked over then and looked down at Errol. She put her arm around his shoulder. "We have cupcakes, you know. They just got put out. I think you'd better grab one before they're gone." Her tone was soft and easy, but Jesse could tell she was tense.

The boy looked back and forth between the glaring faces of the women, then made the exit that Jesse kind of wished he could.

Erika laughed. "Funny. So have you both moved in here now?"

She looked at Jesse. "You didn't tell me you were hiring a whole team for your little shop."

Jesse moved to stand closer to Kerry. He put his arm around her. "No, I didn't," he said, looking Erika in the eye and hoping to end this conversation. He looked down at Kerry and gave her a warm smile. "Listen, I think we're needed up front." He tilted his head toward a couple looking at the baby hats they'd finished. He almost let out an audible sigh of relief when Kerry gave him a warm smile back.

"Sure," she said. "Let's go. Don't want to keep potential customers waiting."

24

KERRY WAS UNUSUALLY quiet over the next week. Though they both should have been over the moon, sexing and laughing and laughing and sexing some more to celebrate the successful opening and relaunch of Strong Knits, there was no laughter. Crazy, right? The old him would be perfectly happy with just sexing. The woman of his dreams was ready and willing and in his arms every night, and here he was not satisfied. He wanted more. No, needed more. Not just her body. Jesse now knew he wanted that *and* her smiles, her laughter and, dammit, even her ire and admonishments. Kerry wasn't Kerry if she wasn't her full and whole self.

And Jesse could tell she wasn't. That she was keeping something from him. Maybe not intentionally, though he suspected as much, but he could tell there was something she didn't trust sharing with him. A part of herself that she was holding back despite the easy fake smiles and light back-and-forth banter at night. But who was he to talk? As for him, he was holding back too. Because, for the life of him, he couldn't bring himself to just ask her. Ask her straight out what was going on. If she wasn't ready to tell him, then the reverse was true too—he wasn't ready for the beautiful fragile bubble he was living in to burst just yet either.

He knew he was being a total coward, but then again, what else was new? He could practically hear Mama Joy scolding him from the grave. The quicker he let Kerry go, the better, was probably what she'd tell him, but whenever he thought of his mother saying those words, they never seemed to sound quite right in his own head.

He wanted to talk to Kerry about things, comfort her like she needed and deserved to be comforted, be there for her like she was for him, but somehow he just kept coming up so fucking short. It wasn't that she intimidated him, it was just that he was afraid of the ultimate goodbye that he knew was to come when and if he let his real feelings out. Jesse thought back to when he'd caught Kerry restraightening Mama Joy's room. He'd caught the look of loss and sadness as she gently refolded the unfinished shawl and carefully sorted the yarns, her tears flowing freely when she thought no one was watching. He should have cared for her then. Should have dried her tears. Made her laugh. Done something, anything, but instead he'd just stood there. Still. He'd watched and let her cry before walking away like an impotent coward. If that wasn't so like him, he didn't know what was. Useless and undeserving.

They'd talked after the party. Or at least he had, trying to explain the presence of so many of his exes, but she didn't want to listen. Not really. It seemed the old Kerry, that girl in the loft, the one by his side who was always there, was gone. This woman was distant, aloof, a shell holding his sweet Kerry Girl captive.

Finally, not sure how to break the ice and get through her wall, he just blurted things out when they were in bed that night. "I did a sort of apology tour. I didn't like all the negative comments, so I wanted to turn them around and make them into a positive. For the business." It sounded stupid already, but there was no going back now, so Jesse continued, this time with a little more desperation in his voice. Maybe she'd get it then. "And it worked. We got so many donations that the bank is now off our back."

Kerry's frown would have been comic if it wasn't so chilling. "Wow, you really do have magical charms."

"Come on, Kerry Girl. It's not like that. This breather is what we need." He reached for her and she pulled away, shocking him.

"I'm not a girl. When are you going to realize that?" she said, then let out a long breath before looking at him again. "You don't owe me an explanation, Jesse," she said. "I don't have any right to you. Not in the past or in the future. Besides, I'm happy for you and your brothers. You're right. This breather is exactly what you need."

You? Your? Shit. When Kerry Girl wanted to hit, she knew just where and how, and the way she twisted the use of "breather" to make it about them when she knew he was talking about the money?

But she was right. Even if he wanted her to be wrong.

He'd already found out from Lucas that the end was getting way too near and that the repairs on her building were perilously close to being done. Kerry could get a call about her apartment being ready at any time. There was nothing and no one holding her here.

So when she opened up and let him back in, if not emotionally then physically, Jesse took what he could and just went with it.

He'd have her this way if it was the only way he could have her at all.

Besides, he should be happy. It was the best of both worlds. Soon he'd have his bed back, his house back, his old life back. Only he didn't want any of it. What he wanted was her. Fuck if what he had always wanted wasn't her.

25

WITH THE SUCCESSFUL turnout for their after-work Knit and Sip event that she'd coordinated, once again Kerry should have been over the moon. But he could see she wasn't. She was going through the motions.

Albeit heavy on the women, save three guys, the Knit and Sip was a hit. Folks showed up to knit, mingle and get their drink on. Too bad it was a disaster for Kerry and Jesse. It was a roller coaster of emotions for many. His boy Craig showed up and got shot down by Val, who, it seemed, had a "one strike and you're out" policy. But Ziggy seemed happy with the scene and deemed it chiller than the club, and with better odds.

Jesse would have been cool with the male count stopping there, but that damned single dad from Kerry's job showed up. He claimed he wanted to learn to knit for his daughter, but the way he kept looking at Kerry and asking a million and three questions had Jesse thinking differently.

Still, he couldn't be mad. Not with the turnout. It was pretty good. Kerry's marketing, for what it was worth, was fantastic. Her idea of putting pics of him and his brothers in various suggestive poses with the yarns and marketing through Instagram was genius.

Jesse watched Kerry mingle with the women, expertly giving advice as she served the fruity sangria they had whipped up along with the cookies she'd stayed up making the night before. He realized this was a sight he could happily and easily get used to. It felt right.

She didn't even seem fazed over the fact that, once again, Erika showed up. Which gave him no small amount of apprehension. If she no longer cared, then was she really and truly ready to move on?

Jesse was ready for a certain amount of tension and the night to be ruined, but instead, Kerry just looked at him and smiled as she took Erika's money and contact info, then handed her a skein of yarn, a pair of needles and a glass of sangria in exchange for her thirty-five-dollar entry fee. The only thing that even slightly gave away that she may have been bothered was the fact that she pulled up a chair for Erika between Sister Purnell and Ms. Cherry, creating quite a tight little sandwich.

It was a reach, but it gave him hope.

The mood lifted easily enough once again when Lucas came in, though he and his brother were still slightly tight lipped over him and Kerry. And who could blame Lucas? As he had predicted, Jesse was totally messing it up. Still, after the successful launch, all his brothers were lightening up a bit and putting business first. He had to thank Lucas for coming through tonight. One look at the hot firefighter who started to demo arm knitting and the women were practically throwing money at them for skeins of heavyweight chunky wool.

Lucas gave Jesse a wink across the room and he laughed at the same time that Erika walked over to him. "You know I would pay extra for a private if you could teach me that arm knitting, Jes."

He looked over at her, careful to keep his expression neutral. Erika licked her lips provocatively.

"Thanks, but I don't do privates," he said, and started to walk forward. "We do have a schedule up front that shows all our group lessons."

Then he paused. Kerry was showing Fake Blair a technique, and he put his hand over hers and ran his thumb across the back of her index finger. *Her index finger!* Jesse took another step forward. He wanted to kill that motherfucker.

A hand on his chest stopped him, along with a low voice in his ear. "Not here. This is not the time or the place," Lucas said.

He turned and looked into his brother's dark eyes; they were full of warmth and understanding and also caution. Lucas was right. Jesse nodded and let out a breath.

He turned back to Erika as the rest of the room came back into focus. Grabbing a blue schedule sheet, he handed it to Erika. "Here you go," he said, deadpan. "All our group classes are listed here."

Jesse snatched up a bunch more schedules then and placed them on the table. He put them in various spots, finally coming around to place some between Kerry and Fake Blair, and that was when he heard it. "I think you'll be a great addition," Fake Blair said. "Please let me know your decision soon. It's time things change, and having you on the team is just what we need."

Jesse froze as he looked from Fake Blair to Kerry. He dropped the flyers and moved on. "Sister Purnell," he said, "you want a personal arm knitting demo? Stand up and let's get close so I can show you how it's done."

THAT NIGHT KERRY tried to snuggle up against Jesse's smooth and hard planes. And though he pulled her in close to him, her naked back to his chest, she could feel him emotionally pushing her away. It was as if she could almost see the little one-inch invisible space between them filled with all their fear and self-doubt. That small space that might as well have been a full mile.

It was fine, she told herself. She had been doing the same to him. And what else could she expect now that things were all coming to a head after tonight and his overhearing what Gabriel had said? At least she thought he'd heard. Kerry gave herself a mental shake. Who was she fooling? Of course he'd heard, and now she knew she needed to tell him about the job offer. She let out a long breath. The job was a perfect opportunity for her. Full-time art specialist for their new satellite school division. They would work in conjunction with the local public school year-round, and with this she'd no longer have as many financial worries; she could still work with the kids in the community and be close to home.

The other big bonus was she'd be working directly under Val, who'd been promoted to assistant department program director. A job she was meant to do. It was terrible to say—okay, not terrible, but honest. Shit, Val was perfect for that job, and Ali could kick rocks. Let her pull her weight for once with her new assignment as Linda's assistant, something far more fitting to her skill set. It was all good. Really good. So why was Kerry holding back?

"Why are you keeping secrets?" Jesse finally said, his voice a low rumble at her back.

Damn him.

"When will you ever not be in my head?" she replied.

"When you finally get out of my heart, so that will be never."

Kerry snorted, trying to shake off his easily said words, but she knew the true gravity of them. The question was, did he know? The image of Erika sidling up to Jesse came to her mind. The smooth way she'd touched his arm earlier, like he was hers. There would always be an Erika in Jesse's life. It was inevitable with him. Just as it had always been. What they had couldn't go on for much longer, and she knew it. She'd seen the end of too many of his relationships, and her time was clearly running out.

Seemed it was the same for Kerry as it had been for her mother and all her bad men, and now bad women. Earlier that day, she'd spoken to her mom, who'd called for yet another role-reversal talk session and cried to her about love on the rocks. It seemed her track record for being a terrible picker would still stand undefeated, gender be damned. Kerry had had it. She had seen so many failed relationships through her mother's eyes, some much worse than others. The far worse ones, full of tears and intimidation, were what sent her out of the house and to Strong Knits in the first place. Her mother was and always would be one for an all-in kind of love. Kerry knew she had that tendency in her blood and had to fight with all her might against it. Thankfully, though it would temporarily hurt like hell, it was probably right on time for saving her heart in the long run. She'd also gotten another call. Her apartment was done. The necessary repairs were made on her building and she could go back to her place at any time.

No more living out of a suitcase. No more infringing on the Strong brothers' private space, and no more falling asleep and waking up in Jesse's warm and, to her, perfect arms. The days and nights of her temporary fantasy were coming to an end.

"So, when are you going to tell me?" Jesse said.

Kerry froze. Tell him. She didn't want to tell him. Not yet. Though she knew it was silly and immature because he probably already knew, telling him would make it real. Make it final. Still he asked. Why did he have to go and ask?

"Tell you what?" Kerry's voice felt thick in her throat. She turned around and looked into Jesse's beautiful, mossy eyes, hoping at that moment that she'd never forget the view. Him above her. Looking at her like she was truly his one and only. Forever.

Kerry swallowed, then finally spoke. "I'm leaving."

Jesse was silent as he only continued to look at her, giving away nothing, his eyes barely even flickering.

"My apartment is ready," she said, then fought to make her voice lighter and brighter. "And I've been given a great opportunity at the center. They finally offered me a full-time job as a teacher and counselor there."

Finally, his expression changed. Kerry watched as his pupils sharpened and the green in his eyes darkened with shades of a deeper evergreen. "They, or him?"

Kerry stiffened. "What do you mean 'him'?"

"There is nothing to mean," he said. She could already feel him emotionally pulling away, and the pain was almost physical. "Forget I said it," he said, then leaned down and kissed her. "I'm happy for you. This is what you wanted. Things are lining up. It's great."

He kissed her again, taking the kiss deeper and then lower to trail down her neck. He looked back up at her. "So, your place is ready, huh?" Jesse let out a long sigh. "I can't pretend to be happy about that, but then again, you do snore like crazy," he joked as he playfully smacked her on her thigh.

She was used to his joking, but this felt different. This wasn't

Jesse playing with Kerry, his old friend and now lover, but Jesse being Jesse, dropping a line to any other woman. His hand roamed from her thigh to her belly and up to her breast. He ran his thumb across her nipple in that way he'd learned, oh so quickly, she'd liked, and against her mind, her body responded.

He smiled. "Snoring aside, since you'll be leaving me soon, I might as well do my best," he said, "to make you sleep well while I still have you. As deep and peacefully as possible."

She quirked a brow. "And how do you plan on ensuring that? You got a Breathe Right strip in your pocket or something?"

Jesse laughed, or maybe it was more a low grumble, as his mouth went from her lips to her breasts and continued its trail down to between her legs. "Let's call it 'or something,'" he said before settling her in for the night.

26

DON'T WORRY, I'LL still be back here to work in the shop for the next couple of weeks. I can do Saturday and part-time Sunday and some of the evening classes. We're still only setting up the new curriculum for the start of school," Kerry said when Jesse was just putting the last of her bags on her bedroom floor.

He stared at her. Who was the woman who was talking to him like he was just another coworker and not the man who'd made her come three times last night and twice just that morning?

Kerry had just come out of her bathroom after having inspected the new sparkling white paint job. She was so pretty as she grinned at him with that big bright smile and those wide, round eyes. She also looked all wrong. Why was she here? Why was he dropping her off here and going back home without her? Alone. All fucking alone.

He walked forward and pulled her into his arms, kissing her, and needing her oh so much. Jesse wanted nothing more than to take her back—no, not take her back, he just couldn't do that. Maybe beg her to stay? He pulled away and looked into her eyes.

"You know," he started, "who knows what kind of job they did here or how safe things are. You could still stay at the house. There really is no rush." He sniffed the air. "And this paint still smells too fresh. Like it's toxic or something."

Kerry frowned. And looked around. He knew he was reaching. "I'm sure it's fine. And I'm sure you're glad to be rid of me. And hey, Damian has his full closet back now." She paused. "I have to remember to buy him new sheets."

"Fuck his closet and his sheets."

"Jesse."

He looked her in the eyes. "You don't have to go, you know."

"I know and I do," she said. Her voice was so soft now but so very clear.

Jesse rubbed her upper arms, wanting to let the feelings of his urgent heart out but too afraid to put a voice to them. What if she still said no?

It was Kerry who spoke. Saving him, again. "This is where I should be. There are plans, and . . ." She paused and looked him in the eye. Her eyes glistened and she blinked. *Don't cry, Kerry. I'm not here to make you cry.* She smiled as if hearing his silent plea. "There is always the danger that I could lose myself in you."

Lose herself? The words crushed him more than a no ever could. He never wanted that. Not when he was so lost himself. Not when he couldn't be trusted to care for her like she deserved to be cared for. She knew him best. If she said it, if she didn't believe he could make her happy, if she didn't believe in him, then it must be true. Lose herself in him, and become what? Nothing? Gone before her time like every other woman who'd ever cared for him. He nodded and took a half step back.

"I guess you're right," he said.

Kerry looked at him in confusion, and then as her smile wavered and a little bit of the light in her eyes dimmed, she reached out and ran her hand along the back of his neck. Her voice was smooth and sweet, soft and placating when she spoke, and he hated every syllable. "Don't worry, Jesse, you'll be fine. And I'll still honor the commitment I made."

He pulled back fully, the anger suddenly as real as the raised hairs on the back of his neck. "I'm not your commitment, Kerry. I never was."

Kerry looked at him, the hurt clear in her eyes. But she didn't lash out. Only nodded. "You're right. And I thought I made it clear that the commitment I made was to the shop and myself, not to you. Don't worry, I wasn't trying to imply anything to hold you down."

He let out a breath. "Ridiculous woman."

"As if a runner like you could ever hold or be held down."

He threw up his hands and turned away from her, heading toward the hall. "Thanks, Kerry Girl. For everything. Truly. We couldn't have made it as far as we have without you."

"SO, SHE'S GONE?" Damian asked.

"Like gone, gone?" Lucas said.

"Really gone?" Noah chimed in from his Skype call.

"What part of the definition of fucking gone do you idiots not understand?" He was back in the shop after he'd dropped Kerry off. It was his first official Sunday open without her, and the fact that he had flipped the sign from closed to open without her there had exhausted him.

"But she'll be back later, right? For the afternoon class? And what about lunch?" Lucas asked. "We were all supposed to have lunch together."

Jesse looked at him like he'd grown another head. "Lunch—what are you going on about? Make your own damn lunch. Stop acting like she was our mom."

"Tell that to yourself," Damian suddenly said.

"What?" Jesse said.

"You're the one who was all torn and confused in your thoughts, not sure if she was some sort of sister, girlfriend or surrogate mother figure. Your head was totally fucked up and you screwed it all up by overthinking."

"He's right," Noah said from the laptop on the desk. "You were both better when you were younger and knew your minds. But I get it. The stress with losing Mama Joy and then taking on the shop has been hard on both of you."

Jesse turned away and picked up his knitting needles. "I don't know what you're talking about."

Damian watched him, his eyes practically heating Jesse's hands. "I think you do. If not, you'll figure it out soon enough."

Lose herself. Jesse looked at the little display hat he was knitting and suddenly thought of Kerry and her words to him. She had done so much for them over the years, silently and not so silently. He thought of her holding that damned recycling when Erika had stayed over and he wanted to kick his own ass again. All her afternoons with the OKG making the shop more than a business, but a home away from home for them. The coffee and snacks always at the ready now for him and his brothers since Mama Joy had been gone. He looked at each of his brothers as they gave him knowing looks back. And now they were freaking hungry and wanted lunch. He threw down his needles. "Fine. I'll make your hungry asses some lunch, but I'm not doing dinner too."

27

KERRY LOOKED AROUND the classroom. Everything was neat and ready. Desks lined up perfectly. Art supplies in place for today's project. The kids would be coming in soon, and she was glad. It felt good being at work. At least here she could pretend that she was happy and busy and not a complete heartbroken wreck who desperately missed a man she hadn't heard from in over a week. For all she knew he'd probably moved on from her to the next.

She let out a long sigh then and got a hard nudge from Val in return for it. "That's the third one, you know, in as many minutes."

"Third what?" Kerry asked, turning to her friend. They only had a few more weeks as teaching mates before they went on break and then came back to take on their new roles. Kerry was still excited about her new job, but it was hard to get as happy as the changes warranted when her heart was being torn in two.

"Third sigh," Val said.

Kerry frowned. "You're actually counting?"

"What else can I do? It's about all I get out of you lately, since you're useless when it comes to conversation. I thought at least if you're suffering and heartbroken, we could commiserate over what a jerk that Jesse Strong is. But you won't even give me that. Just these awful sighs. So I'm counting."

Kerry shook her head as the kids began to file in. She frowned as they all finally took their seats.

This was the second class that Errol had missed. He'd been on track for a perfect attendance award, and now that was ruined. Not that he wouldn't get other awards at the upcoming end-of-season assembly, but still, she couldn't help but wonder what was keeping him from class.

"Did we get a call from Errol's mom about him being absent? It's not like him. You think they may have gone on vacation?" she asked Val when the kids were having some quiet time.

Val shook her head. "I didn't hear that, but I can check in the office." Then she frowned. "Wait a minute, I know they didn't go on vacation, because I think I saw his mother at the grocery store yesterday. I'll make a call."

"Okay, but let's be careful. I remember he was being bullied by some boys about knitting. I wouldn't want to make things harder for him by causing problems at home."

Val nodded. "Yes, but we have to check it out."

Kerry smiled, though her worries were still strong. "Ay, ay, captain," she said, and smiled wider when Val blushed.

"Oh, do go on!"

THE NEXT DAY Kerry was happy to see Errol back and the class complete again. Still, she could detect a change in him; the usual happy spirit that was normally in him seemed faded. Val noticed it too. "So what do you think?" she asked Kerry when the kids left to head for their music program.

Kerry shook her head. "I don't know. He said he's fine, and it was all the right words, but something is not right. When I asked him if he was looking forward to the start of the school year, he seemed pretty down. That worries me, because he is a good student. Then he brought up going out for the basketball team, which is great, but he's never showed interest in it before."

"I know," Val said. "I can't help but wonder if it has to do with Troy and his crew. During free time I heard them saying something to him about him giving up his girly arts and crafts and joining the team."

Kerry sucked in a breath. "Those little jerks."

Val nodded, then shook her head. "I know. But I put a squash on it. They thought they could flex in front of the girls by picking on Errol. Not that it worked, but what do they know at that age?"

Kerry shook her head. "They need to learn and quick."

"That they sure do," Val agreed.

28

WITH THE END of the summer just about here, the kids were excited but so very restless. They were more than ready for their short two-week break before the school year would begin, and they were showing it by being generally rambunctious, and at times downright surly know-it-alls.

Then, to top things off, on this day, instead of it being bright and sunny, or at least just bright-ish enough that they could go outside for free play time, there was practically a mini monsoon, and they were stuck inside bouncing all that pent-up energy off the center walls and back at the teachers and counselors.

Who could blame them? Kerry could admit she was feeling just about as frayed as the kids were, as she tried, along with the rest of the staff, to get everyone quieted down in the assembly room for the special program. They were having a few people from the community come in to talk with the kids about careers, which was great, because it was never too early to get them started.

In New York, the competition was tough, and as early as elementary school, kids had to begin prepping for the rigorous and, in many folks' opinions, skewed high school testing process. Kerry hoped today's program would help them but not add weight to their young, already stressed minds. Still, she wasn't in the mood to smile and play happy teacher today, which sucked and made her feel guilty. The kids deserved much more than her bringing her baggage to work.

Kerry did a little shake. "Get it together," she told herself as a way of jolting her mind and body right.

But sleep had once again skipped over her the night before. She couldn't believe how quickly she'd gotten used to spending the night with Jesse's arms wrapped around her. Just what she'd told herself not to do. At two a.m. she was up flipping channels on her little TV. Picking up her knitting project did nothing but frustrate her all the more. She wanted to bang on the shop's door and beg Jesse to let her in. Though of course she knew that wasn't all she wanted.

Kerry let out a sigh and looked around at the myriad excited young faces. All skin tones, from the fairest of the fair to the most beautiful deep mahogany, sweet dimples and bright brown eyes. Her heart twisted. She needed to get it together. Being tired, stifling yawns and only half watching kids who deserved her full attention was not going to cut it. If this was what being in love did to you, she'd done right cutting it loose.

She guessed?

Despite telling herself not to, she'd gone into the shop last Saturday to work and help out with the lessons. Immediately she knew that the Jesse she encountered was not the man she'd left just days before. He was cool—maybe a little too cool. His smile was there, but each time he sent it her way, there was a slight, brittle chill at the end of it. His words were careful, a little too controlled and measured. As they sat on the opposite ends of the table with the six new knitters between them, the tension was almost more than she could take.

Finally, the class was over, and when the last student left, Kerry let out a breath. She looked at Jesse and smiled. "You did great. You're a born teacher."

"Thanks. I enjoyed it. Hopefully they'll tell their friends and we can expand on the classes even further." He looked like he wanted to say more but instead began to clear off the table.

Kerry knew she wanted to say more but instead started to clear off the coffee mugs and teacups that were left. Jesse's voice stopped her. "Leave that. I can do it."

"But"—she looked at him, and his eyes were cold and unwavering—"I don't mind."

Still he shook his head. "No, I've got it. You don't have to clean up after me anymore, Kerry. Those days are done."

Val nudged Kerry, bringing her mind to the task at hand. "Are you okay? You look done for."

Kerry looked at Val and for a moment she still saw the cold eyes of Jesse. Felt the finality of his words.

Had she made a mistake? "He said those days are done."

Val frowned, then her eyes went soft. "Oh, honey," she whispered and looked around. "I know. But done is never done." She patted Kerry's hand. "Just hang on a few more minutes and this assembly will be over. Then I promise you we'll have him eating his words. I'll make sure of it."

Kerry shook her head, embarrassed for having zoned out like she had. "I'm fine. Just tired. Guess I'm as ready for the break as the kids."

Val gave her a long look. "You sure? Can you make it through this?"

Kerry snorted. "Of course I'm sure. Stop fishing, Ms. Director. There is nothing to see here." She looked over at the doorway, where Gabriel Webb was, and saw him greeting some of the mentors as they began to arrive. She nudged Val. "Looks like you'd better get over there. Some of the presenters are arriving," Kerry said as she spotted Connie Rae and her husband, Raymond, who owned Corrine's Cakes. And there was Becky Bryant, who owned the ironically named Good Hair, which specialized in natural hairstyling. Becky laughed at Gabriel and held on to his hand for an inordinately long time. Kerry held back her own laugh. Now that word was out about Gabriel, it was clear to see they would be in no shortage of single-parent volunteers at the center.

But Kerry froze when she saw the next person come in, followed by two others. It was Jesse, and behind him were Lucas and Damian. "What are they doing here?" Kerry whispered.

"Don't you mean what is *he* doing here?"

"He, they, what does it matter?"

Val shrugged. "I think it matters to you, but whatever." She started to walk forward then. "Pay attention, Teach. You may learn something."

JESSE WAS NERVOUS but knew he had to do this. It was now or never with Kerry. He paused, halting in his tracks when he locked eyes with her across the center of the cafeteria floor. It was like a hush came over the room and everything went still. The workers stopped moving, the kids stopped screaming, everything went quiet and it was only her. But wait, who was he fooling? Was it really now or never? Sure, this felt like it. And yeah, he was scared shitless, but he knew if he fucked up—and it was him, so he prob-ably would—so what? This was Kerry and he wasn't giving up. Not on his life. He'd sure as shit just untangle his mess and start over once again. There was no now or never when it came to Kerry. With his love, their love, he'd never give up. He'd just keep on knitting. He knew this, and he'd probably always known this, which was why he was such an idiot and had lost so much precious time and so many precious years looking at her from afar when he could have been loving and cherishing her from up close.

What a waste. A waste of good time and so much good loving. Damian nudged him in his side. "You just gonna stand here, dummy? Making eyes at her like you're thirteen?"

"Be quiet, bro," Lucas said from Damian's other side. "Don't worry, he's got this. He's not going to screw it up. Not this time."

Kerry only nodded at them. She gave a smile, but it was so bland—lips only—that he could barely recognize her. Staying on her side of the room, she tended to her kids as the other presenters went through their programs. As it got closer to their time to come up, Jesse could feel his heart race faster. He looked at the kids, then looked back over at Kerry. Normally she looked at him with so much easy encouragement, but he couldn't find it today. Today all he saw was confusion and uncertainty in her wide eyes. Once again, though, Damian nudged him forward.

Jesse hardly heard Val's intro, but he did hear when she brought up Mama Joy's name. Jesse blinked then. "Though we'll miss Ms. Joy so very much," Val was saying, "we'll always remember what she's done, the skills and life lessons she's instilled in so many of us in the community. And luckily for us, her legacy will continue on with her sons, the new proprietors of Strong Knits. Today we have speaking three of them, Jesse Strong, Lucas Strong and Damian Strong." She made a gesture for them to begin, and they were interrupted by the sound of a boy.

"Oh look, Errol, it's those boy knitters like you."

Jesse looked over then, for a moment his fear and even Kerry forgotten as his eyes searched for Errol and where the comment had come from. He quickly found Errol sitting by a back table looking straight ahead, eyes bright like he was holding back both his tears and the "eff you" comment he wanted to retort. He stared at Jesse.

Jesse smiled and looked at the assembly. "Yes, it's us, those boy knitters. Sexy, huh?" He winked, and a bunch of the girls giggled, while some of the teachers did too. "I'd like to also introduce a fellow boy knitter and firefighter, my brother Lucas."

A bunch of the kids clapped at that, and one girl yelled, "I know him! He came to my house when our grandmother got sick. They had to do CPR on her."

"And I'd like to introduce another boy knitter—"

"Man knitter," Damian interrupted, and Jesse sighed. "And certified CPA," Damian added as Jesse's eyes went to the sky. *This guy.*

"But can you knit?" a little girl yelled out, not to be deterred.

Damian frowned at the blunt question as he gave the little challenger a side-eye. Not backing down, the little girl folded her arms and just stared. Finally Damian replied, "I do all right. Socks are my specialty, if you must know."

The little girl beamed, satisfied, and the brothers continued, talking about what they had learned from knitting and its values—things like concentration, discipline, coordination. They used Noah as that example and showed a video of him dancing.

"Wow," young Troy, who had teased Errol earlier, finally said. "This must be great for impressing girls."

Everyone erupted into a fit of giggles, and Jesse looked at Kerry. "Um, I don't know. There are definitely worse ways, but we could give it a try. You see, when you make something by hand, whatever you make takes time, patience, concentration and your energy. You should value that. So, when you give a gift, you should do it with a clear intention and your pure heart. And that's the same way you should receive such a gift. That is a lesson it's taken me way too many years to learn, but I think I finally have."

Jesse reached around then, his blood rushing, his heart pounding as he pulled out the now finished shawl made from all the beautiful petal remnants that Mama Joy had knitted and collected over the years, plus the ones he'd added after Kerry had gone back to her place. He knew it was time for him to step up and stop relying on her and others to fill in the missing gaps for him, and for him to take the initiative and put himself out there for those that he loved. He needed for this to be—no, hoped it would be—the first step in showing her the man he was and would now be.

"Miss Kerry?" Shit. Was that him calling her name, or was it young Errol? Dammit, he couldn't let a tween steal his woman!

Kerry looked at him, her eyes wide, beautiful and glistening. Crap, and now he could barely speak. How was it she did this to him when no one else did? If this wasn't love, then he didn't know what was. There was a small shove at his back, and then he was moving forward. "Go and get your girl," Lucas said. Thank God for his meddling brothers.

"Our girl," he heard Damian mutter.

Nosy-assed bastards.

But suddenly he was right there in front of her, shawl in hand. "Kerry Girl." Jesse felt her name come out like a breath from his heart. "Will you accept this? Please." He cleared his throat. The school setting made it feel like he was about to give a holiday report. Talk about pressure. He let out a breath. "Along with my heart, soul and love? Wherever you are and whatever you do, know that I'm always here for you, supporting you and all you are and want to do. I don't want you to get lost in me. Just know that with you I find myself." He was sweating. It was official, he was definitely sweating.

But Jesse stared at her, and Kerry was so very quiet as the kids erupted in cheers. She reached out to touch the multicolored, mismatched shawl. He wondered what she was thinking as she touched it. It was so like him, like his brothers and like the two of them. It went with everything and nothing at all. Where would she even wear it? To Netflix and chill, maybe? A perfect metaphor for his life—and he hoped with all his heart that she could accept it.

Finally, she looked up at him, eyes glistening, and nodded. Lord, could he breathe again?

"I thought I told you I'm nobody's girl."

"Oh Miss Kerry, I know it, but can't you make an exception for me? Throw a dude a bone? Say, trade Kerry Girl in and become my woman. Let me be your man. However you'll have me or want me. Please let me be that or die happily trying?"

She stared at him for a long time—or, who knew, maybe it was just a moment—before she smiled, and it was as if the sun finally shone on him again. She blinked, and he saw the tears in her eyes. "You don't have to try to be anything you're not, Jesse Strong. Don't you know I've always loved who you are, that it was more than enough for me?"

It took all he had not to pass out in the middle of that crowd of kids. But shit if he didn't feel his whole world spin forward, backward, tilt and then right itself again. He may have actually swooned too, because there was Lucas's hand for a moment, righting him, and Kerry laughing as she wrapped an arm around his neck, her fingers lightly caressing his nape.

She grinned playfully then and held up the shawl. "Still, it took you long enough," she said. "I've been waiting for a handknit gift from you forever."

He let out a breath and laughed. "And I've been waiting to tell you I love you for forever."

And just when he thought the noise couldn't get louder, Kerry told him she loved him too and kissed him.

"Get it, Miss Kerry!" a girl whooped.

"I'm gonna take up knitting!" a little boy said.

"Okay, cut it out," Val said in Jesse's ear. "I just got this good job and now I'm gonna have to deal with angry letters from parents. Damn you, pretty-assed Jesse Strong!"

Photograph of the author by Katana Photography

USA Today bestselling author and native New Yorker **KWANA JACKSON** spent her formative years on the A train, where she had two dreams: (1) to be a fashion designer and (2) to be a writer. After spending more than ten years designing women's sportswear for various fashion houses, Kwana took a leap of faith and decided to pursue her other dream of being a writer. A longtime advocate of equality and diversity in romance (#WeNeedDiverseRomance), Kwana is the mother of twins and currently lives in a suburb of New York with her husband.

CONNECT ONLINE

KMJackson.com

Ready to find
your next great read?

Let us help.

Visit prh.com/nextread